D1045338

10/06

that girl
Lucy Moon

that girl
Lucy Moon

AMY TIMBERLAKE

HYPERION BOOKS FOR CHILDREN
New York

First Edition
1 3 5 7 9 10 8 6 4 2
This book is set in 13-point Perpetua.
Designed by Ellice M. Lee
Printed in the United States of America
Reinforced binding
Library of Congress Cataloging-in-Publication Data on file.
ISBN 0-7868-5298-4

Visit www.hyperionbooksforchildren.com

For Phil

CHAPTER 1

It all began with that October 3rd wind—a breeze with a nip that arrived in Turtle Rock, Minnesota, every year, right on schedule at three o'clock. The wind loitered at the top of town, rolling around in the limbs of the old sugar maple on Wiggins Hill, before whooshing down onto Main Street and skipping across the waves on Turtle Rock Lake. Within an hour the wind turned gusty, and a half hour after that, the Arctic rushed in with it. It came quickly, numbing noses, ears, and cheeks, banging drainpipes, rattling windows, and blowing plastic grocery bags high into the air. All over town, people found themselves saying the same three words to one another: "There's that wind."

But this year, the October 3rd wind wasn't finished with just an Arctic gust. No, the gust was followed with ice and then snow on its tail.

* * *

That particular afternoon, Lucy Moon clamped one hand on top of her green-and-yellow woven hat to keep the wind from blowing it off. Then she thought, why bother, and lifted her hand. In junior high school, no one cared about her hat, or why she wore it.

Lucy would not admit this to anyone, but boy, did she miss elementary school. In elementary school, everyone knew why she wore the green-and-yellow hat. Kids thought she *never* took the hat off—not since her mom brought it back from Mexico City. And it was true that Lucy wore the hat every day—on hot days and cold days. Whenever teachers asked her to remove the hat, Lucy educated everyone present about workers in Mexico and how United States businesses took advantage of them. She'd work this into a "And did you know that hemp should be legal?" speech, because the hat was made of woven hemp. Finally, the whole thing would slam to a stop with a simple statement: Lucy wore this hat as a physical symbol of distress around the world.

Then Lucy would sit down.

Some teachers tottered and said nothing. Some stared. Others leaned momentarily on the desk at the front of the classroom, sighed, and went back to their lesson notes. Anyway, after a beat, the class continued with the hat encircling Lucy's head. At the time, it had reminded her of a halo. These days the hat only made her head sweat.

In elementary school, Lucy had felt full of fire and fury. "No frying ants!" she remembered yelling in first grade. She'd take off running toward the perpetrator, and if they weren't quick enough with their magnifying glass, she'd kick it out of their hand. Elementary-school years included outbreaks of petitions about everything from secondhand smoke (wafting from the teachers' lounge) to a demand that girls be taught real baseball and not *Wiffle-Wuss* ball. She even led honest-to-goodness protests, the scariest being the time she and twenty other kids hiked into the forest to prevent Canton Lumber from cutting trees. Everyone except Lucy ran when they heard the rumble of the trucks approaching. Lucy closed her eyes and clung to her tree, thinking she might leave the earth with tire tracks running up her backside. Finally, a big man peeled Lucy from her tree, like skin from an orange.

Today, though (and every single day since starting junior high), Lucy didn't feel any of the old gumption. It's a beat-up hat, she thought. Let it go.

Still, when that October 3rd wind lifted the hat's edges, Lucy couldn't help herself. She caught the hat and tugged it securely onto her head. Junior high was strange enough, she decided, without having to go hatless, too.

Zoë Rossignol, Lucy's best friend, glanced at her.

Zoë and Lucy often walked down the long hill from the junior-high school together, since their houses sat side by side on Fifth Street. Usually they dumped their school bags at their houses and then continued walking down the hill to Main Street, where they both helped out at the Rossignol Bakery until it closed at six o'clock.

Today, Lucy and Zoë were in the middle of an argument. A feather boa floating around her neck, Zoë loped ahead of Lucy and then stopped in the middle of the sidewalk.

"All I'm saying," said Zoë, blocking Lucy's path, "is, how often do you want to write one-page essays about why you shouldn't damage other people's property?"

"I only broke a pencil," muttered Lucy, stepping around Zoë. "And Thomas Duke and Ben Furley started it. It's none of their business whether I wear a bra or don't wear a bra, and whether or not I've 'developed.' And I'm sure Mr. Skoglund can see what's going on from the front of the classroom! As a male, he identifies with their prehistoric, oonga-boonga brains. It's probably a 'boys will be boys' situation. It is so unfair that I have to write the essay!"

Zoë grabbed Lucy's sleeve. "You know that's not what I'm saying."

Lucy pulled free and shrugged.

"Okay, I'll say it plain. You're Lucy Moon! Lucy Moon puts up with it for three days and then writes the essay her teacher tells her to write, like a good little girl? I don't think so."

Yeah, Zoë had a point, but Lucy didn't say anything.

For three days, Lucy (along with every other girl

within pencil reach) had been subjected to Thomas Duke's "daily bra-check." Every morning, Lucy felt a pencil run up her spine. This was followed by "nope," or "yup." Lucy was a "nope," and Thomas Duke liked to whisper loudly about Lucy's "development" (not promising) to Ben Furley.

The first time it happened, Lucy had actually allowed that it might have been a mistake, that Thomas Duke had gestured grandly with his pencil and accidentally swooped it up her spine. The second time, she knew it was a bra-check, but she inwardly panicked—she hadn't said anything the first time, so how could she complain the second time?

Making excuses, inwardly panicking, and hoping—for no good reason—that two lamebrains wouldn't repeat themselves a second day? Lucy didn't do this! In elementary school, she'd have figured out a way to expose them after the first pencil swipe.

Finally, on the third day, Lucy snapped Thomas Duke's pencil in half and yelled, "Will You Stop It?" Yes, this was in the middle of homeroom announcements, but who cared?

Apparently, Mr. Skoglund did. And now Lucy had to write an essay on why other people's property was "sacred." A bra-testing, #2 pencil *sacred*? Oh, give her a break! Worse, Mr. Skoglund explained slowly, as if Lucy were dense, that if a girl *ignored* Thomas and Ben, the behavior would stop. Right.

"I don't get junior high at all. Everyone acts so weird," said Lucy finally. She flipped her hip-length braids over her shoulder and frowned.

What was the *deal* with that place? The only time it had felt okay had been the first week, when all the sixth graders had experienced the newness together, like loose change jingling in the same pocket. They had all felt the looming presence of eighth-grade boys who filled doorways with lumbering frames, and they had openly gaped at older girls with bodies (and outfits) like Barbie, even down to their pointy-toed shoes. That first week, the sixth graders had complained to one another about extra homework, and how they got lost between classes. Everybody had talked to everybody.

But by the next week, the sixth graders had begun to sort themselves into groups, associating only with kids like themselves (popular, band, jock, brain). To Lucy, it made no sense. She had watched it happen—kids splitting and regrouping with all the forethought of single-cell amoebas. As soon as kids found their groups, they avoided Lucy. If the other sixth graders were like pocket change (dimes, pennies, nickels, quarters), then Lucy had always been more like a button, a foreign object. In elementary school, being unique was cool, but in junior high, kids needed a way to define you, or it was the kiss of death. During lunch, Lucy followed Zoë around, waiting to see where she sat. These days, Zoë sat with the oddball, artsy types

(Cape Guy, Quote Girl, the ribbon dancer, etc.). Zoë made things with her hands—knitting, sewing, origami, pastries—and she and this girl named Edna could talk stitches, techniques, and patterns all lunch period. To Lucy, it was like listening to irritating gibberish with just enough English to fool her into thinking she understood what she heard. But she wasn't complaining—at this point she guessed she was lucky to have a place to sit at all.

And the strangeness of junior high didn't stop there. No, as the weeks went on, the sixth graders had developed other signs of junior-high sickness. When teachers turned their back, notes about who liked who traveled palm to palm, and books with dog-eared pages describing people "doing it" were read under the lips of desks. In elementary school—only five months ago—everyone had acted normal. Now, after a summer and a couple of months in junior high, they were clichéd characters from a drippy teen movie!

The epicenter of all this activity was on the third floor, southeast corner of the school, where The Big Six had their lockers—Kendra, Brenda, Didi, Gillian, Chantel, and Eugenie (who everyone called the Genie).

There were advantages to junior high: Lucy *liked* having her own locker and locking it. Lucy *liked* being able to walk to different rooms for classes. (Who wants to sit in the same warm seat all day?)

Still, there seemed to be something off about the place,

or maybe contaminating the air, because even the adults working at the junior high (principal, secretary, janitor, counselor, lunch ladies, and teachers) exhibited telltale signs of junior-high infection. The adults, for some reason, seemed to think of students more in terms of hormones than potential. Potential was all any of the adults talked about in elementary school. Lucy had gotten sick of it back then, but the "potential" mantra sure beat the way some of the adults eyed them here—as if any second a chemical might detonate in their junior-high brains.

The one exception was Ms. Kortum, their social studies teacher. Ms. Kortum liked guesses and crazy ideas. Lucy wrote one of her papers from the perspective of a eucalyptus tree. "An unusual point of view, Lucy," said Ms. Kortum as she handed back her paper. Lucy turned it over and saw "A+ for creativity" written across the front.

Okay, here was a thought: what if her wishy-washy, please-go-away-Thomas-and-Ben squeamishness was a *symptom*? What if it was more than just the creepiness of junior high making Lucy feel unsteady?

But hormones were just chemicals, right? So if her reaction had been caused by a brain-chemical spill, like the Valdez oil spill off the coast of Alaska, there should be some sort of clean-up program to initiate. Maybe Lucy needed to eat some sort of rot-smelling vegetable, like Brussels sprouts. Lucy would ask her mom when she got home. She'd know.

Actually, it might not be a bad idea just to run it all by her mom—the freakiness of junior high, hormones, and most of all, why Lucy just didn't feel like herself anymore. Her mom would give her an honest opinion, without smirks or stupid jokes. That was what Lucy liked about her mom. She took Lucy's concerns seriously.

Suddenly, Zoë ran around in front of Lucy again and held out her arms to stop her. "Okay, if you're not going to fight, you could wear a training bra. Thomas Duke and Ben Furley aren't so bad to the 'yups.' That'll stop 'em."

Lucy moaned and pushed Zoë away. "I can't believe you said that. Why should I have to do anything for those morons? No, no, no! They're the ones that ought to be punished, not me." What was the women's movement for if a person had to wear a training bra in order to go to school in peace?

"Wearing a bra is *not* a punishment," said Zoë.

"I didn't mean you," said Lucy. "I meant I shouldn't have to wear one unless I want to wear one."

The truth was this (and Lucy didn't like to think about it): Zoë was now a "yup," but Lucy was still a "nope." Yes, Zoë wore a bra and had grown about three feet over the summer. So now, Zoë didn't fit into any of her clothes—the Tamarack Books sweatshirt, or the patched jeans, or the hiking boots. Over the summer, Zoë had started shopping at The Wild Thrift, the secondhand store in Turtle Rock. This explained today's purple feather boa.

Lucy, on the other hand, looked exactly like she'd looked in elementary school, still gazing out at the world from her four-foot, eight-inch height. Adults used to call them "two peas in a pod," but now they looked as unlikely as a giraffe chatting with a mouse. No one would even guess that they were both in sixth grade! Secretly, Lucy worried that Zoë wouldn't want to hang out with a puny prepubescent. (And by the way, Lucy hated the word "pubescent." Why was junior-high life filled with medical terminology?)

Zoë glanced at her. "I know you didn't mean me," she said.

Lucy smiled and, feeling guilty for her thoughts, conceded: "Well, wearing a training bra would probably work."

Zoë began to skip and spin down the sidewalk in a wild, limb-flinging dance, and her sweater spun out like a dress.

Lucy couldn't help smiling. "Man, that is a jumbo sweater."

"I know!" said Zoë. She twirled around a few times to watch it. "I knitted it big and grape!"

"Ha!" said Lucy.

Zoë stopped spinning and fell down in the grass. "You wanted to belt someone today," she said. "Admit it."

"I don't hit," said Lucy, imitating the voice their first-grade teacher had used whenever someone in class took a whack at another classmate. They both laughed.

"Anyway," Lucy continued, "I haven't slugged anyone since . . ."

"Since Mealymouth Mickelson kissed you in third grade," said Zoë, standing up and brushing herself off.

"Yeah," said Lucy, smiling. What was a little height difference when the two of them knew everything about each other?

A gust of cold wind interrupted this thought. Lucy tugged at her green-and-yellow hat and looked up. The sky spread out wet and gray, like fresh cement. Lucy remembered it was October 3rd and remembered the October 3rd wind, but she wasn't one for believing that a wind came every year—same time, same place—like clockwork.

A few snowflakes drifted from the sky.

"It's snowing!" Lucy said. She laughed and spun around in an imitation of Zoë.

"Maybe we'll have enough for sledding," said Zoë. She stared up at the sky. One snowflake followed another. "Do you want to go sledding on Wiggins Hill later? If there's enough snow?"

Lucy smiled widely, imagining pushing off on her wooden Flyer from the top of Wiggins Hill. But then she remembered something.

"I can't," said Lucy. She paused and then added, "I can't go sledding and I can't go to the bakery, either—Mom's leaving on a trip."

Most people in Turtle Rock knew that every year or so, Lucy's mom left Lucy and her dad for two weeks to a month to go on a photography trip. Sometimes Lucy's mom followed a whim and shot photos of grebes up on Lake of the Woods. Other times she had an assignment from an editor: when Lucy was in third grade, her mom went to Mexico; a year later, she hiked part of the Appalachian Trail. Between trips, Lucy's mom photographed Turtle Rock families in her downtown studio.

"Where's she going this time?" said Zoë.

"Everywhere," said Lucy. "She's going to take pictures of clouds all across the United States."

"There aren't enough clouds here?" said Zoë, gesturing at a sky packed tight with gray clouds steadily releasing snow.

Lucy smiled. "She says she wants to capture clouds over different landscapes. You know—mountains, ocean, prairie?"

Zoë sighed and shook her head. "I'm just saying . . ."

"*Your* mom is weirder," said Lucy, laughing.

"No use arguing that," said Zoë.

Lucy and Zoë said good-bye when they reached their houses at the end of Fifth Street. Zoë promised to call after she finished at the bakery.

But Lucy barely heard her. Lucy was too busy gawking at the state of their light-blue compact car, which was parked in the driveway of their little red house. A winter parka, flip-flops, CDs, darkroom equipment, and camera cases were smashed up against the car windows like stuff to be won in the quarter machine at the movie theater. A bag of chips and a sandwich sank sideways on a beach towel right under the hatchback.

"Mom?" Lucy called tentatively.

"Oh, Lucy," said her mom, banging out the screen door. She looked a little flushed and her eyes were bright. "Good! You're *finally* home. Stay here and see me off, okay?"

Before Lucy could answer, her mom snapped her fingers and dashed inside the house.

As Lucy waited, she noticed that the snow had already completely covered the lawn. It was really coming down! Her dad was clearing twigs on the yard's edges, his hat and coat covered in snow. Lucy knew what he was thinking— that you couldn't help Mom when she was like this. So Lucy dropped her backpack on the snowy ground, plopped on top of it, and waited. She twiddled one of her braids.

Meanwhile, Lucy's mom whizzed like a balloon freed from its knot, whirling around the car, tucking this in there, moving a box of lenses and filters over here, darkroom equipment in the center, sandwich up front. Car doors opened and shut; the hatchback went up and down with a heave and a clack and a sigh of relief.

"I've got enough equipment to make a mountain out of a molehill or turn cloudy skies blue," her mom said. She laughed giddily.

It was 5:10 P.M. The streetlamps blinked on. Snow streamed out of the sky. Lucy and her dad stood at the side of the car.

"Well," said her mom, grinning at both of them.

A particularly cold gust of wind skidded over Lucy's skin.

"I might as well see how far I can get tonight," she said slowly. She flashed a quick smile. "I'll call and write postcards, and then I'll be home in November." She glanced at her watch. "Oh, I've gotta hop to it!"

Her mom hugged Lucy and gave her a kiss. She lifted the yellow-and-green hat off Lucy's head and handed it to her. "Take the hat off sometimes, okay, Lucy?"

Then her mom planted a quick kiss on her dad's cheek.

Lucy thought the way her mom kissed her dad was a little odd, and not very nice, but when her mom got all happy like this, there was no telling what she'd do.

Still her dad smiled. "You have a good trip, Jo. I love you," he said.

"Yes," she said, glancing between them. "You know I love both of you very much."

Her mom said she would call when she reached Duluth.

Bach blasted from the stereo as the car turned right onto the road. Her mom said listening to Bach gave her the guts to try new things. Lucy hated the word "guts," because of roadkill.

A few moments later, the car disappeared from sight, and all that was left was a gassy cloud.

That was when Lucy realized that she hadn't asked her mom about junior high and hormones, and if she was becoming the wimp of the world.

Lucy kicked at the snow collecting in the gutter. It was rude to be that happy leaving, she thought. Her mom should at least *pretend* to be sad!

"How about pizza for dinner and a nine thirty bedtime?" said her dad, putting a hand on her back.

Bedtime? Good grief, thought Lucy. Couldn't he wait five seconds before laying down the rules? Still, Lucy nodded and picked her backpack up off the lawn.

But before she followed her dad inside the red house, Lucy took a last look at all the snow, and thought of sledding on Wiggins Hill. There was enough snow now, thought Lucy. Too bad Miss Wiggins was such a stickler about sledding past dark.

Then Lucy stepped inside, the screen door slamming behind her.

Not long after the Moons had said their good-byes, a champagne-colored Cadillac lurched backward and forward at the side of the road, its wheels spinning in fresh fallen snow. Finally, the car rolled back, jolting to a stop deep in the ditch. A long moment passed, and then the driver's side door opened. A small foot in a fur-trimmed boot appeared.

The chief executive officer of Wiggins Faucet—Miss Ilene Viola Wiggins—stepped out of the car, holding an alligator briefcase in one hand and her car keys in the other. For a minute, Miss Wiggins stood by the side of her stuck Cadillac without doing much of anything. She wiped at her eyes with the back of a gloved hand and nearly wiped her glasses off her face.

"Idiot driver!" she said as she hit the Cadillac's hood with a kid-gloved fist.

Then Miss Wiggins slammed the car door shut, locked it, and began trudging up, up, up the remaining blocks home.

Yes, Miss Ilene Viola Wiggins lived at the top of Wiggins Hill—the only good sledding hill in Turtle Rock—and she ran that hill just like she ran the town. Miss Wiggins didn't let kids use toboggans (snap your back) or slide past dark (decapitate someone). Sledders dreamed about that extra slide, when the air turned so blue that the whole world looked like it was underwater, and the only light came from the reflection of the dusk moon on the blue-white snow. Those blue-lit runs were crazy, out of control, rushing, rushing, with roots of trees, clumps of snake-grass, and gopher holes taking on different shapes.

When a bold someone finally tried one of their schemes, they found out that Miss Wiggins was a force unto her own. Their friends would quickly tell them that if they didn't stop sledding, Miss Wiggins might not pay for the new school auditorium, or the machine for the hospital that mapped out a person's insides. Or if they didn't get off the hill, that movie theater with "all-around sound" was a pipe dream. For those undeterred—and there were always a few every year—they would find out that Miss Wiggins could see through snowsuits and ski masks, and that she knew the names (and more important, the *stories*) of that person's parents, grandparents, and extended relations. Even five-year-olds who couldn't tie their own shoes got the hint: there was no messing with Miss Wiggins.

An hour after her car got stuck in the ditch, Miss Wiggins sat in her kitchen (still wearing her coat, water puddled around her boots), speaking to a police officer.

"It was Josephine Moon," she said. "You know who I'm talking about—the postmaster's wife." She cocked her head and crossed her arms. "Driving like a maniac. She forced me clear off the road."

"Are you sure, ma'am? Josephine Moon?"

"That woman turned and waved at me—while driving, I'd like to point out. Minnesota plates 1PHT0GRL."

The police officer nodded and wrote it down. "Certainly must've been upsetting."

Miss Wiggins snapped her head up to look him in the eye. "At sixty-eight, I'm beyond needing any psychological mumbo jumbo," she said, pointing a finger. "Just do your job."

"Yes, ma'am," said the officer, quickly stuffing his notebook in his pocket.

He was halfway out the door when he turned and said, "Ma'am? You've got some sledders on your hill—right near that big sugar maple. They might rip it up with those sleds."

"Sleds? It's October. . . . Oh, for heaven's sake. Well, arrest them."

"What?" said the police oficer.

"You heard me. Arrest them and charge them with trespassing," Miss Wiggins said.

"They're only kids . . . and this is the sledding hill."

"I don't care," said Miss Wiggins, reddening. "It's my hill. Those kids know not to be sledding past dark in an October snowstorm."

At eight thirty that same night, Lucy Moon put down her pen, straightened her hat, and read through her essay:

Why Thomas Duke's Bra-Testing #2
Pencil Is Sacred
by
Lucy Moon

It's hard to figure out why Thomas Duke's pencil is "sacred," but that's what you said to write about, so I am trying to do it.

"Sacred," according to the dictionary, means, "set apart for worship," or "dedicated to a single use," or "worthy of reverence and respect." You probably didn't mean the first two meanings, because in the first case, no one wants to worship Thomas Duke's tooth-dented pencil. And in the second case ("dedicated to a single use"), if Thomas had only used his pencil for schoolwork, I wouldn't be writing this now. I am not kidding when I tell you that Thomas used his pencil for a second purpose—the daily bra-check.

So now, all I've got is the third meaning: "worthy of reverence and respect." But I'm having trouble feeling reverent about Thomas Duke's pencil—even if he didn't sit there and run it up and down my back, hoping for a bra bump day after day after day. (I don't even respect <u>my</u> favorite pencil, and that pencil is made from recycled Christmas trees!)

But let's say Thomas kept his pencil to himself: I agree that he would have had a right to use his pencil as long as he wanted, without me breaking it. I agree with that.

Here's what I think is sacred: justice, fairness, friendship, loyalty, truthfulness, and a place to live and learn without bullies. Mr. Skoglund, why should I have to wear a training bra just to sit through homeroom in peace? (Though, even a training bra might not stop Thomas and Ben completely.)

I know you're going to make me write this essay again, but at least I told the truth.

Lucy grinned. Mr. Skoglund probably didn't mean that the pencil was really "sacred," but he *had* said it, and anyway, it was a lot more interesting to write about. Clearly, Lucy had some fight left in her! Maybe it just took a little impetus, like a bra-check, for Lucy to start acting like herself in a brand-new school.

"Ha!" Lucy said, putting the paper down.

She pulled off her hat, rolled the brim, and listened to the snow outside. The snow fell in sheets—*shh, shh, shh.* This time of night, Lucy's mom was usually clanking around in the kitchen, cleaning. She'd be singing along to the music Ken and Julie played on WBRR, North Country Radio. But tonight, Lucy heard only the groans of her dad's lounger. If Lucy listened hard enough, she might hear the page of a magazine turn!

The blue walkie-talkie on Lucy's bedside table jingled.

"Lucy? Are you there? Lucy? " A grainy-sounding voice came through the speaker. A bit of static followed, and then silence.

Lucy grabbed the walkie-talkie.

"Hey," she said. Lucy got up off her bed and looked out her window. Light streamed out of the diamond-shaped window of the yellow house next door. Zoë stepped into the window and waved.

Lucy waved back.

"Sooooooo," said Zoë, stretching out the word, "sledding tomorrow?"

"We've got *tons* of snow," said Lucy.

"Early?"

"Of course."

"Over and out."

CHAPTER 2

It was either very late or very early when moonlight finally filtered through a parting in the storm clouds. Around this time, the walkie-talkie on Lucy Moon's bedside table jingled.

A bit of static followed and then, "Lucy? Lucy? Aren't you up yet?"

Lucy snorted and rolled over.

When she finally opened her eyes, the walkie-talkie voice was going on about a cave collapse: "Fifteen minutes of air left. Aaron glanced at his spelunking companions. Sheila gingerly touched an ankle that would later prove broken. Bill, farther back, breathed with difficulty— four broken ribs . . ."

Was it that late? When Zoë used the walkie-talkie to wake Lucy, she usually started with talk, moved to hypnosis, sang camp songs ("The Lonely Loon Wails for You" was a Zoë classic), and *then* started reading from her "Saved from Certain Death" books. Lucy glanced at her alarm clock. 5:30 A.M. 5:30 *A.M.*?

Lucy sat up and pressed the button on her blue walkie-talkie: "How did they know there was only fifteen minutes of air?"

She let go of the button and sank back into her pillow, rolled over, and closed her eyes.

"Is that you?" came the voice on the walkie-talkie. "I've been reading to you for ten whole minutes! Do you want to be first on the hill or not?"

After thirty minutes of hard slogging through drifting snow, Lucy and Zoë stared up at Wiggins Hill and knew they weren't the first sledders. Piles of fresh snow lay on the hill, but underneath the new snow an experienced eye could see trails left by sleds and divots made by boots from the night before.

Still, it would be one of the first runs of the year, and they'd settle for that. This was Wiggins Hill, after all. Tough Minnesota grass bent over by the snow waited for a chance to pop up like whips. Land a trip into the blackberry brambles lining the hill's edges, and a nylon jacket came out looking like confetti. But the hands down best danger during first-of-the-year runs was the giant sugar maple in the center of the hill. It stood its ground, thick as a small silo, its limbs cross-hatching the sky, and its roots lacing that hill like a boot. Early in the season those roots surfaced unexpectedly, and a sledder hitting one sailed on a trip they weren't likely to forget anytime soon.

And since it was morning, Miss Wiggins wasn't likely to bother them at all.

Zoë kicked Lucy on the behind and took off running up the hill. Lucy chased her. Pretty soon they were sledding. Lucy and Zoë flung themselves down Wiggins Hill for more than three hours that morning. They sledded backward, forward, belly-up, belly-down, and cross-legged. They surfed, they water-skied, and they tried horseback-riding tricks they'd seen at the circus. They made snow ramps to jump their sleds. They exaggerated their falls: jumping, rolling, somersaulting, and then playing dead. At the bottom of the hill, they lifted their bodies from the snow, raised their arms in triumph, and tromped back to the top to do it again.

It was later that morning—while Lucy and Zoë sat in their long underwear in the Rossignol kitchen, eating day-old pastries and rehashing the morning's near-death, Wiggins Hill experiences—when the phone rang. Zoë picked it up and then signaled to Lucy to get on the other line. It was Edna—Zoë's make-it-by-hand friend from the cafeteria. Had they heard the news? Last night two junior-high students were arrested for sledding on Wiggins Hill.

What? Lucy's heart raced. She asked Edna who had been arrested. Edna said she didn't know.

Lucy and Zoë hung up, unable to believe what they'd heard. People did not get *arrested* for sledding! Then they began to call one person after another—anyone who they thought might know something—to find out more.

Lucy and Zoë weren't the only ones phoning that morning. As the midday sun melted the snow, word of the arrested sledders seeped out. The news trickled through Turtle Rock on phone lines not downed by the storm, over neighborhood fences and coffee cups. Junior-high students awakened by the ringing found parents whispering into the phone, covering the receiver with their hands so the story wouldn't escape (though spoken word has a tendency to slide up air ducts, underneath doors, and between cupped fingers, finding waiting listeners). By midafternoon, when thoughts had strayed to the Saturday Afternoon Special (fresh double chocolate–chunk cookies) at the Rossignol Bakery, nearly everyone in Turtle Rock knew that two unidentified students had been arrested, and every kid found themselves sternly told that they were *not* to go sledding on Wiggins Hill.

In the end, it seemed no one quite believed that the police had done this on their own initiative. People had sledded on Wiggins Hill for as long as anyone could remember without getting arrested! So everyone came to the same conclusion: if it had happened at all, Miss Wiggins had a hand in it.

For a lot of folks, the rumor was enough, satisfying in itself. But for Lucy and Zoë it wasn't. Lucy, in particular, felt an outrage that stirred her deeply, at the DNA level, and boy, did that feel good. Her anger at the daily bra-check had felt like a start of something, but this? Lucy welcomed the feeling like an old, old friend.

Now Lucy turned to Zoë, who stood next to her flipping through the phone book. "We've got to do something!" said Lucy.

Zoë snapped the phone book closed and grinned. "Lucy Moon is back."

As they walked downtown that afternoon, they discussed all the possibilities, went back and forth, and forth and back, and came to one conclusion: they'd wait until the *Turtle Rock Times* came out on Thursday and see what it had to say about the incident. That might help them decide what needed to be done.

Lucy did think about what it might mean socially if she organized a protest at the new school, but she brushed the thought aside. Anyway, if everyone wanted a definition of who she was, well, at least she'd be providing it.

That week, Lucy found herself waiting not only for the *Turtle Rock Times*, but also for a chance to teach Thomas Duke and Ben Furley a lesson. Nothing seemed to have happened with the "Why Thomas Duke's Bra-Testing #2 Pencil Is Sacred" essay. At the very least, Lucy expected Mr. Skoglund to ask her to write it over, but instead he remained silent. Meanwhile, Thomas Duke and Ben Furley continued their extracurricular pencil activities.

Lucy spied her chance as she and Zoë were making their way to English class. Thomas Duke and Ben Furley were leaning against their lockers, rating the passing girls. Lucy met Thomas Duke's glance, and he held up two fingers. He leaned toward Ben Furley and whispered something. Ben Furley's eyes zipped up and down Zoë's body and he held up seven fingers.

"Did you see that?" said Zoë. "Yuck!" Zoë stuck her tongue out at them.

Then Lucy saw an opportunity in the hallway ahead, and everything fell into place. Yes! Lucy made a U-turn and walked up to Thomas and Ben. "I dare you to bra-check the new girl." She nodded in the direction of a petite, black-haired girl who was having an animated discussion with another student.

"You dare me?" said Thomas Duke.

"I double dare you," Lucy said.

Thomas Duke looked at the girl's thin back, and smiled slightly at Lucy.

"Bra-check!" yelled Ben Furley, and, pencils out, the two of them strolled over to the girl and dragged their pencils up her back.

"Yup," said Thomas Duke.

"A genuine bra-wearer," said Ben Furley. "Yes-siree-bob."

And that's when "the new girl" turned around. It was the eighth-grade accelerated math teacher who came in on Tuesdays from the high school. Though small, she competed in triathlons, and at one time was the All-State Swimming Champion. She grabbed Thomas Duke and Ben Furley by the ears and dragged them into Principal Adams's office.

"By the *ears*," said Lucy, clapping her hands to her mouth.

"I can't believe anyone really does that," said Zoë. "It's so Dickensian."

Then they looked at each other and laughed until they cried.

CHAPTER 3

The *Turtle Rock Times* was published only once a week, and it hit the newspaper stands and the front steps (and hedges) of houses every Thursday. On Thursday, October 9th, the headline blared "THE BLIZZARD ISSUE—28 INCHES!" (Some people thought that it was overstating the case by calling twenty-eight inches of fluffy snow a blizzard.) Folks had been stranded in their cars on the highway—a lesson to all who did not have kitty litter, candles, canned soup, bars of chocolate, and old sleeping bags stowed in trunks. Pastor Leeson's column told how a family found hope that stormy night by singing "Warmed by the Spirit's Holy Fire." There were articles about the old north section of Turtle Rock losing power: how Miss Eneborg of Ives Lane nearly lost all of her venison rump roast until she realized that it *was* snow, so why not just stick the rump out in God's snowy handiwork? The *Times* even interviewed Clare, of Clare's Meats & Foodstuffs. "I had to post a sign, 'Leave snowshoes outside,' if you can believe it."

Ken, of the *Ken and Julie Show* on North Country Radio, WBRR, declared the *Turtle Rock Times*'s blizzard news "old and moldy."

"The snow is almost gone!" moaned Ken. "You betcha, I've moved on—I'm a man of the future."

Julie snorted and said slyly: "Okay, listening audience, check out the man-of-the-future's playlist: up next, the Whistling Bulgarian puffing his way through 'Greensleeves.'"

After school that Thursday, Lucy Moon and Zoë Rossignol walked into the Rossignol Bakery. Zoë headed to the back to make piecrusts—Mrs. Rossignol swore that no one made crusts as tender as Zoë's—and Lucy hurried through her bakery chores, sponging down the front tables, refilling the sugar packets and the napkins, and today, grating fresh ginger. Then Lucy shook off her duck shoes, settled on the big red couch, and began to read the *Turtle Rock Times.*

After reading the paper three or four times, front to back, back to front, Lucy tossed it on the coffee table and crossed her arms.

The story of the arrested sledders wasn't there.

What was a *news*paper if it didn't report the *news*?

Zoë plopped down next to Lucy on the red couch.

"What did the *Times* say?" she said.

"Nothing," said Lucy.

"No!"

Lucy picked up the newspaper and tossed it to Zoë. "You see if you can find it. I've read everything. Did you know that the junior high is fund-raising for a new school gymnasium and erecting a 'Fill the Pencil with Lead' sign to keep track of the money? Did you know that our third-grade teacher is selling a fortune-telling moose at his garage sale, or that there's a talk about 'The Twelve Secret Wives of Shakespeare' at the VFW? I do. Look, my skin is tarred with newsprint!" She spread her ink-covered fingers in front of Zoë's face.

They sat silently for a second, Lucy frowning as she stared off into space, and Zoë paging through the newspaper.

Then Lucy raised an eyebrow. "You know what it is?"

Zoë glanced up and, seeing the look on Lucy's face, grinned.

"It's a . . ." began Lucy. Zoë and Lucy said the words together, ". . . cover-up."

Zoë clapped her hands. "What are we going to do?" she said.

"Something . . ." said Lucy, rubbing her hands together, ". . . communicative."

Zoë gave her a high five.

The two of them grabbed their stuff and got going. "Piecrusts are in the walk-in, Mama!" Zoë yelled on the way out, the doorbell dinging behind them.

Since the *Turtle Rock Times* had decided *not* to reveal the story, Lucy and Zoë decided to tell it themselves. They would interview the arrested sledders.

The only trouble was that no one seemed to know exactly who had been arrested. At school, rumors and wild stories spread like weeds: twelve names were bandied about as possibilities, and three of those named actually claimed the honor. These boasters told stories about how they beat back a police officer with sleds and snowballs, how they tried to escape by driving off in the police car, how they spent the night in a Turtle Rock jail cell jam-packed with murderers, arsonists, spies, and counterfeiters, and how they heard their parents begging the police to spare their "dear children" an adolescence of sewing vinyl wallets at the juvenile prison.

Lucy and Zoë heard these stories and laughed. "As if," said Lucy. They decided to find the sledders' identities by employing a more methodical approach.

Since they were both serious sledders, Lucy and Zoë knew the Wiggins Hill regulars. So one by one they eliminated each possibility. Then they spotted Lisa Alt arriving at school with her shoulders up near her ears, shivering.

She carried her coat balled up in her arms, and no won-der—this was a granny coat with a wide fur collar and enormous plaid buttons. Worse, the coat was the color of . . . ? Well, the only descriptor coming to Lucy's mind was "puppet flesh." They watched Lisa hurriedly stuff the coat into her locker.

Lucy frowned. "Where's that brand-new, powder-blue ski jacket?"

"That's what I was thinking," said Zoë.

It didn't take long for them to realize that the new ski jacket—the one Lisa had been showing off at the start of school—had disappeared around the time of the snow-storm. And now that they thought of it, wasn't it odd that Lisa didn't seem to be talking about the loss of her jacket or about the arresting of sledders on Wiggins Hill?

If Lisa Alt was involved, Sam Shipman was too. The two of them always sledded together.

After an hour of serious cajoling, Lisa and Sam admit-ted it—they were the arrested sledders. But both of their parents had threatened to punish them if they talked, emphasizing how Miss Wiggins did not need to be both-ered with this. (Lisa's mother had added: "We certainly don't need our name brought to Miss Wiggins's atten-tion.") Lisa and Sam both thought their parents were acting strangely, but seeing how serious their parents were, they'd kept quiet about the whole situation.

"You weren't arrested?" said Lucy, confused.

"Not technically," said Sam, "but close enough!"

Then Lisa and Sam glanced at each other, and shut up.
Lucy began to lose all hope for an interview.

But Zoë worked a minor miracle: she sold Lisa and Sam
on the idea of an interview by explaining that if they did
it, the story of the arrested sledders would die down, and
it wouldn't be so hard to keep quiet. Lucy quickly added
that no names would be used and that the story would
only be circulated among junior-high students. "I promise,
your parents will never find out," Lucy told them both.
Finally, Lisa and Sam agreed.

After school on Friday, Lucy conducted the interview
in the basement of Lisa Alt's house. This is the story Lucy
heard (and saw in her mind's eye):

*As usual, Lisa and Sam fought about sleds while they
trudged up Wiggins Hill on Friday, October 3rd. The
wrong sled ruined—utterly ruined—a good run. This
they agreed upon. But the problem was that each of them,
according to the other, owned the wrong sled. According
to Sam, Lisa's plastic saucer spun out of control and had no
padding. (Padding was essential because of all those roots
on Wiggins Hill.) But according to Lisa, Sam's inner tube
was too bouncy, and impossible to grip. She called it an
"overblown butt pad," because it looked a lot like what her
grandmother had to sit on after a doctor removed her
hemorrhoids. At this, Sam turned red and walked faster.*

But as was often the case on Wiggins Hill, within a half an hour of sledding, all arguments were forgotten.

Time passed. Snow fell harder and harder. Sam and Lisa dimly registered that the streetlamp had flickered on, illuminating the snow pink and blue. Lisa and Sam sledded and sledded and sledded and sledded.

When the police car came, Sam was standing at the sugar maple, waiting for Lisa to push off from the top. Through the falling snowflakes, Sam saw the spinning lights as the car pulled up to the side of the hill. The red of brake lights flashed. Then the car door opened and a police officer got out. He slammed the door shut and walked toward the hill.

Sam pulled the inner tube close to his body and stood tight against the sugar maple, hidden by its thickness.

That was when Lisa came over the edge of the hill on that orange saucer sled, bright enough for deer hunting season.

Oh, no, Sam thought. Right toward the police officer!

As discreetly as he could, he tried to wave her down and get her to stop. But Lisa didn't see him, it seemed. He even tried sending psychic messages: POLICE! POLICE! STOP! HIDE!

He was screaming (in his mind), but it did no good. Lisa was screaming for real—a happy yell, a yodeling— the usual sound of someone traveling down Wiggins Hill at breakneck speed. It was just inappropriate now.

INAPPROPRIATE! Sam yelled in his head. *(It was the first time he had used the word, and later he reflected that maybe "inappropriate" had too many syllables to be a good psychic message.)*

Sam saw the police officer moving toward the place Lisa's orange saucer would eventually land.

"Liiiiiiisssssaaaaa!" yelled Sam, abandoning his inner tube and hiding place. He ran, tripping on the snow and grasses.

Lisa turned to look for him, and that's when one of those maple roots got her. The saucer banked and she soared into the air, a powder-blue alien wrangling an orange saucer.

Lisa went up high, higher, and higher still, and Sam knew he was seeing something legendary, especially when, suddenly, Lisa . . . stuck.

The saucer banked and whirled off, riderless, down the rest of the hill.

For a moment, it seemed the whole hill stood still. The snow came down in sheets, and Sam heard the wind rattle the limbs of the maple above him.

And Lisa hung on a stout maple branch, like a great blue fruit.

It was her brand-new, powder-blue ski jacket that kept her suspended in midair. This was the jacket—the jacket that was supposed to hold new ski lift tags when she got her first downhill lessons at Blizzard Bluff.

Now the new jacket groaned under the strain of holding Lisa four feet above the ground.

Sam was at Lisa's dangling feet in an instant. So was the police officer.

The jacket gave a final tearing sound, and Lisa was caught in the man's arms.

"My jacket!" Lisa cried.

"You're lucky that tree didn't take your head off," the police officer said, putting her down. "You okay?"

Lisa gazed up into the tree. The collar of her new jacket now hung twelve feet in the air, impaled on a branch. "Oh," she said, touching the frayed fabric around her neck. "My mom is going to kill me."

Then another thought occurred to her.

"What did that look like?" she asked Sam.

But the officer didn't let them continue.

"Excuse me, guys," he said, "but I've got to take the two of you down to the station."

This stopped Lisa and Sam cold.

Sam was about to ask if they were under arrest or something, but then all three of them heard a noise—a scream from somewhere at the top of the hill.

This wasn't a scream of pain or of surprise—no, this scream sounded wild, half out of its mind.

"Move," said the police officer, grabbing Lisa and Sam by the shoulders and pulling them closer to the trunk of the sugar maple.

And out of the white came the front of a sled—round, wooden, shined, made of boards turned up in a curl. They saw the soles of snow boots sticking out to either side. . . .

It was a toboggan with a single rider.

Several years ago, a Turtle Rock Times headline declared, "TOBOGGANS KILL!" The headline ran through Sam's and Lisa's minds, along with the accompanying illustration of seven skeletons riding a toboggan into the fiery pits of H-E-double-hockey-sticks.

Dressed in black (black snowmobile suit, black leather gloves, and a black knit ski mask), it seemed that this rider had rocketed straight from those fiery pits. The only detail that didn't suggest "demented" was the purple tie on the neat black ponytail trailing from the nape of the rider's neck.

But this seemed a small point. Lisa and Sam gaped in awe.

The toboggan skidded around the sugar maple and swooshed to the bottom of the hill, up the culvert, and over the road, before disappearing from sight.

"Come on," said the police officer. Sam and Lisa found themselves trying to sprint down the hill after him.

Within minutes, they had hauled their sleds into the trunk of the police car, climbed into the backseat, and were on the chase of the toboggan. The car fishtailed onto the street, went around the block, and ended up at a lilac *bush—Tom Berg's prize lilac bush, the one shipped from France. It had a toboggan-sized hole in it.*

The toboggan and rider were gone.

Sam and Lisa found themselves thinking about one thing—how to get themselves a toboggan.

Lucy typed up the interview on a library computer and then gave it to Zoë, who worked on the design on the Rossignol Bakery's back-office computer. Late in the afternoon, Zoë handed Lucy a copy. *"Voilà,"* she said.

It looked just like the *Turtle Rock Times*: the headline, *The Turtle Rock Times Shuts Its Eyes,* was in a font similar to the newspaper's. There was even the same image of a sawmill in the upper right-hand corner. The weather report was there: "Friday, October 3rd, Wiggins Hill, SNOWSTORM—28 inches of the white stuff!"

Lucy smiled as she read through the interview, finally reaching the last bit of the story:

INTERVIEWER: So what happened down at the station?

BOY SLEDDER: We sat in a kind of waiting room while the police officer called our parents. Then she *(he points at the girl sledder)* told the officer at the front desk that she needed to be locked up.

GIRL SLEDDER: I got locked up!

BOY SLEDDER: She begged to get locked up.

GIRL SLEDDER: And this other police officer in the back

hears me begging and he takes us to a cell and puts us in it.

BOY SLEDDER: He won't lock the door, though, because he says the cell is not a toy.

GIRL SLEDDER: And I take the top bunk and he takes the bottom.

BOY SLEDDER: I wanted the top bunk.

GIRL SLEDDER: The toilet was indecent—you had to do it in front of everybody. It was just sitting there. We didn't have anything to bang on the cell bars with—that was kind of irritating, but we yelled, "We want out! We're innocent!"

BOY SLEDDER: We want OUT! Innocent! Innocent! Innocent! *(Both sledders get up and demonstrate. They are jumping around, waving their arms.)*

BOY SLEDDER: And then the other police officers come by and they bring orange sodas and cookies and weird snacks, like soy nuts. They tell us stories about who was in the cell that we were in. There was even a ghost in that cell once. . . .

INTERVIEWER: Really?

BOY SLEDDER: Yeah, the ghost wanted the bottom bunk. In the morning, the prisoner woke up on the top bunk.

GIRL SLEDDER: That is such a lie.

BOY SLEDDER: Truth—he said it was the truth.

GIRL SLEDDER: Lie.

INTERVIEWER (interrupting): And then what happened?

GIRL SLEDDER: The officer who arrested us came in and got mad at the guy who put us in jail. Anyway, our parents picked us up. They weren't very happy. My mom practically screamed when she saw my new coat.

As she read, Lucy felt her happiness spark and then roar into a bonfire.

"Yes!" yelled Lucy, holding the paper in the air. "You've totally outdone yourself with the design, Zoë. This rocks. The truth will not be ignored!"

CHAPTER 4

School Bus 260—the one that took the Country Road D loop around Turtle Rock Lake—arrived first at the junior high that Monday. It wheezed to a stop beside two girls (one with braids down to her hips) who stood on the sidewalk. "Arrested sledders!" Lucy Moon held a flyer above her head as she yelled at the students getting off the bus. "Arrested sledders!"

"*The Turtle Rock Times Shuts Its Eyes*. . . . Read about what happened to two of our own on Wiggins Hill!" Zoë Rossignol said loudly, a few feet behind Lucy. Of course Zoë was with Lucy—they'd been inseparable for as long as anyone could remember. Zoë's smile suggested that nothing was more amusing than watching reactions to the two of them.

The sixth graders pushed past Lucy Moon. The curious

ones pinched a copy from the pile stacked next to Zoë. Most of the seventh and eighth graders pretended that they couldn't be bothered. Yet, one or two stopped in front of Lucy, glared down at her tiny, birdlike frame, and held out their hand. Lucy met their gaze and handed them a copy. As they headed inside, kids huddled around single copies. That was when some of them circled back to get their own.

By the time the fourth school bus came to school that day, Lucy Moon and Zoë Rossignol had run out of copies of *The Turtle Rock Times Shuts Its Eyes.*

All morning, Lucy saw *The Turtle Rock Times Shuts Its Eyes* in back pockets, folded into books, or passed hand to hand in the hallways. The copies appeared and disappeared like light from fireflies. Lucy breathed deeply. Even the air tasted sweet!

The *Turtle Rock Times* had ignored the story, but she, Lucy Moon, had stepped in and filled the gap. Yes!

In the cafeteria, Lucy found Zoë sitting with the odd-balls (as Lucy had come to think of them). Lucy swung her sack lunch onto the table and plunked down next to Zoë.

Edna leaned back and said, "Everyone is reading *The Turtle Rock Times Shuts Its Eyes.* Everyone—even the seventh and eighth graders."

Quote Girl interrupted them: " 'Her joy with heaved-up

hand she doth express. And, wordless, so greets heaven for her success.'"

It seemed a sort of pronouncement.

When Quote Girl raised an eyebrow at her, Lucy forced a smile.

"It's Shakespeare," Quote Girl filled in. Then she picked up her fork and began to separate *some* Tater Tots from *other* Tater Tots.

Lucy glanced at Zoë, who shrugged, amused.

A moment later, someone else told Lucy she wasn't a bad writer; Edna began to ask more questions; Cape Guy gave her a thumbs-up; and another kid patted the top of her hat on the way to his table.

Obviously, her status had gone from nonexistent to somebody, and Lucy couldn't help herself—she started grinning like an ape. For once, Zoë ate in silence.

After lunch, when she and Zoë were alone in the hallway, Lucy said, "I did it, Zoë. I can't believe it. I did it! I did it!"

For a moment Zoë frowned at Lucy. But then Zoë's face broke into a tiny smile. It was the kind of smile a parent gives a small child, though Lucy barely noticed because zings of happiness were Rollerblading up and down her spine.

When Lucy took off skipping, she heard Zoë's laugh echoing in the hallway behind her.

* * *

By the time the cafeteria workers had finished serving up roast beef, Tater Tots, and cheesy green beans, *The Turtle Rock Times Shuts Its Eyes* was all anyone was talking about—very few of those flyers ended up in the recycle bin.

And so, like dandelion seeds in a good wind, those pieces of paper strayed far beyond the junior high. One even found its way to Miss Ilene Viola Wiggins.

CHAPTER 5

Lucy Moon actually became popular! And Lucy stared into popularity's headlights like a deer at dusk on a country road. She gloried in the mind-numbing dazzle; a mantra skipping through her head: *I did it! I did it! I did it!* Lucy's mouth muscles ached from all the smiling— entire *days* of smiling. A few kids actually sought her opinion, and Lucy gave it freely and generously. It made her feel like someone out of a novel: an aristocrat tossing gold coins into a crowd of peasants. It was delicious.

But then, a few days into popularity, Lucy passed Thomas Duke and Ben Furley in the hallway. Thomas and Ben eyed her up and down and flashed a rating of six out of ten, instead of the usual two or three. Lucy felt a surge of pleasure. She thought, I'm up three points! Wasn't Zoë a seven?

That was a shock. The blinders fell off Lucy's eyes, and she saw what an absolute dolt she had become. Was this what she wanted deep down—to be popular?

Of course not, Lucy told herself, stopping abruptly in the middle of the hall, so that a girl with a stack of library books nearly slammed into her. "Watch it!" the girl said. Lucy ignored her and continued thinking: Lucy wanted the truth set free. This was the story of kids getting arrested for sledding on Wiggins Hill!

Then she admitted more: okay, yes, she had harbored the idea that putting out the flyer would force kids to make up their minds about her. But she had honestly thought she was kissing her chances of a junior-high social life good-bye.

Yet, instead, she had stirred the populace. She was *good* at this. This was what adults meant when they called kids "talented," or "gifted," right?

Lucy had never thought about it this way. In elementary school, Lucy's need to take action had been something she did impulsively, almost a gut instinct. She did it in order to release the pressure that injustice created inside her. Still, maybe it was more than that. . . .

But the bell rang and interrupted her thoughts. Lucy dashed up the stairs, late for class.

Lucy's popularity lasted nine school days, and when it was gone, Lucy found herself relieved—though she had to admit life in junior high had gotten a bit better. She had gained some respect—kids acknowledged her existence, and Lucy didn't end up the butt of jokes, or as a living, breathing morality lesson. (Let this True Loser be an Example to Ye!) The oddballs accepted Lucy on her own terms (and not just as a friend of Zoë's), so Lucy had people to talk to during lunch. And whenever kids wanted to talk about Wiggins Hill, they came to Lucy.

Lucy would have thought these changes perfectly rosy, but around this time, there were some bumps in her friendships. Zoë, for instance, was becoming more and more impatient with the Wiggins Hill talk. She'd tap her foot and grab Lucy by the shirt and say things like, "We're late, come on," when they weren't late at all. Finally, Zoë blurted: "I wish they'd remember that I had something to do with that flyer, too." Then she looked at Lucy. "You don't remember it either, you know. It doesn't help." Lucy tried to protest that Zoë had it all wrong, but by that time Zoë was down the hall, and anyway (though Lucy felt ashamed to admit it), she knew Zoë was right. Lucy saw the truth flash like a bit of metal at the bottom of a creek: deep down, Lucy wanted every bit of the attention for herself. It wasn't as though she denied Zoë's role if it came up—Lucy simply didn't mention it.

Lucy thought in her defense: well, why couldn't Zoë let her have all the attention? Was that too much to ask? Had she been blind when everyone was ignoring her? It seemed pretty clear that Zoë couldn't take it when Lucy got more popular. Maybe Zoë didn't care about Lucy's welfare.

No, Lucy thought. It wasn't true! Zoë was her best friend—The End. Lucy apologized.

Then there was Sam Shipman and Lisa Alt.

Lucy had been genuinely surprised when adults found out about *The Turtle Rock Times Shuts Its Eyes*. Her stomach rolled like a log the first time she overheard the true story of the arrested sledders told by an adult drinking tea at the Rossignol Bakery. Soon after this, Lucy heard adults talking about the arrested sledders at the gas station, and twice in Clare's Meats & Foodstuffs. Once she heard an adult actually say, "My kid brought this flyer home from school called *The Turtle Rock Times Shuts Its Eyes*. . . ."

Lucy hoped that Lisa Alt and Sam Shipman's parents hadn't seen the flyer, but one day Lisa came to school looking glum and told Lucy that her mom and dad had found out and grounded her for a month. "They said it didn't matter that my name wasn't on it; by the details, it's obvious that it's us—which is true because everybody at school figured it out. . . ." Lisa must have seen the look on Lucy's face, because she added, "It's okay. I don't care. I mean, who wants to be quiet about getting stuck in that tree on Wiggins Hill?

"Anyway, I guess I'm lucky," she said. "Sam got it worse. He's grounded, and his dad won't take him deer hunting. His dad told him that a kid unable to follow orders shouldn't be out in the woods with a rifle."

That explained the frost Lucy felt from Sam. They'd talked a lot lately, and the more Lucy talked to him, the more she liked how his smile seemed to burst upon his face like a firecracker. But then suddenly he went cold, avoided her. Lucy swore he glared at her in the hallways. Now, finally, she understood what was going on. He could have told her! If she'd known, she wouldn't have tried to get his attention by throwing spitballs in social studies, causing Ms. Kortum to assign one hundred lines of "I will not throw spitballs in class," due tomorrow. Sam had smiled at her then; Lucy glared in return. And the whole thing was over *deer hunting*? Like he was missing something by being stopped from killing a graceful, sentient creature? Lucy filed the friendship under "good riddance."

And so, Lucy was glad that November had come so she could shift her focus in another direction: "Killing Season," more commonly known as "Deer Hunting Season."

Lucy shared her dislike of deer hunting with a small chunk of the Turtle Rock population, including city folks (who didn't have a family tradition of hunting) and schoolteachers (who hated how their classes emptied out in November, causing endless paperwork of makeup assignments and tests). However, most people who did not care for the sport simply tried to ignore it. That's how a person got along with others nicely, without too much fuss. But Lucy rarely felt she could let the season go by without something to counter the blaze-orange celebration. One year, she and Zoë secretly stuffed the Rossignol Bakery's hunters' boxed lunches with flyers, hidden under the napkin, describing the last moments—millisecond by hideous millisecond—of a deer's death. (They were so successful in making chicken and tuna fish croissants unappetizing that Lucy and Zoë were forever banned from touching the hunters' boxed lunches.)

This year, though, Lucy and Zoë were going simple. They tied bloodred bandannas around their necks. The bandannas would stay on until the season closed (exceptions: showers and sleep). Anyone asking about the bandanna would get an earful of deer-hunting "facts and massacres."

This year, Quote and Edna joined them. Of course, Quote didn't say anything she was supposed to say. Asked about her red bandanna, Quote settled on an ominous: "'For murder, though it have no tongue, will speak.'" She'd pause and add, "It's from *Hamlet*."

After about a week of this, Lucy couldn't stand it anymore. "Why can't you just do it right?" she pleaded.

"It's Shakespeare," said Quote, as if that explained things. "When *your* words have lasted hundreds of years, I'll use them, okay? But since you can't appreciate my contribution, I'm done." Quote took off the bandanna and dropped it at Lucy's feet, adding: "'The smallest worm will turn being trodden on.'" Then she pivoted on her tiny, pointy shoes and strode away. Quote, Lucy decided, had style.

And with this, Lucy and Zoë's life at the junior high settled into a comfortable rhythm: they ate lunch with the oddballs. They walked down to the Rossignol Bakery together after school. They wished it would snow again so they could go sledding. And they told each other everything. (Or almost everything.)

As for Lucy's life at home, well, that had changed. Lucy could not figure out why, but every time her mom left on a trip, the silence of their little red house seemed to sneak up and surprise her. After returning from the Rossignol Bakery in the early evening, Lucy would see their red house a block away, and swear she could smell simmering onions and hear the chop, chop, chop of her mom's knife as she made dinner. When her mom was home, Lucy would barrel through the front door, pull a kitchen stool up to the counter, and talk and talk and talk. But with her mom gone, Lucy opened the front door and heard nothing, except the rattle of the refrigerator. Lucy felt a pang of missing her mom. It had gone away quickly enough at the beginning, but it had begun to grow stronger as her mom's trip extended into November. (The month she said she'd be home!)

Lucy checked the mail pail every afternoon. Every three or four days, Lucy would find a postcard or a letter from her mom. Her mom also phoned two or three times a week. Lucy wished her mom would get a cell phone so they could call her, but her mom didn't like to be interrupted. She said cell phones "impinged on her creative space."

So Lucy was left with her dad, which was kind of like being left with a relative seen only on major holidays, maybe like an uncle who is an officer in the army and is used to a little authority. Lucy's dad worked as the postmaster at the Turtle Rock post office, and he stood six-foot-ten with a barrel chest. When he was angry (which was not often), his voice shook the house down to its foundations.

But the worst was this: as soon as Lucy's mom left on her trips, Lucy's dad doled out rules for Lucy to follow. The nine thirty bedtime was only a start. He had rules about phone calls, the radio, TV, and the stove. Shoes, boots, coats, and backpacks were not to be left "lying around" downstairs. At the dinner table, Lucy needed to say "please pass . . ." and "thank you" after her dad handed over the dish. He expected Lucy to keep an eye on the garbage cans and to empty them when they got too full. The sidewalk and driveway were to be shoveled and her room picked up. He even had rules about her shirts—no words. (This happened after he saw her go out with a

T-shirt that said "Well-Behaved Women Rarely Make History.") Lucy wondered what he was afraid of—that she would tear up the carpet and chew the furniture?

But all was not lost. Until her mom returned, Lucy committed to a tried-and-true strategy: obey the rules and blend. Lucy's dad lived in a kind of self-contained eco-system, and as long as Lucy didn't interfere with its cycle of life, all was well. For instance, here is what Lucy's dad did on Saturdays: he ate his cereal. He rinsed his bowl and set it in the sink. He went for a bird walk. When he returned, he sat at the kitchen table and wrote bird names in his bird journal. Then he tossed a load of clothing in the washing machine and went to Clare's Meats & Foodstuffs for groceries. For lunch, Lucy and her dad ate peanut butter and jelly sandwiches. (They ate in silence punc-tuated by the slosh of milk going down her dad's esoph-agus.) After lunch, her dad picked up a magazine, stretched out in his lounger, and started reading. That's where he stuck (body to lounger, hand to magazine) for the rest of the day.

So Lucy kept her grades up, told him where she was going, wore plain clothing, went to bed by nine thirty, and kept the volume on her radio low. Believe it or not, this left Lucy free to do what she wanted. Lucy had no idea if he'd heard about *The Turtle Rock Times Shuts Its Eyes,* but he hadn't said anything, and she wasn't going to bring it up.

The only thing Lucy absolutely hated was the food

situation. Lucy opened the refrigerator after her dad's first trip to Clare's Meats & Foodstuffs, and it was so empty, white, and glowing, Lucy swore it looked like a portal to the pearly gates. Two gallons of milk? That's it? Then Lucy opened the freezer and saw frozen foods of nearly every persuasion (low-cal, low-carb, vegetarian, vegan, soy, and family-size). Lucy moaned.

"You *have* to teach him how to cook," Lucy said to her mom during one of those October phone calls. "First it was Puddle Jumper Cafe Pizza until it fell out my ears. And now it's frozen food. Mom, tell him about nutrients! Tell him how food can't be kept forever and still be good to eat! Tell him cardboard is for boxes, not for twelve-year-old girls to consume!" Lucy's mom laughed and said she'd mention it to Dad, but did Lucy know that her cookbook was sitting on the shelf in the kitchen?

"I can't cook!" said Lucy. She hated it when her mom turned the situation around on her. She had a legitimate problem, something that needed fixing by an *adult*! And anyway, her mom knew what kind of kid she'd given birth to—and Lucy wasn't a chef.

"Well," her mom said slowly and with a little amusement in her voice, "maybe you and your dad could make something together."

"Mom, it would interrupt his magazine time," said Lucy. "He reads all night long—*The Overachieving Birder*, or *Scientists at Rest*, or *Centuries of Post Office Delivery*."

"Have you asked?"

"No," said Lucy. And she didn't want to ask. If she did, her dad would find something else Lucy needed to be responsible for, and he'd give her a rule explaining how and exactly when it was to be done.

Of course, there was the added problem that she'd have to find the recipe and write down every single ingredient. And she couldn't write any ingredient on a shopping list without checking to see if they already had it on a shelf somewhere. For everybody's information, Lucy's mom didn't know how to keep an organized pantry—the dried basil could easily be behind the bin of corn flour or sideways underneath a bag of dried apricots! Lucy had important things to do, and cooking was what parents did, not kids.

Lucy determined to eat the frozen food.

It was in November, during one of these meals, that a car drove down Fifth Street and pulled into the Moons' drive-way. Lucy was picking at a Frozen Fiesta dinner (third this week), and her dad was scooping up a gluey hump of his Manly Lumberjack Meal. Lucy heard the car and jumped up to look out the window. She sat down, dejected.

"Finish your dinner, Lucy—every bite," her dad said pointedly.

So Lucy put another brown forkful of "Tostada-arriba! Hot! Hot! Hot!" in her mouth, tried to keep her tongue off it, and then washed it down with milk. Her whole body shivered. Yuck.

That was when the knock came at the front door.

Her dad wiped his mouth, opened the door, and there stood Mr. Gustafson, the owner of Gustafson's Wild Nature Gallery. He owned the store directly below her mom's downtown photography studio.

"Oh, it's a bad time," said Mr. Gustafson. He glanced at Lucy and the frozen-dinner trays on the table. "I'll come back. I shouldn't interrupt your dinner hour."

"We're finished," said her dad.

Lucy thought about throwing the rest of her "Tostada-arriba!" in the garbage as soon as they were out of sight.

Her dad glanced at her. "You eat up, Lucy."

Then Lucy's dad ushered Mr. Gustafson into the living room.

Lucy sighed and stared at the last lumps of tostada—pasty lumps, speed-bump lumps, maggot-rump lumps. Her throat closed up like a camera shutter. Rot! Rot! Rot!

Lucy listened to the conversation in the living room as she stared blankly at the food before her. Mr. Gustafson was looking for Lucy's mom, but when he realized that her dad couldn't help him, not even with a phone number, Mr. Gustafson sighed loudly and said, "I guess I've got to talk to you, then." Mr. Gustafson continued on, talking about an "opportunity" and that the "Turtle Rocks Arts Committee has chosen the gallery as the location for traveling exhibitions." And then something "unfortunate" and "I need the studio space."

What? Lucy gulped down the last tostada lump, turned her chair toward the living room, and leaned in to listen.

"You need the wall space?" her dad said. "I'll have to ask Josephine how she feels about taking down her portraits."

But Mr. Gustafson continued: "No, not that. I need Josephine to *move out* of the space. I'm talking major renovation, Don. I'm expanding. I'm going to renovate the gallery and the studio into one space. It'll be beautiful. But, unfortunately, I need Josephine to move out ASAP. I was real lucky and got the contractors. So the good news is that everything will be renovated for a holiday exhibition called 'Snowy Wilderness.' You guys should come to the opening."

"You want her to move out?" said her dad. "Do you know how much money and work she's put into that place? She put in walls, a darkroom, a special sink. . . . There's the rent, too. Now you're giving her a few weeks' notice and she's not here to say anything."

"I've given that some thought and I want to pay for the remodeling she did. I can offer a thousand dollars."

"A thousand dollars doesn't come close."

"Okay, thirteen hundred, then. But I need her out of there 'cause I've got an opportunity that's never going to come this way again." Mr. Gustafson laughed a little laugh.

There was a pause.

Mr. Gustafson broke the silence. "No joke," he said. "It's Miss Wiggins. She's putting up half and she says it's now or never. You know how she is—she loses interest if you don't snap up her offers. So thirteen hundred or nothing. Sorry."

There was another pause.

Mr. Gustafson added: "Take the fixtures. I'm not going to need them."

"Pitiful, Jerry—it's pitiful. I can't believe you'd do this to her—*years*, Jerry—it must be six years since she moved in."

"Don, I'm sorry, but she was renting, you know? Her lease ran out a year ago, and we never renewed it. It's tough luck for poor Josephine that this is the way it worked out. What more can I say? Look, I gotta go now."

"That's all you're going to say? Your final words on the subject?" said Lucy's dad.

"I gotta go with the times," said Mr. Gustafson. He glanced at his wristwatch. "Oh, jeez, I got to run."

"You run, Jerry," said her dad.

Mr. Gustafson didn't even say good-bye to Lucy as he sprinted out the front door.

Lucy waited for the screen door to slam behind him and then ran into the living room.

"We've got to get in touch with Mom," said Lucy, a little desperately. "He can't just take away her studio!"

Her dad looked down at her and ran his hands through

his hair. "You know what I think about you listening in on adult conversation, Lucy."

"But, Dad," Lucy said. "Do you know where she is? We've got to call her."

Her dad sighed. "I don't know where she is," he said. "I'll tell her when she calls." He put his hand on Lucy's shoulder. "Lucy, this is business for an adult, not for a child. This is my business. Are we clear?"

Lucy stiffened feeling his hand on her shoulder. Lucy hated that he didn't talk. He just decided and did. Lucy's mom would have talked to her. It was like Lucy didn't even count. She had a brain, you know!

He looked at her. "I don't want another word," he said. "I mean it."

Then he walked out of the room.

Lucy plopped down on the couch. From the living room, she heard him pull out the phone directory in the kitchen, and start calling. Within minutes, Lucy knew he was looking for packing supplies. Lucy banged her feet against the front of the couch and tried to think. What could she do? There must be something she could do!

But all she ended up thinking about was Miss Ilene Viola Wiggins. It was the second time in a month she had thought about her. First, Lucy thought about Miss Wiggins because of the arrested sledders, and now, Miss Wiggins was indirectly responsible for kicking Lucy's mom out of the studio.

Surely it was a coincidence and nothing more. No one could tell the police what to do! They took an oath, right? And as for her mom's studio, well, the lady was being generous. It had bad consequences, but so what? No, Lucy was mad at two people: Mr. Gustafson and her dad. Mr. Gustafson was taking her mom's studio away. . . . And her dad? Well, her dad was the one who was doing nothing—nada, no, not one single thing—about it.

Lucy grabbed her walkie-talkie off her belt.

"Zoë? Are you there?"

The walkie-talkie jingled when she let up her finger on the button.

Zoë answered, and within minutes, Lucy yelled her plans up the stairs to her dad, grabbed her books, and went over to Zoë's house.

Hauling, stacking, shoving, wrapping, taping, marking, and kicking—that was Lucy's weekend. Yes, they got a lot of Josephine Able Moon's Photographic Studio packed up, but it was irritating all the same. (This was where *kicking* came into the process—it soothed Lucy to line a box up with the other packed boxes by kicking it.)

Zoë came by with lunches from the Rossignol Bakery, and this cheered Lucy up some. But after lunch, Lucy's anger returned. Lucy knew that as soon as her mom found out about the studio, she'd talk to Mr. Gustafson and stop the eviction, and then every single one of these boxes would have to be unpacked. But until her mom called, Lucy had to pack boxes because her dad said she had to. (Luckily, her dad didn't catch her kicking them.)

The weekend came and went without a phone call from Lucy's mom, and not one message on the answering machine, either.

On Sunday night, Lucy stayed up, read her mom's last letter, and waited for the phone in the hallway to ring. The letter was sent two weeks ago from Yellowstone National Park, written on a piece of notebook paper: *All the gods seem to be for me, Lucy!* Her mom's handwriting looped like a roller coaster and it scrawled across the page in thick, green marker. *As soon as I got to the end of the walkway, Old Faithful blew to high heaven, as if it had been waiting for me to arrive. And I feel I have arrived. This is a rich, rich place, Lucy, and I wish you could see it! This is going to be a good trip. I've sent you some photographs. Be good to your dad. Hugs, Mom.*

Lucy flipped through the five photographs tucked into the letter. She had never been to Yellowstone, and couldn't get her mind around all the spurting, boiling places, so she rubbed her fingers over the glossy surface and began to think.

Hands down, Lucy's mom had the best job in Turtle Rock. Lucy wouldn't mind having her mom's life when she grew up. Lucy's mom traveled all over; she got paid to do what she loved; she owned her own business; and she lived in northern Minnesota (lakes, trees, wild animals, lots of snow). Her mom's photographs turned up in magazines, books, and art galleries. Around Turtle Rock, everyone liked Lucy's mom. When adults didn't know what to say to Lucy, they'd talk about what a "hoot" they had getting their family photograph taken at her mom's downtown studio. Close-ups of bobcats, bears, and wolves never failed to impress kids, especially when it looked like the photographer had come close to being mauled. Lucy, though, was glad that the subject of this trip—clouds—lacked teeth.

And that was the problem with the entire scenario. Lucy's mom was her *mom*—not some woman in a book, or a byline under a photograph, but a living, breathing mom. It was at the end of these long trips that Lucy invariably wondered if it would be so bad to have a mom who stayed home baking gingersnaps and crocheting hot pads, living solely for unending conversations with Lucy.

Nah, Lucy decided—too boring. She did not want a boring mom.

Still, she wished her mom would come home! Right now, the little red house was the land of self-enforced silent treatment, since Lucy avoided her dad as much as possible. As soon as her mom banged through the front door, Lucy planned to pull her over to the couch and tell her everything. She hadn't told her mom about *The Turtle Rock Times Shuts Its Eyes* yet, or asked her how a person knew if they were good at something. Lucy wanted to wait until her mom came home. Then they could talk about it forever, poring over it piece by piece.

It was only a matter of days now. It *was* November.

With this thought, Lucy turned off the light and slipped down under the covers. She lay on her back with her right foot off the bed. She figured this way, if the phone rang, she'd be ready to sprint. And in this position, Lucy fell asleep.

The phone did not ring that night.

Lucy's mom finally called Monday during dinner. Lucy raced up the stairs to answer the phone.

"Hello?"

"Hello, Lucy-love, it's me!"

"Mom, where are you?" Lucy had been storing up things to say for so long now, the words splattered without any regard to sentence structure. Lucy told her about the studio and how Dad started packing up the place and Lucy thought he shouldn't. She ended with, "And when are you coming home?"

It wasn't until she stopped talking that Lucy heard all the voices in the background on the other line. She heard laughter and the clinks of silverware, plates, and glassware. Someone close to the phone said, "Come on, Josephine!" And her mom laughed a sparkly laugh and whispered, "I'm talking to my daughter."

"Are you listening to me?" said Lucy. "Where are you? Are people eating? What's that sound?"

"Oh, Lucy," said her mom in the same sparkly voice, "I'm in this restaurant called Aubergine with a few friends I haven't seen in *ages*. And we are having so much fun catching up!"

Lucy heard someone whisper something on the other end of the line, and her mom responded, laughing loudly. It reminded Lucy of the ancient question of the tree falling in the forest and whether or not the tree made a sound if no one heard it fall. Who was her mom when Lucy wasn't there to witness her?

Lucy decided that she never wanted to think that thought again. Her mom was her mom was her mom. Lucy *knew* her mom.

"Mom," said Lucy, irritated. "Are you going to do something about the studio?"

"What, honey?"

"The *studio*, mom?"

"Oh, yeah," said her mom, sighing. "There's probably not much that can be done about it. I'll give Mr. Gustafson a call. Thank you for helping your dad pack it up." She paused for a moment and then added: "Maybe you should get your dad now. I need to talk to him, and it looks like we'll be seated at a table soon."

Lucy, feeling her time on the phone was nearly over, rushed out with her next sentence. "When will you be home?"

"Well, I'm in Banff now," her mom said, and then there was a pause that sounded like she was thinking things through. "I'm probably not going to be home this month. I've got so much to do. I'm making great contacts and seeing all my old M.F.A. buddies. The opportunities have been astounding!"

"So, *Thanksgiving?*"

"Probably not," said her mom. "Very unlikely."

"So when will you be home?"

"*Soon*, Lucy," her mom said, sounding amused. "Now go get your dad. I need to talk to him."

"Okay," said Lucy. She didn't know what else to say. So her mom wasn't coming home in November, not even for Thanksgiving? Her mom had said November.

"I love you," said her mom.

"I love you, too, Mom," Lucy said. The words crumbled on her tongue, but she said them anyway.

CHAPTER 6

On Thursday, November 13th, the construction workers at the base of Wiggins Hill listened to WBRR from a portable radio at the side of the road. Julie was finishing the local news.

"The Turtle Rock PTA reports they've reached only a quarter of their fund-raising goal for the new junior-high gymnasium," said Julie. "They'd like me to remind you that 'healthy children are happy children with outstanding SATs.'"

"SATs?" said Ken. "What kind of baloney is that? Shouldn't healthy and happy be enough?"

"Ken," said Julie sharply. "Please, folks," she said, in a voice thick as honey, "write a check today to the PTA. The kids need a bigger place to play."

Ken sighed audibly. "Let's have that oldie but goodie, shall we?"

"Snow Drifts, Ski Lifts, and a Hot Chocolate," an old melody from the '40s crooned through the radio as the workers erected the ten-foot chain-link fence around Wiggins Hill. The ground was near freezing now, but Miss Wiggins had paid extra for the job, and they had the equipment. It took a week. Every day they came back and dug more holes, poured cement, put in the metal poles, and attached the chain link. Each segment of fence held a sign: PRIVATE PROPERTY: NO TRESPASSING.

The construction chief lived a few towns over, so she'd never seen this hill. Man, what a beautiful piece of land— four or five maples surrounding an enormous maple in the center of the hill. Who knew they grew that big? Something about the wildness of the place made the construction chief think of her grandparents, and great-grandparents, and wonder how they'd found northern Minnesota when they settled here all those years ago.

The wind blew harder, and the air nipped colder as the construction chief attached the last sign to the fence. That's when the first snowflake fell, and then another and another and another.

She saw a boy taking pictures then, but she didn't think much of it.

The boy was Sam Shipman. He took a picture of the construction woman attaching the last PRIVATE PROPERTY: NO TRESPASSING sign on the Wiggins Hill fence, as snow fell from the sky. He snapped another, and for good luck, two more after that.

He stepped behind a tree then, to check the digital photos he'd taken, and finally found one that looked right: there was the NO TRESPASSING sign, the construction worker in front of the fence, and Wiggins Hill. He couldn't wait to see what Lucy Moon would do with this!

A fence on Wiggins Hill? Sam was so mad he could spit. Losing deer-hunting privileges was nothing to losing sledding on Wiggins Hill. (Sam liked deer hunting, but it also had its mind-numbing parts, like sitting in tree stands for hour after hour after hour.) He knew what his parents would say about the fence: "That's disappointing, Sam. We're sorry." And his teachers wouldn't care, just "Get that homework done." But Lucy Moon would get indignant, and then she'd go after Miss Wiggins.

Sam was going to pit two evils against each other, like the ancient rivalry of the mongoose and the cobra. That was Sam's plan.

Lucy Moon and her fake promises! Every parent he knew was talking about *The Turtle Rock Times Shuts Its Eyes*. "No one will know it's you," Lucy had said, solemn as a priest. Sam had looked into those brown eyes and believed her. What a dummy! He could kick himself for it. Sam had decided never to talk to Lucy again.

Until this happened. Fencing Wiggins Hill was plain

cruel. Snow and no sledding? Look, but don't touch? Miss
Wiggins was the cobra. Lucy was the mongoose.

Out of the two, the mongoose was Sam's favorite animal. If he were truthful, he'd have to admit that, before
she cost him deer hunting, Sam had kind of admired Lucy.
She was fierce. He liked how her eyes burned when she
talked about things that were important to her. But Sam
supposed the thing that really made him think about Lucy
was that interview. She had *listened*. She didn't tell stupid
jokes or make wisecrack comments while he and Lisa told
their story.

Not that he wanted her as a girlfriend.

But if she took care of this fence, he'd be so happy, he'd
forget about missing deer hunting.

She was still going to have to admit that her promise
had been bogus.

Anyway, first things first—they had to deal with the
fence.

Lucy Moon and Zoë Rossignol sat on the big red couch in
the Rossignol Bakery. Lucy had spread her math book out
on the coffee table in front of her, and Zoë sat nearby knitting an orange-and-olive cable sweater. Every so often Zoë
asked Lucy what answers she got. "Good," said Zoë. "I got
something like that, too."

That was when Lucy felt a small tug inside her. She
looked up. And through the big plate glass window, she

saw snowflakes blowing sideways, puffed out like the sails of boats. Snow! In her mind's eye, Lucy took a nosedive down Wiggins Hill—the rush of air, her cheeks numb with cold, her braids blown backward, and plummeting, plummeting, plummeting down the hill.

Lucy whispered very, very quietly (she might scare it away): "It's snowing."

Zoë lifted her eyes to the window and stared, the knitting needles frozen in the middle of a purl stitch. "Is that really snow?" she said. Zoë finished the stitch and stuffed the knitting into her bag.

More and more snowflakes began to fall, lines of them, filling the windowpane with white.

Lucy grabbed Zoë's hands, pulled her off the couch, and the two of them ran for the front door.

Mrs. Rossignol yelled: "Lucy and Zoë, you wear your coats!" But it was too late for that. The bakery door dinged, and Mrs. Rossignol watched them run full speed up the sidewalk.

Lucy and Zoë ran with all their might up and down the sidewalk, yelling and wailing. They were a sight: Lucy wearing her favorite wool shirt and hiking boots, and Zoë slipping around in a pair of ballet shoes, teal tights, and fuzzy blue skirt. (Grover fur, Zoë called it.) Finally, they stopped to catch their breath, stuck their tongues out to taste the snowflakes, and started shivering. So they ran back inside the bakery and begged Mrs. Rossignol—please, please, please—for another hot chocolate.

Drinking their hot chocolate (and wrapped together in a blanket Mrs. Rossignol found in the back office), they sat on the couch and stared out the window.

Lucy said, "It looks like it'll be enough."

Zoë absentmindedly kicked one of her wet ballet slippers. "If it snows all night."

"Will your mom let you, after the arrested sledders?"

Zoë grinned. "Oh, she doesn't care about that."

Lucy smiled. At that moment, nothing—not one thing—felt insurmountable. Not even the fact that her mom would not be home for another month. Who cared? Now she could finally go sledding on Wiggins Hill.

That's when the door to the Rossignol Bakery dinged, and in walked Sam Shipman.

CHAPTER 7

After that first November snowstorm, the clouds continued to bring snow to Turtle Rock—no blizzards, but steady, steady, workaday snow. There was light, dry snow—barely visible, but making the air and everything seen through it sparkle. There was the kind of snow that came assembly-line fashion, one snowflake rushing after the next. This snow lasted all day and into the night. And then there were the big flakes that floated out of the sky, drifting like daisy petals—"She loves me . . . She loves me not . . . She loves me." The snow piled up in curls, outlining trees, causing the tops of pines to bow under the weight. When the wind blew, long strands of snow combed over land and road.

The largest sugar maple on Wiggins Hill held out its snow-festooned limbs, and the five smaller sugar maples reflected the larger tree's glory, while the surface of the hill smoothed downward in polished rolls. The perfection of the hill's snowy surface was a sledder's dream. No footprints, no sled tracks, only wind shivered across its surface.

At first, many adults found themselves feeling rather huffy about that fence. Who did Miss Wiggins think she was talking to when she posted PRIVATE PROPERTY: NO TRESPASSING every five feet, like they didn't get it? They were not "trespassers," thank you very much. Oh, they knew that *technically* Miss Ilene Viola Wiggins owned that hill. It's just that Wiggins Hill felt like communal property, as close as a piece of land could come to being a public park without actually being one.

Then they sighed and recollected that time (a decade ago, at least) when that young Doug what's-his-name from Duluth had tried to get the city council to ask about buying Wiggins Hill. They called him "citified," and said that he was "raised suspicious."

"No," the city council had said. Turtle Rock was a *community*: a place where people worked together for the common good. There was no need to own Wiggins Hill, and they had better places to spend their severely limited funds.

But no one wanted to hurt anyone's feelings by reminding them of *that* missed opportunity—no, there wasn't a thing to be gained by dredging up the past.

Then Turtle Rock residents reminded themselves of all Miss Wiggins did for Turtle Rock: the hospital, the reference wing of the public library, the pipe organ at the Lutheran Church, the movie theater (with all those wholesome G-rated movies), and the Baroque music concerts. Every other week she appeared in the newspaper for helping out with something. Wasn't that worth trading a little sledding for?

But even after all was said and rationalized, a primal injustice stirred in the hearts of many in Turtle Rock, seeing that hill and that sugar maple noosed with a chain-link fence.

The kids stared at the fence, the hill through the fence, the snow falling from the sky, and found life and its promises unfair. Here they'd waited weeks, while weather forecasters promised snow that never came, and then when it finally snowed, the hill was fenced—NO TRESPASSING. Now they'd never be able to try out their new saucer sleds on the best hill in town, or find out if Lisa Alt had been telling tales about getting snagged by that sugar maple. Suddenly, kids found wool sweaters itchier than normal, board games wimpy, and television blundering and stupid.

Sam Shipman came up with the idea for the postcards. Lucy Moon thought it was genius.

After taking the photos of Wiggins Hill, Sam had walked into Turtle Rock, turned left on Main Street, and continued on until he arrived at the Rossignol Bakery. He passed Mrs. Rossignol at the counter and headed toward Lucy and Zoë, who were bundled together in a blanket on the red couch. Then he reached into his backpack, got out his camera, and turned it on.

"Look," he said, pointing to the display. He held the camera out to Lucy.

Lucy saw the camera, but ignored it. She stood up, dropping the blanket, and crossed her arms. The Rossignol Bakery was her territory. If he had come here to yell at her, she'd never let him forget it.

"Will you look at this?" Sam shook the camera in front of her face. "It's important."

"I thought you weren't talking to me, remember?" said Lucy.

Zoë stood up and grabbed the camera from Sam's hand.

Sam put his hands on his hips. "Remember making me a promise?"

That was when Zoë, who stared down at the tiny screen on the back of the camera, gasped. "Oh, no," she said. "Is that Wiggins Hill?"

In an instant, Lucy was at her shoulder. Sam took up on the other side, and all three of them stood in complete silence gazing at the image on the camera. Then Zoë slumped on the couch, Lucy crashed next to her, and Sam plopped down on the overstuffed chair opposite them.

Sam broke the silence: "Well, you're going to do something, right? Because this is bad, you know." His eyes found Lucy's.

Lucy looked away. She stared out the window at the falling snow and tried to think, but ideas were not coming. Each falling snowflake felt like a pebble dropping into her pocket, sinking her into a deeper state of despair. A fence on Wiggins Hill?

Finally, Sam picked up Zoë's hot chocolate, slugged the last of it, and banged the mug down on the coffee table. "But what are we going to *do*? There isn't a law against a person who fences their own hill."

"Don't you treat my dishware like that," Mrs. Rossignol yelled from across the bakery. "I've got plenty of jobs to do for people who break things."

Two pink spots appeared on each cheek of Sam's face.

Then Sam's eyes brightened. "Hey, I got it! What if we send Miss Wiggins a postcard every time we want to go sledding?"

Lucy blinked. She looked at Zoë. Zoë stared at Sam. And then it all fell together in Lucy's mind.

"Yeah," Lucy said slowly. She clapped her hands. "Then we're only asking. Anybody can *ask* anything."

Suddenly, Lucy found herself thinking about being "gifted" and "talented" again—if Lucy led this protest, and if it all went well, she'd know she was "gifted"!

"Okay," Lucy said, slapping her hands down on her

thighs. "We'll print up the postcard and put your photo-graph on the front, with a saying like . . . I don't know, we'll think of that later. . . . And then on the other side will be Miss Wiggins's address and some space for sledders to ask if they can go sledding. We'll pass them out at school and tell everyone to send them. Zoë, you'll design the postcard. And Sam, you'll get your friends involved, right?" Lucy narrowed her eyes at Sam. "You're not going to bag out on me, are you?"

Sam hesitated, the pink spots reappearing on his face. Then he said, "No! Why do you think I came here?"

Zoë seemed to be regarding Lucy. "We'll all be in this *together*, right?"

"Of course," said Lucy quickly, thinking that there was no need for Zoë to know that she had designated herself as leader. Wasn't that the way it usually worked out anyway?

Zoë rolled her pencil between her fingers. "Okay," she said. "I'm in." Then she added (almost defensively, Lucy noted), "And the saying should be, 'Free Wiggins Hill!' "

"Yeah, that's perfect!" said Lucy. The phrase captured Lucy's feelings about that fence.

The postcard campaign began pronto. Lucy cringed as she read the article in the *Turtle Rock Times* titled "Safety Calls for Fencing of Wiggins Hill."

"It's nothing personal," said Miss Wiggins. "With property

comes responsibility. Unfortunately, I can't continue watching over those children sledding on my hill, and I would hate to see anything happen. It was an extremely difficult decision."

As if they were *babies*, thought Lucy.

So Lucy determined to make the postcard campaign a priority, despite all the other things going on in her life: first, deer hunting season didn't end until Thanksgiving, and so Lucy and Zoë faithfully wore their Killing Season bandannas every day. (Though after the first week, no one even came close to mentioning the bandannas.) Second, Lucy and her dad were still packing up her mom's studio, working on weekends and sometimes on weeknights. Her dad said that Mr. Gustafson and his construction crew would throw out anything left inside after Thanksgiving, and Lucy didn't want Mr. Gustafson's grimy, greedy hands on anything belonging to her mom. And of course there was always homework. In Lucy's estimation, junior-high teachers loved assigning homework a little too much.

But now Lucy also carried the "Free Wiggins Hill!" postcards, trying to find ways of putting them in students' hands. Sam and Zoë did the same, as well as Edna, and Lisa Alt. (Quote said she'd send a few postcards, but refused point-blank to take part in handing them out after the "debacle" of the bandanna.) The story of Lisa Alt hanging from that maple tree on Wiggins Hill had given her something of a legendary status. "My whole sledding reputation is based on Wiggins Hill," Lisa said, grabbing a pile of post-cards.

For Lucy, the postcard campaign turned out to be more work than she'd expected. Lucy found out quickly enough that kids would rather gripe about no sledding on Wiggins Hill than actually do something about it. Still, as disappointed as she was in her fellow students, she didn't give up. Anyone who gasped a breath of a sentence about Wiggins Hill, or snow, or sledding, found a postcard stuffed into their hands and was told, "Just write something like: 'Wish I could sled on your hill,' and sign your name at the bottom. Don't threaten! All we're doing is asking—it is her hill, after all." If two or more kids were gathered in the hallway, Lucy homed in. Spying someone staring out the window, she would say, "I feel exactly the same way, since Miss Wiggins fenced that hill—please send a postcard!" And a "Would be nice to spend a Saturday sledding on Wiggins Hill, wouldn't it?" was said to any kid talking about weekend plans. More than one kid jumped after finding Lucy Moon at their elbows.

Over the long haul, Lucy was by far the most dedicated. Sam came in second, Lisa Alt third, then Edna and Zoë. Lucy couldn't believe how quickly Zoë had petered out. She'd lasted *two* weeks—that was it. Instead, Zoë spent her time altering clothes from The Wild Thrift and talking fashion. She'd even knitted a pair of shoe-laces! Then one day Zoë told Lucy to give it a rest. Okay, so it *was* after school and Zoë *was* waiting for Lucy, but still.

"Everybody in this school knows about the postcards," said Zoë. "If they want a postcard they'll find you."

This made Lucy angry. "Do you want to go sledding or not?"

Zoë rolled her eyes and retorted: "Do you want to be late to the bakery or not?"

Lucy glanced at her watch. Zoë had a point. "Okay, I'm going." Then she added: "Man, I can't seem to stop."

"I noticed," said Zoë pointedly. She started walking toward her locker.

Lucy mumbled at Zoë's backside: "Better than knitting shoelaces. What do shoelaces cost—five cents?"

Zoë rounded on Lucy. "What did you say?"

"Forget it," said Lucy. "Let's go to the bakery." When Zoë continued to stare at her without making a move, Lucy added: "Do you want to be *late?*"

They walked down to the bakery in silence that day.

But overall, the effort seemed to be working. The post-cards even made it into the hands of The Big Six in the southeast corner of the third floor. Lucy stepped out of her science class and saw Sam giving a postcard to the Genie. Sam smiled. Then his smile widened. Lucy stopped in her tracks and took in the scene. Bile rose in Lucy's stomach. The Genie had *everything*—body, hair, head, face, and clothes. Her shoulder-length black hair shone and turned up at the edges, reminding Lucy of cursive hand-writing found in ancient love letters.

Sam and the Genie exchanged a few words. Sam laughed.

Lucy watched while absentmindedly picking up one of her braids and finding a dozen split ends.

Then the rest of The Big Six blocked Lucy's line of sight. Kendra, Brenda, Didi, Gillian, and Chantel rushed up to Sam and the Genie, asking for postcards too, *please*. That "please" was so sweet it would have killed laboratory mice, thought Lucy Moon. Lucy tossed the braid over her shoulder, adjusted the Killing Season bandanna on her neck, and continued to walk down the hallway. This was a test of her principles. Even though Lucy was ninety-nine percent sure that The Big Six would use their postcards as lipstick blotters or to clean dirt from under their nails, it was good for them to have the postcards just in case they had a bout of conscience and sent them. The more people that sent those cards the better, even if it was Kendra, Brenda, Didi, Gillian, Chantel, and, yes, the Genie.

Thanksgiving arrived. Lucy's dad invited two new postal carriers over to their house for dinner.

While many Turtle Rock Thanksgiving spreads included venison or deer sausage, meat was not on the Moons' Thanksgiving menu. Lucy built her own tofu turkey! She used tofu for the body, created the head out of a carved potato with a pistachio beak and a tomato wattle, and the feathers in the back were celery and carrot sticks. Finally, Lucy covered the whole thing in soy sauce. ("Turkeys are *brown*, Dad," she explained, when her dad tried to stop her from pouring the entire bottle on the tofu.) Okay, it did look a little sickly, thought Lucy, in retrospect, but that was no reason for the postal carriers to joke. Even so, everything would have been okay if that guy hadn't poked her turkey with his fork! The turkey trembled. Then big bricks of tofu began to slip like wet soap. Lucy had to jump up and commandeer every wine and water glass to shore up the sides of her turkey. Then she gave those postal carriers a piece of her mind, which apparently, she shouldn't have done, because her dad gave her a look.

From there on out, the dinner proceeded with little noise except for the scraping of silverware on plates. It seemed to Lucy that her dad was the only one comfortable with the silence. Lucy wanted to make their guests feel welcome, but A. she didn't know what to say to two grown-ups, and B. she had just yelled at them. Anyway, the postal carriers ate a lot of canned cranberries, and said good-bye immediately after dinner. Lucy and her dad were left with mountains of dishes. Doing dishes was not one of Lucy's passions.

Worse, she was stuck in the kitchen with her dad. Lucy found being alone with her dad more unsettling than usual. Yes, she assumed that once they were alone she'd hear it for yelling at their dinner guests, but there was more to her discomfort than that. The truth was that her relationship with her dad was out of kilter, off balance. It had happened right after that phone call with her mom—the one about the studio, where her mom had been laughing and said that she'd call Mr. Gustafson, but that "probably not much could be done about it." What? Hadn't Lucy seen her mom refinish those floors and put up walls? What about the window boxes filled with flowers? And how about those times when Lucy discovered her mom there, asleep in her yellow plaid chair with a novel splayed on her lap? She loved that place!

Like a flash flood, her mom's response washed away Lucy's anger at her dad for packing up the studio. When the phone call ended, she was left with hollowness and a sense of bewilderment. Her mom was not acting like Mom. And her dad was right, when Lucy had been so sure he was wrong. It felt like the sun was the moon and the moon was the sun.

The end result was that Lucy didn't know what to say to him. Not that she'd had a lot to say before, but at least they'd had rules of engagement (avoidance and pleasantries).

In addition, ever since that phone call, he'd been talking to Lucy more, coming up with ideas for her. It was his idea she help with Thanksgiving dinner, and when she suggested building a tofu turkey block by block, he'd grimaced, yes, but then he'd said "sure." He probably regretted that now!

Lucy stared at the pile of dishes around her, and her dad's thick forearms elbow-deep in soapy water. He rinsed off a ladle and set it in the drying rack. Lucy picked it up, rubbed it dry with the dish towel, and put it in its drawer. She wished they'd turn on the radio. But they continued on in silence until her dad said, "Anything you're thankful for, Lucy?" He handed her a wineglass to dry.

Good grief, thought Lucy. She rubbed the wineglass down like it was a wire-haired dog coming out of a bath, and clunked it on the counter with the other wineglasses.

"Careful," said her dad.

Lucy ignored him. "Dad, we're not religious, so no Thanksgiving thank-yous, okay?"

Her dad gave her a look when she clunked another wineglass on the counter.

"It's not about religion, Lucy," he said. "It's about being grateful. So tell me."

"I don't know," she mumbled, threading a dish towel through a drawer handle and then pulling it back and forth.

"Come on—what are you thankful for?" Her dad passed her another dish. Lucy pulled the dish towel out of the handle, dried the dish, and put it in the cupboard.

"You want to hear what I'm *not* thankful for?" she said suddenly, snapping the trash can with the dish towel. "That's easy."

"Lucy . . ." said her dad.

"Okay, okay, okay." Lucy balled up the damp dish towel in her hands, sighed loudly, and began: "On this Thanksgiving Day, I, Lucy Moon, am thankful that . . ." There was a long pause as she tried to think thankful thoughts. It was like waiting for a herd of tortoises to climb a hill. Eventually, the thoughts came: ". . . the deer don't have to be shot at anymore. I'm thankful for Zoë. I'm thankful for free leftover éclairs from the bakery. I like my teacher Ms. Kortum. I'm glad we finished packing the studio. . . . And I'm thankful that Miss Wiggins hasn't figured out a way to keep people from snowshoeing, cross-country skiing, or starting snowball fights."

Her dad chuckled. "Yup," he said. "That sounds about right."

"Okay, well, what are you thankful for, then?" Lucy said. If he made her do it, he sure wasn't getting out of it.

Her dad smiled at her, meeting her eyes. "That's easy," he said. "I'm thankful for you."

Lucy felt something stop inside her. She turned away from him, wiping dry a dish. Why would he say that? She complained about his frozen dinners; she got mad at him for packing up the studio; and today she yelled at his dinner guests, and it was *Thanksgiving* of all days. They couldn't eat that canned cranberry and scoot out the door fast enough!

"Dad," she said, "I'm sorry about the studio." Lucy kept rubbing the same dish, polishing it, really. "I thought you weren't trying hard enough to keep it. I didn't know that Mom—"

"I know," he said, interrupting her. He half smiled at her.

Lucy asked the question that was in her mind. "Did you know Mom wasn't that excited about the studio anymore? Before, I mean?"

"Not really," he said. He picked up some silverware and put it in the soapy water to soak.

Lucy stared at him. "But you knew *something*?" She had never pressed her dad this much, but she wanted to know.

There was a pause while Lucy watched her dad gently set the gravy boat in the soapy water and then slowly work a sponge around a ring of soy sauce.

"I had a hunch," he said finally. "She never came right out and said it." He rinsed the gravy boat and handed it to Lucy.

"Oh," said Lucy.

A stretch of silence passed. It lasted through the washing and drying of water and wineglasses, forks, knives, spoons, and plates. Lucy contemplated her mom and the studio over the last summer, searching for clues. But she came up empty. If anything, her mom seemed to hang around the studio more this summer. It didn't make sense.

Lucy's dad broke the silence. "What did you think of your turkey?" He pointed at the tofu rubble spilling off the platter onto the counter.

Lucy smirked a little and shook her head. "Ha!" she said.

Her dad frowned at her. "You didn't eat it? Who did?"

"You," said Lucy. She grinned. "How was it?"

Her dad took a deep breath. "Challenging," he said.

Then he handed her the tray with the remains of the tofu turkey and motioned for her to dump it in the garbage, and they both began to laugh.

CHAPTER 8

December 5th—the grand opening of the "Snowy Wilderness" exhibition at Gustafson's Wild Nature Gallery and, like idiots, Lucy Moon and her dad sped right to it in the family station wagon. The windows of houses passed in front of Lucy's eyes (living rooms, kitchens, front hall-ways), spilling yellow light onto the snowdrifts outside. Of course, Lucy did not want to go. But because her mom had a photo in the show, her dad had insisted, saying, "We should support your mother."

This was plain dumb all around. First, on her mom's side: her mom submits a photograph to the place that kicks her out? What was that? Second, on her dad's side: how did her dad come to the conclusion that viewing a photograph meant they "supported" Mom? Her mom wouldn't be attending the show, because she wasn't physically in Turtle Rock, Minnesota—no, they'd be "supporting" a photograph. Third, her dad made Lucy put on a dress. So Mr. Gustafson takes away her mom's studio, and Lucy has to wear a *dress* to celebrate it!

Lucy doubted that her mom would appreciate the sacrifice she was making. In general, Lucy didn't know what to make of her mom these days. Whenever she called, she sounded so la-de-da and cheery. She didn't have much time to talk.

And then, in one phone conversation, her mom says she's not sure she wants to take portrait photographs anymore. Portraits "make her tired." What did that mean? All work makes a person tired. Lucy didn't like spelling tests, but she still studied her word lists. "*Nebulous*: vague, hazy, indefinite." Spelled: *n-e-b-u-l-o-u-s*. See? What was so bad about that? And spelling lists had to be worse than taking photos of people, talking to them and making them smile. People told jokes. Spelling lists lacked any sense of humor! Plus, what other job was her mom going to do in Turtle Rock? Waitress? A person had to keep a schedule to be a waitress, and her mom said she liked being her own boss.

And what about the house? Was it fair that Lucy and her dad were knee-deep in boxes marked "studio"? Her dad even bought a storage shed to accommodate the extras. There was no more Ping-Pong in the basement, or easy access to the washer and dryer, because of all the studio boxes packed floor to ceiling. Then there were all the stray boxes that had somehow wheedled their way into the upstairs portion of the house, like in the hallway by the bathroom. Lucy was sure the boxes were reproducing, like amoebas, breaking bits of themselves off and then the bits swelling into bigger boxes. They needed an eco-friendly spray—a box-icide—to fend them off.

Clouds, clouds, clouds—ever changing, puffing, pulling, stretching, fuming, steaming clouds. Lucy pictured her mom in the light-blue compact car driving across the country. "There's one," she'd say, turning to drive down a country road. There's another, she'd think, and make a quick detour. She'd chase clouds in loops of road, like a flycatcher snatching insects out of the air. Or maybe her mom was more like a red-tailed hawk; she'd find her spot and spend hours waiting for that singular cloud to be birthed above a half-collapsed barn. Who knew? Anyway, the clouds kept coming. Clouds scuttling over the plains, clouds puffed above a weathered house, clouds speared by a mountain, clouds stretched like cotton. Clouds, clouds, clouds—promises of clouds—only a little more time; only a drive around that bend; only, only, only.

Lucy's heartbeat raced a little.

She calmed herself by reciting the types of clouds: cirrus, cumulus, stratus, nimbus. There were only four kinds. Realistically, how much longer could this go on?

If only Lucy could go sledding on Wiggins Hill!

Lucy shook herself a little. It was this dress that had set her off—and her dad forcing her, dragging her, to go to this gallery opening. Well, Lucy hoped no one would see her in this dress—prickly pink lace over even pinker cotton, little prissy collar and puffy sleeves. Obviously, Lucy could not remove her mom's long winter parka, which covered every last, lacy inch of pink. People would see Lucy's green-and-yellow hat, her mom's parka, and her hiking boots—that's it.

Lucy put her hand in her pocket and felt her walkie-talkie. If it got bad, she could call Zoë. Gustafson's Wild Nature Gallery was only two miles from the Rossignol's house—well within the walkie-talkie's three-mile radius.

Lucy glanced over at her dad, whose profile stood out against the light from passing streetlamps. Everything about her dad was long and formidable, and from the side, Lucy thought he looked like a rocky precipice: wisps of hair, furrowed forehead, bushy eyebrows, long bent nose, jut of chin, and the line of jawbone.

But her dad wasn't as unyielding as he looked. Last week, he took Lucy and Zoë to a movie, and made them a tofu-loaf with mashed sweet potatoes on the side. Recently, he'd decided that Lucy needed a salad and a multivitamin every day. (Lucy tried to tell him that she didn't need the children's chewable in "barnyard" shapes, but this went over his head. "You don't like the taste?" he said, concerned, tapping one into his palm and then popping it into his mouth.) And now, Lucy's frozen dinner came served up with three questions: "What did you do in school today?" "Anything new at the bakery?" and finally, "How's Zoë?" Lucy sometimes answered the questions before he'd even asked. Once, Lucy made her dad laugh at her imitation of a bakery customer with one too many dinner rolls. His laugh rolled out of his chest, making every molecule resonate, and Lucy felt warm, as if she were sitting in front of a fire.

Now Lucy pressed her face against the car window and found the Big Dipper, Cassiopeia, and the North Star. Lucy's dad told her to "be nice" at the gallery. Please. What did he think she was going to do?

Then they were there, parking the station wagon on Main Street, Turtle Rock. A big banner spanned the entire top half of Gustafson's Wild Nature Gallery: SNOWY WILDERNESS: PHOTOGRAPHS OF THE WILD, DECEMBER 5– JANUARY 11. Little white lights ran around the big windows in front. A tiny sign was posted in a corner of the window: "See local photographer Josephine Able Moon's photograph inside!"

As if that makes up for it, thought Lucy.

"Come on," said her dad, glancing at her.

Sandblasted, sanitized, scrubbed—those were the words that came to mind when Lucy stepped into the Moose Call Gallery (what Josephine Moon's ex-studio was officially named). This was despite the fact that people packed the space. It was a forest of bodies in church clothes. Glasses clinked, adults talked and laughed loudly while eating thumbnail-sized food. The stereo piped in music of a lone guitar, and the air smelled fresh, like mint leaves at the supermarket. And not one, single, identifying thing remained of Josephine Able Moon—no clutter, no color, no rag rugs, no wooden toys, and no plants. Moose Call Gallery was a vast room with white walls and two or three starved-looking metal chairs. (A person would only sit on those, thought Lucy, if they were desperate.) In a way, it made the whole thing easier for Lucy.

Lucy pushed past the adults, two of whom were Mr. and Mrs. Sovil. Lucy noted happily that they had come without their daughter, Eugenie, aka the Genie, of The Big Six. (Lucy didn't need to be reminded of Eugenie's perfection while wearing this stupid dress.) Then she began viewing the photographs. A wolf showing its belly to another wolf . . . A sunset on a frozen lake . . . A pine martin hanging off a branch . . . Two ravens in the snow. Soon the whole show felt like the same photograph lined up into infinity. Sweat beaded on Lucy's forehead, but if she unzipped the coat, she would expose the lace collar. She wished she could find her mom's photograph!

Lucy grasped her walkie-talkie deep in her coat pocket.

But just then, two women stepped away from the line

of photographs, and Lucy saw Sam Shipman standing by a picture of tracks in the snow. Lucy ran over and took a leap. "Mountain lion!" she said as she landed right next to him.

Sam screamed a little, which made Lucy laugh.

"Can't you ever be normal, Lucy?" he said.

"Nope," said Lucy, smiling at him. "I'm glad you're here. I'm dying of boredom."

Then Lucy peered at the little card next to the photograph. "I was right! That is a mountain lion! Ha!" She flashed a self-satisfied grin.

"Big points for you," said Sam.

"I bet you didn't know it was a mountain lion."

Sam didn't say anything. Instead he fingered her coat. "Aren't you hot? It's got to be a hundred degrees in here."

Lucy stepped over to the next photograph and pretended to look at it intelligently. "I'm nude underneath," she said.

"What did you say?" Sam tried to snatch the edge of the coat.

Lucy whacked his hand away. "Stop that!"

"Did you say you were nude?"

"I'm not saying anything to you anymore." She stepped between two adults. Sam followed and tried to catch the coat's edge again.

Lucy sidestepped him. "Don't touch my mom's coat!" Lucy said. "I mean it."

"Why?" Sam strolled a few steps closer. "Is it poisonous?"

Lucy dodged two adults talking, and then darted around a group of three, and between another clumping of two. Sam followed. Lucy started laughing, and they chased each other, zigzagging this way and that. Lucy avoided Sam by inches. A few adults protested, and then finally Sam made a big grab, succeeded in flipping up the edge of the coat, and stopped.

"That was a dress," he said. He panted a little. "Lucy Moon is wearing a pink dress." He shook his head. "Pink!" he said, laughing.

Lucy turned on him. "You can't tell anyone," she whispered. "I'm serious."

"About the pink or the dress or the fact that you told me you were nude?"

"Well, the nude part is okay, but not about the dress. My grandmother gave it to me because she wants me to be more ladylike. But all it does is make me sweat because I've got to wear a coat over it." Lucy paused, aggravated by how amused Sam looked. "Shouldn't you be wearing a suit or something?"

"I only have to wear suits to funerals and weddings."

"Well, I couldn't help it with the dress—my dad made me."

"I thought no one made Lucy Moon do anything."

"You don't know my *dad*," said Lucy. People were so dumb sometimes. Lucy thought about getting out of there. She was boiling, and Sam was annoying.

Maybe Sam could tell Lucy was about to leave, because he pulled out a ball of fabric from his pocket and let it unroll in front of her eyes. It was a tie covered with wild-eyed smallmouth bass.

"*That* is the world's ugliest—" said Lucy.

"It's my only clip-on," Sam said, interrupting her. His eyes darted around the room. "I'm supposed to be wearing a tie. Tell me if you see my mom coming."

There was a pause. Lucy stuck a finger down the collar of her coat to get some air in without unzipping it. "Hey, have you seen my mom's photo? I can't find it anywhere."

Sam stared. "Are you kidding?"

Then without saying a word, he grabbed Lucy and pulled her through the crowd. Lucy felt Sam's hand on hers—the joints of his fingers, the smooth surface of his palm, the pad of his thumb. Lucy's face got hot, and everything around her grew sluggish and still. When Sam let go of her hand on the other side of the room, Lucy felt dizzy and knew one thing: she could not look at Sam. Lucy was sure her emotions scrolled ticker tape, letter-by-letter, across her forehead in Day-Glo green: "I like you! I like you! I like you!" It was too humiliating, because it was not true. She did not *like* Sam!

So Lucy looked up at the gigantic photograph in front of her.

Oh. My. Gosh.

"Found," as her mom titled it, hung four feet by six feet from the ceiling. It was the largest photograph in the room. The title of the show "Snowy Wilderness" hung above the photograph.

This was why her mom wanted to be part of the show. Lucy had never seen one of her mom's photographs featured like this—never. A mountain goat peered downward, appraising the photographer (and not in a friendly way, thought Lucy). After looking closely, Lucy saw a tiny cloud—like the dot over the letter *i*—drifting above a distant mountain peak.

It was good, as in, better than anyone else's, and there was a small part of Lucy that felt validated by it. *See*, she wanted to yell out, *my mom is a real photographer. She's not just driving around the United States doing nothing. She's making art!*

And then Lucy's thoughts switched direction: *Another monster photo?* (This is what Lucy called the photographs where her mom risked her life to take a photograph.) In this case, the mountain goat clearly wanted to trample or head butt the photographer. Lucy had thought that the clouds trip meant an end to all this crazy, life-risking photography. But now, Lucy saw that her mom had been able to risk her life *and* include the clouds.

"You don't like it, do you?" Sam interrupted Lucy's thoughts.

"No, it's amazing," Lucy said flatly, removing her eyes

from the photograph and smiling at Sam. "But what I want to know is how I missed it. It's humongous!"

"You're too short," said Sam. He imitated Lucy walking right by the photograph without seeing it, making her seem like Dopey of the Seven Dwarfs.

"I'm telling about the clip-on," said Lucy. She did an imitation of a wild-eyed smallmouth bass caught on a line.

Sam waved his pinkie in the air. "I'll tell about the pink."

"Okay, truce!"

"Truce."

Then Lucy realized with great relief that she had just spoken to Sam without going all goofy. Good. Things were back to normal. She was probably overheated. She needed to get outside and cool off.

That's when Lucy saw Miss Wiggins standing in the middle of a group on one side of the room. She nudged Sam and pointed. Up close, Miss Wiggins reminded Lucy of a falcon, a small bird of prey with a tendency to watch every movement closely.

"Let's ask her about Wiggins Hill!" said Lucy. She walked toward Miss Wiggins, and was halfway there before she realized that Sam was not with her. Well, so be it, she thought. She was the one in charge of the postcards, so she should be the one to talk to Miss Wiggins.

It took some serious wiggling to penetrate the circle of adults, and when she finally got to the center, Lucy found her elementary-school gym teacher describing the ice-hockey arena in Burnham to Miss Wiggins.

"Excuse me," Lucy said loudly, as soon as the gym teacher paused. "Excuse me, Miss Wiggins. I've got a question."

Slowly, Miss Wiggins turned.

As Miss Wiggins's gaze landed on Lucy, the heat in her mom's parka rose by about a hundred degrees, and Lucy felt like a French fry under a heat lamp. Still, she would not be stopped. "Me and my friends want to sled on Wiggins Hill. Would that be okay?"

"My friends and I," Miss Wiggins corrected. Then she sighed. "What's your name?"

"Lucy Moon," she said. "So will you let us?"

Miss Wiggins didn't answer her at first. "And how old are you?" she finally asked.

"Twelve," said Lucy. "It's just sledding!"

"So you should have no trouble reading the signs." Miss Wiggins looked at her dismissively. "Your age surprises me. I would have guessed eight."

Lucy frowned. Read the signs? That's all she had to say about the sledding? And that Lucy looked like she was eight, a *third* grader?

Then Miss Wiggins looked at someone behind Lucy, and Lucy felt hands on her shoulders.

"Excuse us, Miss Wiggins," Lucy's dad said. He started to guide Lucy away.

Miss Wiggins gestured for her dad to stop.

"Have you heard from the photographer?" said Miss Wiggins.

"Two days ago," said her dad.

"She's fond of risks, isn't she?" said Miss Wiggins. She nodded in the direction of "Found." Lucy felt something tighten in her chest. She didn't like it when an adult spoke her private thoughts like that, least of all Miss Wiggins.

"Well, she is a professional," said her dad, taking Lucy's hand in his. He gently tugged Lucy away from the group. Lucy felt Miss Wiggins pat the top of her hat. She clutched the hat defensively.

On the way out, Lucy twisted around and saw Sam standing by his mom. His clip-on tie hung at an odd angle from his collar. Sam waved and jerked his head at a huge fur coat piled on top of one of the emaciated metal chairs. Miss Wiggins's pillbox hat sat on top of the coat. And on top of the pillbox hat sat a "Free Wiggins Hill!" postcard.

Lucy grinned.

Then it occurred to her that Miss Wiggins would now associate those postcards with her. It made her pause.

But that's the way it should be, Lucy told herself as she got into the station wagon. She was the one in charge, after all.

Once her dad had buckled his seat belt, he said, "I asked you to be nice. I expect you to respect your elders."

"I was nice," said Lucy. "It was a *question*."

"I think you understand what I mean," said her dad. "Tell me you won't do it again."

Lucy stared out the window without responding. How could she tell him that she wouldn't do this again? Lucy didn't even understand what he meant by "respecting her elders." Did he mean she couldn't talk to older people? Okay, Lucy knew it was cheeky to talk to Miss Wiggins the way she did. She knew it. But why couldn't she ask? She could hear what her dad would say if she tried to explain this: "Do as I say, Lucy." So now he was forcing her to promise something that she wasn't sure she even understood. Lucy wished her mom would hurry up and come home! If Lucy agreed to this, she would be lying in some way, because she was sure to break it. And Lucy didn't lie to her parents. If they asked, she answered truthfully.

Lucy watched people leaving the gallery opening and mumbled: "Okay, I won't do it again."

"I need to *hear* you, Lucy."

"I won't do it again."

Then her dad started the car. Lucy stared out the station wagon window, her fists clenched in her lap like two stones, all the way home.

CHAPTER 9

It was a Monday morning—a full week after the "Snowy Wilderness" opening at Gustafson's Wild Nature Gallery—when Lucy Moon was called to the principal's office. Principal Adams wanted to see her. So now Lucy found herself sitting on a stiff couch watching a secretary page through an office-supply catalog. The door to the principal's office was closed. Lucy thought maybe her dad had left a message for her, or maybe she'd forgotten something from home. Lucy had asked the secretary several times why she was here, but the secretary wouldn't say. She just repeated the same two sentences over and over: "When Principal Adams is ready for you, he'll ask for you. Sit down, Lucy Moon."

Lucy didn't particularly want to be face-to-face with Principal Adams. Between classes, during what Lucy heard him call "the running of the students," Principal Adams tended to stand in the hallway outside his office, surveying the rushing students while twisting an end of his red mustache into a curl. He wore cowboy boots, a bolo tie, and a pearl-buttoned shirt so tight, Lucy swore she could count the striations of his biceps and pectorals at fifty yards. If a boy attracted his attention by smirking, running, or jarring another kid so his books spilled, Principal Adams grabbed that boy out of the hallway, clamped him in his arms, whispered a word or two in the boy's ear, and let him go with a head nuggie. Even though Principal Adams didn't seem to do these things to girls, Lucy didn't trust him.

Finally, after the minute hand on the wall clock jerked its way through forty-two minutes, Principal Adams called her into his office.

"Ah, Lucy Moon," Principal Adams said when Lucy entered. He did not smile. He stacked some papers, put them into a tray, and gestured for Lucy to sit in one of the puffy chairs in front of his wooden desk, which was roughly the size of an SUV. A large print of a cowboy warming his dinner by the fire hung on the wall behind him. Lucy also noticed a closet, which she assumed was the legendary "Confiscation Closet," where squirt guns, whoopee cushions, banned superstrong glues, electric shockers, and clown noses found their final resting place.

Lucy sat down on the nearest puffy chair and sank lower and lower, giving her the distinct feeling that she was being digested. She scooted to the chair's edge.

"I've heard about you," he said, tugging on the tips of his mustache.

Lucy furrowed her brow. She opened her mouth to ask what—

"Ah-ah-ah," he said, shaking his finger at her. "I don't want to hear it."

Then Principal Adams opened up a folder with her name on it and held up his finger. She was not to speak. It was a long five minutes while Lucy watched him flip slowly through each piece of paper in her file. He'd sigh at some bit, tap his finger there, write on another piece of paper, erase something else. Lucy decided that Principal Adams was faking it. She couldn't have that much material in her file—she'd only been in junior high a couple of months. Everybody started out with a blank file at a new school, right?

Finally Principal Adams closed the folder, leaned back in his chair, and put a cowboy-booted foot on his desk.

He stared at her for a second.

Lucy smiled encouragingly.

He opened his top drawer and held up a "Free Wiggins Hill!" postcard. "Does this look familiar?" he asked.

"Yeah," said Lucy.

Principal Adams watched her, and Lucy gazed back. He

held the postcard in one hand and batted at it with the thumb of his other hand. As it flicked up and down, Lucy swore she saw a stamp.

Principal Adams continued: "According to this file, your teachers like you fine. The teachers I've asked all say you're smart and interested, and they like having you in class. But you've just started here, and frankly, I don't know what to make of you. . . . Of course you bring your reputation with you. But this isn't elementary school anymore, is it, Lucy Moon? You will not—and I repeat, will not—get away with the same behavior at Turtle Rock Junior High School. I let *The Turtle Rock Times Shuts Its Eyes* go by, but I can't let this postcard campaign continue. I don't want any more of these schemes of yours to take place on school property. Do I make myself clear?"

He gestured for Lucy to speak, and in the process, turned the postcard over.

"Oh wow," said Lucy audibly. There was a *postmark* as well as a stamp on the postcard. This meant the postcard had been through the mail, arrived at its destination, and now, somehow, this postcard had ended up here in the principal's office. This meant . . . Lucy felt a tickle of joy. It meant that Miss Wiggins had complained about the postcards. She complained about the postcards!

"Not 'Oh wow.' *Yes*," he said, correcting her.

"Yes," Lucy said. She met his eyes and realized that she was smiling. Smiling wasn't appropriate. Somberness—

think somberness, grief, Dutch elm disease, she thought, while trying to suck the smile in. But the ends of the smile kept escaping. The postcard campaign was working!

"Yes, *sir*," he said. He gestured for Lucy to say it.

"Yes, sir!" she said. She felt like kissing him.

"You may go," he said.

"Thank you, sir!" she said. Lucy hopped off the chair.

As she opened the door, Principal Adams raised his voice again: "Lucy?"

She stopped and turned around.

"Yes, *sir*?"

"Starting Tuesday you have detention until winter break. Report to Study Hall Room 103 with your home-work ten minutes after the last school bell. If you are even thirty seconds late, you will add another day of detention. I'll call your parents to notify them. I hope you choose to learn from this experience."

"Yes, sir!" she said. "Yes, sir!"

Lucy practically ran out of the office, slammed the door, and yelped in the hallway. Free Wiggins Hill! Free Wiggins Hill! Miss Wiggins complained to Principal Adams about the postcards! Yes!

That lunch period, Lucy sat at the end of the oddball table in the cafeteria with Zoë, Edna, Quote, and the rest of them, when an announcement came over the loud-speaker: "Attention, all students—a quick announcement. Anyone found with 'Free Wiggins Hill!' postcards on

Tuesday will find himself—or herself—in detention. I will not put up with students from this school harassing citizens of our community. I am giving you this one warning. So I suggest you remove any such items from the school today, and do not bring them back. I repeat: anyone found with postcards tomorrow will receive detention. Thank you for your attention."

"It's official," Lucy yelled. "Miss Wiggins knows!" Lucy threw her green-and-yellow hat in the air. Zoë and Edna whooped, and Lucy heard Sam whistle from a table near the back.

A few people clapped and cheered; others pointed, shaking their heads; and some outright laughed at them. The Big Six glanced casually in their direction and shrugged. But Lucy didn't care.

"'O world, I cannot hold thee close enough,'" mumbled Quote.

Lucy agreed. "Yes! That's it!"

Quote nodded. "Edna St. Vincent Millay."

Needless to say, Lucy's dad didn't find the news as exciting. Normally, Lucy's mom took calls from school. But Lucy's mom wasn't home, was she? When Lucy got home that afternoon, her dad let loose a stream of verbiage so steady and strong, it felt like water from a hose. He paced as he talked. The intensity of it all seemed to swell her dad's monument-like height (all chest and legs), until

Lucy felt like she had been squashed into the corner of the couch, unable to move. She held on to the armrest.

The lecture started this way: "Didn't I tell you to respect your elders, Lucy? And with Miss Wiggins again! I thought I made myself perfectly clear the night of the gallery opening. I don't know what kind of game you think you're playing." Lucy's dad didn't want her "bothering adults." This was because: "Adults have their ways, and you're too young to know what you're getting into." Then there was the bigger issue: it was time for Lucy to "grow up and learn to get along with others." "Getting along" seemed to be a major theme.

Finally, after all the words, the walking back and forth, and on and on and on, her dad said he'd decided not to ground her.

That was surprising. Lucy started to ask why, but then her dad started talking again: "I want you to write a letter of apology to Miss Wiggins."

"No, Dad," Lucy said. The words rushed from her lips.

"Do you have any idea what it must have been like for Miss Wiggins to receive all those postcards, Lucy?"

"She fenced Wiggins Hill!"

"She *owns* the hill, Lucy! She can do whatever she wants, including flattening it with bulldozers. Take some paper and pencil and sit at the kitchen table and think about it. If I ground you for this, it will be for a very long time."

Lucy sat at the kitchen table for two hours. Finally, she managed to put this on the piece of notebook paper:

Miss Wiggins,

I understand that you didn't like getting all those Free Wiggins Hill postcards. I wish you would let us sled, because there are a lot of people who miss sledding, and it's hard looking at the best sledding hill through a fence. But I didn't mean to harass you, which is what adults keep saying I did. I only meant to ask **a lot**. My dad says I have not treated you with respect, and if this is true, I am sorry. I didn't mean to do that. I won't send you any more postcards asking to sled.

Lucy Moon

Lucy read it over and thought *at least it's not a lie.* She handed the letter to her dad, who was sitting in his lounger, went into her room, and slammed the door.

Her mom would have been proud of her. Lucy's mom believed in "standing up to the fray," "fighting the good fight," and "speaking for the voiceless." Her mom never told her to "get along"! What kind of mind-melding, turn-your-daughter-into-a-zombie talk was that? Her dad *got along* so well with Mr. Gustafson that now her mom didn't have a photography studio in town. Not that her mom wanted it, but still. Anyway, her mom wouldn't have messed with Lucy's affairs, like her dad did. She would have let Lucy fight it out! *When* was she coming home?

Lucy threw herself across the bed and lay there, waiting and listening. If her dad came up the stairs, the letter was a failure (not sorry enough), and she'd get punished forever, starting now. And if he stayed downstairs, he'd send the letter.

So this was the way the postcard campaign ended—with no sledding, and a fence around Wiggins Hill?

As hard as Lucy found the end of the postcard campaign, detention turned out to be not too bad. Lucy decided to wear her punishment like a badge of honor. After all, she'd earned it. She had engaged in civil disobedience and got arrested for the cause (well, it wasn't quite getting arrested, but close enough). In addition, it was only a couple of weeks to winter break. Lucy got her homework done, and she now had something to do after school, like the rest of her friends. Zoë had started taking Tuesday and Thursday afternoons off from the bakery to make bowls and candlesticks with the art club. Sam Shipman played scales on his trombone in the band room every day. And Lucy attended detention—an after-school club for the activist!

Since Lucy's detention began, Sam waited for her at her locker every afternoon. He admitted he felt guilty about Lucy getting detention and having to write that letter to Miss Wiggins. Lucy figured this was why Sam appeared.

But frankly, Lucy didn't care why. She just felt happy about it. She packed her backpack, put on her coat, and then together they walked down the big hill, turned left on Main Street, and continued on toward the Rossignol Bakery.

During their walks they talked about everything: Wiggins Hill, random animal facts (one male mountain lion needs 175 miles of space), and Sam's latest description of a jazz riff by an "amazing trombonist." Lucy gave Sam updates on her mom's cloud adventures (now in California). And Sam told Lucy about how his mom secretly wanted to start a theater troupe in Turtle Rock, but knew Miss Wiggins and the Turtle Rock Arts Committee would never approve. They also did impressions. Sam did impressions of Lucy's dad as the postmaster (reading a magazine while sorting the mail), and Lucy pretended to be Sam's mom acting out the parts in *Macbeth*. They talked about what they would do during winter break. They both moaned about no sledding on Wiggins Hill. And they always ended their walk with Sam's favorite argument about one of the world's great to-the-death battles: who won more often—the mongoose or the cobra?

This had developed into a silly game. As soon as they reached the bakery, they ran to the big red couch to ask Zoë the question: "Cobra or mongoose?"

Then Zoë chose one randomly (in theory, anyway). "Mongoose," she said.

Sam raised his hands in exultation.

"No," said Lucy, whining a little, "you can't always pick the mongoose, Zoë. In real life, the cobra has to win sometimes."

"Not today," said Zoë.

"Yeah, I am so good," said Sam. He stretched out on the couch with his hands up behind his head.

Lucy moaned and sat down limply.

"Poor Lucy," said Zoë to Sam. "She didn't win today." Zoë grabbed one of Lucy's knees right where she was ticklish.

"Stop it!" Lucy said, laughing. "Stop it!"

"Settle down," said Mrs. Rossignol, "or the hot apple ciders go down the drain." They sat up, and Mrs. Rossignol set the three hot apple ciders on the coffee table in front of them. They said thank you, and then they talked. If it weren't for the fence around Wiggins Hill, all of them would've agreed it was a nearly perfect time. Despite everything, thinking about the three of them together made Lucy smile.

CHAPTER 10

In December, winter had begun in earnest. The lake froze and refroze with wailing moans and cracks that sounded like shotguns gone off unexpectedly. Temperatures dropped, dropped, and then dropped further still. Night came on strong, like a second shift, the moon rising as soon as business owners hung CLOSED signs on doors at five o'clock.

And expectation of the holidays shimmered in the air like the snowflake-shaped lights strung up and down Main Street. Every night another Christmas tree sparkled in a front bay window; every night more lights flickered in yards, or outlined houses. And, like every Christmas before, Mr. and Mrs. Lundgren's house was lit up like an airport landing strip, complete with singing bells; thirty-six light-up crèches; twenty-two of Snow White's dwarfs, and ninety-eight waving, belly-laughing Santas. The Turtle

Rock Police Department had to send a police officer out to Spruce Street just to keep the traffic moving.

Some of the churches tried to get their yearly Nativity pageants together. But several found unforeseen obstacles with their choice of Mary, as reported by Jessica Ar'dour in her "Ear to the Door" column in the *Turtle Rock Times*:

Who will play Mary at the Lutheran, Presbyterian, and Catholic Nativity plays this year? That is the question. Three Turtle Rock churches have asked the same girl to play the part: eighth grader Eugenie Sovil (known as "the Genie" to her nearest and dearest). With Miss Sovil's long black tresses, her lavender eyes, and bow-shaped lips, it's no wonder. You couldn't want for a prettier Mary.

For the past few years, Miss Sovil has played Mary at two or three churches during the holiday season. But this year, she says she is unable to combine her social schedule with the dates of all those Nativity plays. Miss Sovil says she is forced to choose one church, and is making the churches bid for her services. "I'm an experienced Mary—that's worth something," she says. "But, I've promised the churches I'll consider all offers equally."

So far, the offers being considered include her own dressing room at the Presbyterian Church, a hand-tailored peasant costume at the Catholic Church, and a donkey processional at the Lutheran Church. Miss Sovil has also read all three scripts.

("They're basically the same plot," says Miss Sovil.) Miss Sovil seems most excited about the donkey.

"Riding on a donkey—that's authentic," she says. "I think I might be persuaded by the Lutheran Church, if they'd allow me to leave by donkey too. The angels could hold up my train." As an afterthought, Miss Sovil added: "Trumpets would be nice."

Miss Sovil plans to give her final answer over the weekend.

. . . Always listening in, Jessica Ar'dour.

Everyone kept busy with holiday preparations, except the Moons. Lucy Moon didn't think much about holiday decorations. She liked to look at them on her walks down to the Rossignol Bakery after detention, and she and Sam always tried to outdo each other by finding the tackiest decoration, but Lucy didn't decorate. Decorating was something that *happened* to a person. One night, Lucy's mom would make an announcement, and then suddenly the whole house was turned inside out, upside down with activity. The next thing Lucy knew, a fake Christmas tree stood in the living room (Lucy had never liked cutting down trees), a wreath was hung on the front door, and someone was warming eggnog in a pan. Okay, Lucy helped with the decorations, but she wouldn't have *started* them.

Lucy did do the one thing that was required of her: her Christmas shopping. For her dad, who always complained that by the time he learned a particular warbler's song, the warbler had moved on, she bought a CD of warbler warbles so he could study up before spring. And for her mom, who always seemed to be warming her hands under her armpits, Lucy bought a pair of fingerless gloves so she'd keep her hands warm and still be able to turn camera lenses. (She got them at the Lutheran Church Christmas Bazaar, and they were so cheap that she'd bought a pair for Zoë, too.)

But then one day, Lucy gazed out at the backyard through the picture window in the living room and realized that it looked too perfect, with the snow covering the ground and the boughs of the small pine.

The bird tree! Every year after Thanksgiving, Lucy and her mom decorated that small pine. By now, the small pine tree should have been packed with bird food ornaments. Chickadees, redpolls, and juncos should be hopping in and out of the branches. Woodpeckers should be hanging off the suet ornaments. Lucy should hear birds chirping from the roof of their house. There should be a pair of binoculars, a bird guide, and a notebook on her dad's little table by the lounger. And Lucy should be checking it to see if a McKay's bunting showed up. Years ago, Lucy swore she saw one, but no one had believed her. Her dad had said it probably was a snow bunting.

But instead, the small pine sat green and white, without even a footprint in the snow around it.

Lucy couldn't decide what to do. Her mom always announced decorating the bird tree, and then they worked on it together. The bird tree started off the whole sequence of Christmas events: the bird tree led to snapping together the Christmas tree; the Christmas tree led to making braided bread; the braided bread led to the Winter Parade in downtown Turtle Rock; the Winter Parade led to the Hallelujah Chorus sing-along; the sing-along led to the candlelight service; and the candlelight service led to chocolate-chip cinnamon buns, hot apple cider, and presents on Christmas morning. Every year, it happened this way. Every year, it was a tradition between the two of them. It didn't seem right to start anything, not without her mom here.

Wherever she was in California, her mom probably felt the tug of that bird tree, too, especially since they were already a few weeks behind schedule. Lucy imagined the light-blue compact car driving across the country. Her mom rubbed her eyes and reached for a giant travel mug of coffee while she drove, drove, drove. Drove all night long, barely slept. Oh, yeah, maybe she was going to surprise them and come home without telling them! Well, whenever she arrived, Lucy planned to help her unpack, and then the two of them would get started on that bird tree, and then Christmas events would overtake them like a snowball pushed down a hill, until it collapsed happily on Christmas Day. Yay!

* * *

One night, the phone rang during dinner. Lucy scooted back her chair and ran up the stairs for the phone. It was her mom!

"Mom, where are you?"

"Sacramento," said her mom. "And I have news!"

"Why are you still in California?" Lucy sat down on the chair in the hallway. It would take at least three days to drive from California to Minnesota—she should get started now.

"I'm getting to that," said her mom, "if you'd let me finish." She sounded like she was happy.

"Okay," said Lucy. She waited.

"I think we should be able to talk every single day on the phone now until Christmas! Isn't that fun? I've decided to spend Christmas with Grandma and Grandpa in Nevada. I'm leaving tomorrow morning, and I should arrive tomorrow night. I've missed hearing about your day, Lucy. I know I'm missing out on all sorts of stories."

Lucy sat up in her chair, trying to wrap her mind around what she'd heard.

"Wait," said Lucy. "You're not coming home for Christmas? You're spending Christmas with Grandma and Grandpa?"

"Oh, I'm sure you'll do fine without me," said her mom. "You know, I haven't seen my parents for a year now, and they're getting older, and I've got this idea for cloud portraits using Grandma and Grandpa. Oh, it'll be spectacular. Clouds age as people do, only a cloud's life is shorter. I'm imagining a photograph of a cloud above the landscape of a human face. And, Lucy, the landscapes in your grandpa's face are awe-inspiring!"

"Mom—wait," said Lucy. "When are you coming home?" Lucy's mind reeled.

"I'm not sure, Lucy," she heard her mom say across the line. "But I'd say things have almost run their course. So, soon."

Soon? Did she say "soon" again? Lucy felt confused. In fact, the entire idea sounded strange. Lucy couldn't even imagine Grandpa sitting long enough for one of her mom's portraits, let alone trying to get a suitably wrinkled cloud to line up behind him. Anyway, Lucy would rather go for a desert walk with Grandpa than make him sit still for an hour. . . .

And then Lucy thought of something.

If her mom wasn't going to be in Turtle Rock for Christmas, maybe Lucy could be in Nevada. . . . Yeah. Lucy hadn't seen her grandparents in a while, and they always wanted her to come out and see them.

Lucy saw just how it would be. Every morning, Grandpa would yell at Grandma for fussing in the kitchen while he made his jalapeño eggs. Her grandma would put Lucy to work wrapping presents and making beaded ornaments. After Grandpa's nap, he and Lucy would play cribbage. (There'd be a running score all vacation long.) And every evening, Lucy would stand in her grandparents' kitchen and watch her mom chop vegetables for soup. Lucy would tell her mom about the arrested sledders, detention, and Wiggins Hill. It was perfect. Yes!

"We'll talk every day on the phone," said her mom, breaking the silence on the line. "I promise."

"Can I spend Christmas with you and Grandma and Grandpa?" Lucy blurted this out.

There was a pause. The pause felt solid.

"Oh, Lucy," her mom said finally. "I don't know."

"Why not?" said Lucy. "All we need is a plane ticket. I haven't been to Nevada in forever."

"Think of your father," her mom said. "He'll be all alone."

"He's fine," Lucy said. "He's got his magazines." (Later, Lucy felt guilty for this betrayal of her father.)

Her mom replied suddenly, almost interrupting Lucy: "We can't afford it, Lucy. We simply cannot afford it."

"I'll pay you back," Lucy said, with a tinge of desperation. If Lucy couldn't go to Nevada, that meant she would have to consider the alternative, and Lucy didn't want to consider the alternative—alone, with her dad, eating in silence on Christmas Day. Christmas was for families—for the *whole* family, not shards of it. Lucy couldn't stay here.

She wouldn't stay here! No! Lucy begged, she pleaded, she whined. She tried it all.

"But what about the birds?" said Lucy finally, in a small voice.

"What?" said her mom.

"The birds," said Lucy, feeling suddenly angry. There were promises her mom wasn't keeping, things that were important, Christmas things. "You're *supposed* to help me decorate the bird tree."

"Lucy," said her mom. "I'm sorry. That's just not going to work out this year." The words by themselves could have been construed as warm, even a "sorry" tucked into them. But Lucy knew her mom wasn't really sorry. Her tone was flat. It said something like this: *You've gone too far. This is the way it will be and I don't want to hear another word about it. Do you understand?*

Lucy couldn't believe her mom would use that tone about Christmas. And in that moment, Lucy thought a bad thought: maybe her mom didn't want her to come to Nevada for Christmas.

Lucy banished this thought immediately. Her mom was driving across country photographing clouds, and who did Lucy think was paying for this trip? They were paying for it. And Lucy's dad was a postmaster, and he couldn't be making all that much, and who knew how much her mom had saved up. This trip had to cost a lot, didn't it? Driving across country?

The phone line was quiet. Lucy's mom seemed to be waiting for Lucy to say something, but Lucy couldn't think of anything to say. So instead, Lucy put the phone receiver on the chair in the hallway and went to get her dad, who seemed to be waiting for her in the kitchen. He got up and went to the phone.

"Josephine," she heard him say. "What's this I hear about you not coming home for Christmas?"

Lucy felt a tiny prick of satisfaction knowing that her mom had some explaining to do.

Soon afterward, Lucy decided that Christmas held no interest for her. She was over it. Good thing she got her shopping done, because now she could forget about Christmas. Let the snap-together tree sit in its box. She could wait Christmas out. Why pretend it was more than it was? Twenty-four measly hours of gimme-gimme gluttony—that's it. It would pass.

Of course, trying to forget about Christmas made Lucy think about it obsessively, and not in a nice way, either. Christmas lights wasted electricity. Ax murder was what happened to Christmas trees. (Don't even ask about Christmas tree farms!) She'd see an image of Santa and think lies, lies—all lies.

Lucy knew better than to say these thoughts out loud. Instead, she was giving Christmas, and the rest of the celebrating world, the cold shoulder.

For two days Lucy sat in her anti-Christmas, anticheer funk, and at the end of it, she found herself sitting on the big red couch at the Rossignol Bakery, watching Sam and Zoë secretly discuss something up at the counter as they waited for Mrs. Rossignol to finish steaming their hot apple ciders. Lucy didn't like how they leaned in together, and then each of them looked her way. Anybody would be grumpy if friends did this, she thought.

"Hey," she yelled over to them. "Don't forget my cinnamon stick!"

In reply, Zoë twirled three cinnamon sticks over her head. She leaned in to listen to Sam like he was a fount of wisdom. Zoë probably liked Sam, or something. Oh, good grief, that was it! Zoë was tall, all fashionable in her Wild Thrift clothes, and Sam liked her! Lucy was doomed to spend the rest of their friendship being the third wheel in some sort of adolescent romance. Great.

Finally, they brought the three mugs of apple cider over, and Lucy was just about to grab hers, when Zoë said "Now!"

Suddenly, Lucy found her shoulders pressed into the back of the red couch. Sam held her left shoulder and Zoë, her right.

Lucy felt like an insect pinned for display. "What?" she demanded, struggling under their palms.

"Ah, yes," said Zoë, peering down at Lucy. "The patient seems unwell. I need to perform a few tests. Lucy, say the first thing you think after hearing the following words."

Oh, give me a break, thought Lucy. She hated it when Zoë insisted on playing games like this. Sometimes Zoë was such a freak.

Zoë continued: "Sugar cookie?"

Lucy sighed, rolled her eyes, and said, "Cholesterol."

"Ornament?"

"Eyesore."

"Christmas music?"

"Buy, buy, buy, buy, buy, buy, buy, buy, buy, buy, buy, buy some more!" Lucy sang to the tune of "God Rest Ye Merry Gentlemen."

"Angel?" asked Sam.

"Tree up my butt."

Zoë and Sam laughed and let go of her shoulders. Lucy did not see what was funny.

Then Zoë stood up and paced back and forth, shaking her head. "You see what I mean, Samuel? There is something wrong with Lucy. She has lost her Christmas spirit."

Lucy looked between Sam and Zoë and finally understood. "It doesn't have anything to do with you two! Okay?" Lucy yelled this—surprising even herself. "Are you satisfied?"

Zoë backed up with her hands above her head. "Just trying to help," she said.

A bakery customer grabbed her bag and hustled out the door.

Lucy glanced over at Mrs. Rossignol, who looked more than a little perturbed. "Those were rosettes, Lucy," she said. "I'm sure she'll be back in half a second when she realizes that she crushed them all trying to escape you!"

"Sorry," Lucy said. And she meant it.

Sam looked shocked.

Then Lucy started to cry, and between gulps, told them all about her mom and Christmas and not going to Nevada. Zoë put her arm around her shoulder and Sam sat forward to listen.

And then Mrs. Rossignol swooped down and scooped Lucy into her arms.

"It's dumb," Lucy kept saying. "It's stupid." She tried to push her fingers against her tear ducts to stop the tears. But they kept coming, so Lucy kept crying.

"It's not dumb. It's not stupid," said Mrs. Rossignol. She rocked Lucy back and forth. "It matters because it's Christmas."

Mrs. Rossignol kept rocking Lucy long after she finished crying. But getting free of a woman who wrangles pastry every day is no easy matter. Lucy wiggled this way and that, but Mrs. Rossignol kept patting her on the back, thumping her the way a baker thumps bread dough. "Have a cry," she kept saying. "It's good every once in a while."

"*I fink I'm dun cryung gnow,*" Lucy said as loudly as she could into the enormous aproned bosom pressed up into her face.

Sam and Zoë burst out laughing, and Lucy couldn't stop herself from laughing, too.

That's when Mrs. Rossignol let Lucy go.

"Well, if all you're going to do is laugh," she said sternly, "I've got customers who *need* me!"

The next night, a Friday night, Zoë called on the walkie-talkie to see if Lucy wanted to go to a movie, but Lucy told her she had "a family obligation she needed to attend to."

"Are you sure?" Zoë's voice sounded tinny and far away on the walkie-talkie.

"Another time," said Lucy.

"Okay. Over and out."

Lucy stared at the blue walkie-talkie, half hoping Zoë would buzz back and beg her to come to the movie. But instead, Lucy heard the Rossignols' garage door open and close, and then tires crunching over snow in the driveway. Lucy felt a little like crying. No, she thought, shaking off the tears. This was the beginning of a hard new life, where mothers did not come home for Christmas and do the things they were supposed to do. Lucy cared, and so she must shoulder the world's burdens alone. This very night she would begin a lifelong path of sacrificing her happiness for the good of others. Eventually she would die, shriveled up and forgotten like a raisin rolled under an edge of linoleum, but who cared? She needed to decorate the bird tree. Lucy gritted her teeth. For the birds.

Lucy popped some popcorn and began to thread it together with a needle and thread. She sat in the kitchen, a big bowl of popcorn in front of her and WBRR, North Country Radio playing softly in the background. She heard her dad turn a magazine page in the other room—probably *Stories of the Pony Express*, which had just come in the mail.

When her fingers began aching, and she had finished only one strand of popcorn, Lucy dropped her head onto the table. She couldn't stand it. She couldn't do it. Only one hour had passed—one lousy hour into her mission of self-sacrifice—and she was already wrinkling and pruning like that forgotten raisin.

"Dad," she said weakly. "Help!" Lucy said this so quietly, she was sure he hadn't heard. She imagined the sound wobbling to the end of the table and puffing off into nothingness.

"Did you call?" he said.

"Yes," Lucy said weakly again. She closed her eyes. Her strength was spent, gone. She was a rattling old sack of bones.

Then she heard the lever release on the lounger. The next thing Lucy knew, her dad was laughing. Lucy kept her eyes closed and tried not to respond, though she could feel her lips twitching into a smile.

"Looks like it's a Christmas emergency," he said finally. "Remain calm and stay where you are. I'll get help."

Lucy heard synthesized Christmas carols start on the stereo in the living room. And when he began to bang around in the kitchen, Lucy opened one eye to watch. On the stove, he stirred a bar of chocolate into fresh milk. Finally, he set a mug of hot chocolate in front of her. Lucy sat up, took a sip, and smiled.

"In the nick of time," she said.

"I thought so," he said.

Then they both got to work.

That night, as they sat at the kitchen table, Lucy forgot all about the cold, hard life she was planning. Lucy watched her dad struggling to thread the popcorn, tiny in his large hands, and she thought the happiness inside her just might break a bone—maybe a wishbone. Did people have wishbones? Or did only chickens get to be that lucky?

CHAPTER 11

During winter break, Lucy kept herself busy at the Rossignol Bakery. No time to think, and that's the way she liked it. Customers called on the phone to reserve mincemeat, apple, or pumpkin pies for Christmas, and place orders for holiday parties. Mrs. Rossignol enforced strict guidelines for the fragile baked goods. Sandbakkels, a kind of buttery cup that melted in a person's mouth, were too fragile to leave the bakery and were for in-store eating only. Krumkake (a thin cookie rolled into a cone), pizzelles (wafer cookies pressed with an iron), and rosettes (a batter deep-fried into crisp, delicate stars and covered with powdered sugar) were allowed to leave the bakery, but only after the buyer got a lecture about how these were *sensitive* baked goods (think a bad thought and they might break) and that the Rossignol Bakery couldn't replace the broken ones, even for blood relations. Buy at your own risk! Lucy was good at lecturing, so she liked that part. She'd be whistling happily by the time she'd packed up the order, rang up the sale on the big cash register, and sent the customer on their way. But Lucy didn't always get to be out front. Often she found herself helping in back, peeling apples, grating chocolate, and scooping out the insides of cooked pumpkins. She also cleaned the tables in the seating area and made sure there was enough turbinado sugar for the coffee in the condiment rack.

After lunch, Lucy and Zoë would go on strike, demanding a break.

"I'm not keeping you here," Mrs. Rossignol would say, rolling her eyes for the benefit of the customers. Then they would run in and out of the downtown stores. They'd meet Sam, Lisa, Edna, and Quote and go ice-skating at the elementary-school ice rink, or cross-country skiing; or sometimes they'd climb on the mountains of snow the snowplows left behind the bakery.

It was on one of these excursions that Lucy and Zoë ended up at The Wild Thrift. Zoë dressed Lucy up in a sequined cocktail dress, and Lucy made Zoë put on a tuxedo over army-issue long johns.

They stood side by side admiring their outfits in the shop mirror when Zoë said, "Don't take this the wrong way, okay?"

Lucy froze. Never once had she ever liked what people said after that kind of statement. "Say it," said Lucy.

"If you're going to be like that . . ."

"Like what?" said Lucy. "You brought this up. Say it!"

"Okay, you were bossy during the postcard campaign. Everyone had to do it your way. No one worked hard enough. I mean, come on, it's just sledding. No one's dying here."

Lucy stared at herself in the too-big slinky dress that fell to her ankles, and realized she didn't want to explain about how she was trying to find out if she was "gifted and talented" at something, and how she had failed because the hill was still fenced, and that meant . . . But Lucy wasn't thinking about that right now.

Zoë continued: "I don't mean to be harsh, but you get too serious sometimes. I mean, don't you ever want to be happy and not so worked up? You make life a lot harder than it has to be. You know what I mean, right?"

Lucy stood speechless. This is what Zoë thought? Lucy wanted to shake her. Zoë knew that most people spent their whole lives numb to everything outside their immediate life. They didn't see. They didn't hear. They didn't taste, smell, touch, or feel. Miracles and disasters exploded on the right and the left, and these people went on plodding ahead, oblivious to it all. So if a few people responded with passion, wasn't that cause for celebration?

"No!" said Lucy finally. "No, I don't!" Lucy pushed

herself into the changing booth and put on her clothes. Lucy had thought Zoë was for her, through and through, one hundred percent.

Lucy didn't talk much as they walked back to the bakery. Zoë kept stealing looks at Lucy again and again and again.

"You *are* my best friend," said Zoë, after a few blocks of silence.

"Yeah, okay," said Lucy. "I just didn't think you wanted me to change into some happy-go-lucky bimbo with no brains."

"I don't," said Zoë.

"You do! Admit it!"

"Admit you judged me during the postcard campaign," said Zoë. She stopped walking. "You thought I wasn't working hard enough."

"Okay, yeah," said Lucy. "But the worst was that you found cable needles, types of sewing machines, and your latest jeans rehab so much more fascinating."

"What if I did? Is that so bad?"

They walked in silence. Then Zoë said, "Okay, as long as we're being all honest, I've got another question for you: are you comparing yourself to me? I might be making this up, but sometimes I swear it feels true!"

This one took Lucy by surprise. She started to say, "No," and then she realized it was true. She hadn't been able to get over the fact that Zoë's growth spurt had left her in the dust.

"I guess it's clear, then," said Zoë quickly. "Neither of us is a perfect friend." She pushed open the bakery door.

This incident blew over, they apologized to each other, and they didn't speak of it. Everything seemed normal (they laughed and talked), except that Lucy couldn't get the conversation out of her head. And neither of them ever asked the other to go to The Wild Thrift again.

Lucy's mom kept her promise to call nightly from Nevada during winter break. It amounted to her mom talking and Lucy listening. Sometimes Lucy said a few things, too. Lucy tried to work herself into being a good person by thinking the right sort of thoughts: wasn't it true that they didn't have the money to fly Lucy to Nevada? And why shouldn't her mom be with her parents over Christmas? She had a family, too, and she missed them. But about ten, fifteen minutes into their conversations, Lucy would notice how lame their Christmas tree looked this year, or realize she hadn't had a sip of eggnog, and couldn't think of anything to say to her mom. A long pause, and then good-byes ended the conversation.

Lucy's present from her mom arrived a few days before Christmas in a thin envelope. When her mom called that night, she told Lucy to open it.

Lucy gasped. The present rated a ten on a scale from one to ten. Slipped inside the envelope was a gift certificate for a pair of mukluks, the hand-sewn boots worn by

Native Americans. Lucy remembered the knee-high boots she'd seen in the mukluk store window in Burnum as a second grader. She had fallen in love then. Every year since, Lucy had checked to see if the woman still made them—the ones with the Navajo blanket tops in red, yellow, and black that went all the way up to the knees. With those boots, Lucy could cross snowdrifts and never get snow in her pants. She wouldn't take them off ever! But the boots cost hundreds of dollars, and Lucy's mom had always said that she wouldn't buy her a pair until Lucy reached her adult height.

Lucy said, "But, Mom, my feet haven't stopped growing."

Lucy heard her mom laugh. Then she said she had paid for the mukluks with the money from "Found," the mountain goat photograph.

"Thank you," said Lucy, staring down at the gift certificate. "Thank you!"

Even with mukluks in her future, Lucy thought that Christmas day would surely be the most shoe-shuffling, tick-tock-went-the-clock day of her life. Luckily, Mrs. Rossignol invited Lucy and her dad over for Christmas.

Christmas at the Rossignol house was Christmas bursting at its seams. Relatives sat in every chair, stood in every corner, and leaned on every counter. Their cars lined the length of Fifth Street on both sides. Arguments broke out and apologies were accepted with the regularity of the chiming of the kitchen clock. Lucy gaped happily at the commotion, until the aunts chased all the able-bodied relations out the door, one of them bearing a spatula, and another, a whisk, saying that a woman couldn't cook in such a din. Lucy and Zoë, along with all the others, donned their cross-country skis and took off into the park. When they got back, the aunts corralled them into the basement, where they were told to stay until Mrs. Rossignol called them. They waited, waited, waited. Stomachs moaned and stretched. One of the uncles swore he'd swallowed a cat, and if they listened, they could hear it mewing. They listened, and they could!

"It's time," Mrs. Rossignol yelled finally.

Everyone stopped midsentence, midknit, mid–Ping-Pong serve, and sprinted to the Christmas table.

They ate for hours. Lucy lost track of the courses—vegetables, cheeses, meats, pastas, mushrooms, and on and on. The courses arrived from the kitchen in swishes of aproned women, each one initiating rounds of low murmurs and gasps, teasing, and stories. The men let out their belts.

When it was all over, Lucy sank in her seat, one hand resting on her belly. She saw her red socks under the table and wiggled her toes. Her feet ached from skiing. She imagined her feet snug inside those mukluks. It made her feel sleepy to think of all that warmth. Lucy closed her eyes then and there, and a question sauntered into her head, like a cat checking out an unfamiliar room: Why did her mom choose this year to finally give in to the mukluks?

Lucy's eyes opened. She sat up. It was strange. For years, her mom had stood firm. Lucy's feet needed to stop growing before she bought her a pair. It was almost a joke when Lucy begged. Why was this year different? Did her mom feel guilty? Was it a bribe for not coming home? Then the questions pounced on something in the corner of her mind. Mukluks were expensive. A pair of mukluks cost as much as a plane ticket.

Lucy felt sick to her stomach.

"Are you okay, Lucy?" said Zoë.

Lucy broke away from thoughts of her mom and said quickly: "Too much food."

Zoë laughed. "It happens to everyone the first time they eat Christmas dinner with us. Next year will be better. Your stomach learns."

At nine thirty that night, Lucy and her dad cut across the Rossignols' yard to their little red house. Lucy leaned against him, grateful for the solid presence of him here, now—her dad. He gently straightened her green-and-yellow hat and asked how she liked Christmas.

"Fine," said Lucy quickly. She didn't want to talk. Her stomach felt upset.

When they got home, a message on the answering

machine from her mom, grandma, and grandpa awaited them: "Merry Christmas!" they said. Then they sang "Jingle Bells."

"We'll call them tomorrow," said her dad. "You look like you could use some sleep."

Lucy nodded and went upstairs to her room.

It took a while for Lucy to fall asleep that night. She twisted in the sheets for at least an hour, but eventually all that food had its soporific effect. Lucy fell asleep in spite of the fact that one thought kept circling like a goldfish in a bowl: *Mukluks cost as much as plane tickets. Mukluks cost as much as plane tickets. Mukluks cost as much as plane tickets.*

CHAPTER 12

It aggravated Lucy Moon that her mom left places and never told them, like her family didn't play a part in her decisions, which, okay, apparently they didn't. Lucy's mom had left her grandparents' house early the day after Christmas. She was now driving toward New Mexico. This is what her grandparents said when Lucy called them. Lucy's dad didn't know a thing about these travels, either.

When Lucy woke up the day after Christmas, she wanted to ask her mom one, single, solitary question. It was the question that woke her up at 5 A.M.: Why did her mom buy a gift certificate for mukluks instead of buying Lucy a plane ticket to Nevada? A person would think a mom could answer a question. It wasn't too much to ask.

Lucy remembered how her grandma described her

mom's destination: "We think she went to Santa Fe," her grandma said. "She did go on about a girlfriend and a dog—some enormous dog that liked to sleep on people's bare feet. I believe it was a Newfoundland." The phone muffled and Lucy heard her grandma yell: "Ernie, do you remember what kind of dog?"

Great, Lucy had thought. So her mom left Nevada to visit a big dog. Maybe Lucy should practice fetching and rolling over.

The next morning, two days after Christmas, Lucy ate her cereal and thought about what she knew of Santa Fe: Georgia O'Keeffe's round buildings, longhorn skulls, and black crosses; and a big dog jumping up and licking her mom's face. Every time Lucy imagined the dog jumping up, she thought, Oh, you'd like that, wouldn't you? She was in a rather grim mood. She needed to talk to her mom about the plane ticket. But who knew when. Maybe her mom would call. Maybe she wouldn't call. Could be today. Could be days. Heck, why not a month?

In the middle of these thoughts, Lucy heard a knock at the door.

Lucy clanged her spoon down on the kitchen table and opened the front door. It was a police officer.

Oh, no, Lucy thought. She didn't mean it. She was grumpy in the morning. Ask anyone! Please, don't let it be her mom. Lucy remembered what Miss Wiggins said about her mom at the gallery opening: "She's fond of risks, isn't she?"

Lucy saw the scene in her mind: the compact car swerving off the road. Her mom lying facedown on the roadside, camera equipment splayed around her. Passing cars skidding on lens filters and developer fluid.

Or it could be something else. Something like her mom running, glancing behind her. A grizzly bear catching her, striking and slashing with its claws. Oh, yeah, that was something her mom might do—get between a mama grizzly and her cubs.

What if there wasn't a body? What if her mom was just missing? Lucy couldn't stand that—she knew she couldn't stand that. Lucy waited for the police officer to say something, anything.

"Is there a parent at home?" said the police officer. He stepped inside and glanced around.

Later, that's all Lucy remembered him saying. Maybe the police officer had said something before that. Maybe he'd shown a badge—weren't they supposed to? But if any of that had happened, Lucy didn't remember. What she heard was the squeak that meant her dad pulled the lever on the lounger to sit up. And then Lucy's dad was at the door.

In a daze, Lucy followed the police officer and her dad into the living room.

The police officer dug around in a briefcase and

then handed Lucy a "Free Wiggins Hill!" postcard.

Lucy stared at the postcard for a moment. It didn't make any sense. Then all her theories about the police officer's visit fell like rows of dominoes.

"Is this about me?" asked Lucy.

The police officer nodded. "Do you know what these are?" he asked her.

"Oh, yeah," said Lucy. She relaxed. "Why didn't you say so?" All Lucy could think was that her mom was okay. Her mom was alive!

That's when her dad took the postcard out of Lucy's hand and stepped in front of her.

"What's this about?" her dad asked. "You don't ask my twelve-year-old daughter questions until I approve it. Is that clear?" He stared down at the police officer. Lucy gazed up at the solid plank of her dad's back and felt a little sorry for the police officer.

The police officer sighed. "There was an act of vandalism on Wiggins Hill on Christmas night. A 'Free Wiggins Hill!' postcard was found on the scene. So we need to know where Lucy was that night. She's not the only one we're questioning."

Her dad's hand gripped Lucy's shoulder. "My daughter was sleeping in our home," he said slowly.

"She didn't leave for any reason?"

"No," he said.

The police officer smiled quickly, apologetically, and

added. "You don't happen to have a toboggan around, do you?"

"No," her dad said firmly.

"Sounds good," said the police officer. He flipped a notebook open, wrote something down, flipped the notebook closed, and tucked it in a pocket.

Lucy glanced up at her dad. He patted her shoulders.

"Okay, that's it," said the police officer. He shook her dad's hand. "Thank you for your time." Soon after that the police car's engine turned over and the police officer drove away.

Her dad patted Lucy on the shoulder one more time and then went upstairs. By the slope of his shoulders, Lucy knew she hadn't been the only one worried about her mom.

By the time the *Turtle Rock Times* reported on it on New Year's Day—"Christmas Night Vandalism on Wiggins Hill!"—everyone knew most of the story: how Miss Wiggins saw a light on Wiggins Hill, that she drove her car to the bottom of the hill and arrived in time to see "five or six" sledders running away (one pulling a toboggan) through a freshly cut hole in the fence. Miss Wiggins claimed that all of the sledders disguised themselves by wearing big, bulky winter coats, and covering their faces with scarves and ski masks. "This was a premeditated, malicious action," said Miss Wiggins. "The police had better see to it that the culprits are caught."

It was a good read. Lucy spread the *Turtle Rock Times* on the floor in front of her, while her dad watched the football game. She chuckled at Jessica Ar'dour's "Ear to the Door" column:

A neighbor, who shall remain unidentified, heard a scream that sounded like "Merry Christmas to you, too" on Christmas night. When he peeked out his window, he swears he saw Miss Ilene Viola Wiggins in the middle of the street waving her arms. He also says she "wore only a satiny red nightdress and fuzzy blue slippers."

"You don't think of this sort of thing happening in Turtle Rock, let alone on Christmas night," said the neighbor.

This reporter then called Miss Wiggins to verify that she was, in fact, wearing a red nightdress. Miss Wiggins said, "Anyone thinking I wear skimpy clothing on a subzero night is clearly half-cocked, and that goes for those who print this rubbish in the newspaper, too." Miss Wiggins then hung up on this reporter. . . . Always listening in, Jessica Ar'dour.

The police had questioned Lucy, Zoë, Edna, Sam, and Lisa Alt on December 26th. Lucy didn't blame them. Of course the police thought they had done it: a "Free Wiggins Hill!" postcard had been left at the scene of the crime. All five of them had been within walking distance of the hill on Christmas night. But none of them had done it.

Lucy glanced at her dad, sitting forward in his lounger

watching the game. He had asked her about the vandalism. Lucy told him what she knew, which was nothing. The last thing Lucy would do is cut Miss Wiggins's fence, sled on Miss Wiggins's hill, and then skewer a postcard as a calling card!

The crowd at the football game roared on the television, and Lucy looked up to see a streak of gold on the green turf. The University of Minnesota had scored a touchdown.

"A quarterback sneak!" said her dad, shooting a palm into the air.

When the phone rang, Lucy raced up the stairs to answer it.

"Happy New Year!" said her mom. "I'm in Santa Fe."

"I know," said Lucy. "I talked to Grandma."

"Oh, good," her mom said. She jabbered away. Lucy learned that her mom nearly drove off the road because of a cumulus cloud that looked like a face, that her friend's house was made of adobe, and that she owned a "spectacular" Newfoundland dog named Rufus.

Lucy sat down on the hallway chair and let the words tumble until they were only sounds and rhythms. She grew angrier and angrier. First, her mom hadn't called for a week. Second, her mom had had enough money to fly Lucy out to Nevada for Christmas and didn't do it. And finally, Lucy was supposed to sit here and listen to her mom's litany of happiness, joy, and fun? Enough was enough.

"Sounds great, Mom. Now can I say something?" Lucy said.

"I guess I go on and on," her mom said, chuckling. "It's been real fun."

"Okay," said Lucy. She paused and then came out with it. "Mukluks cost as much as plane tickets, Mom. How come you didn't buy me a plane ticket if you had the money?"

"You didn't like the mukluks? I thought you *wanted* mukluks."

Lucy tried again, spelling it out slowly and with emphasis. "Mom, that's not the point. I wanted to have Christmas with you and Grandma and Grandpa in Nevada, and you said we didn't have the money to pay for it. But you *did* have the money to pay for it! You bought me a pair of mukluks. Why didn't you buy me a plane ticket to Nevada instead?"

The pause on the other end of the line was immense.

Lucy waited. She heard nothing . . . nothing . . . nothing.

"Mom . . . ?" said Lucy.

"I'm sorry," her mom said softly.

"But, Mom, you said I couldn't come because we didn't have the money," Lucy continued. "Mukluks cost lots."

Another pause.

"Yeah," said her mom, with a sigh that sounded like an orca breaking the surface of water to catch its breath.

And then the answer finally came. It was scrunched together on a squeak of air: "I couldn't be a mom this Christmas."

The words crashed into Lucy. Time grew sluggish. Lucy realized that she hadn't thought about how her mom might reply. She had been obsessed with just asking the question.

Then she felt a dull ache. But hey, there was something to be said for hearing the truth, right? The truth was good.

The ache grew into a raw hurt.

Somehow Lucy's mouth began speaking. "But you *are* a mom. You're *my* mom. You're supposed to be a *mom*."

"Lucy," said her mom.

But Lucy didn't let her talk. "I thought you were taking photographs. You're not taking photographs? You're escaping *me*? At Christmas?"

"No, I didn't mean that!" said her mom. What followed was a waterfall of words: "I can't do without you, you know that. I love you. I need you. I love being your mom and I'm real proud of you." On and on and on it went. But Lucy couldn't understand. It made no sense. And anyway, she couldn't hold the phone up to her head anymore, because her face seemed to be slick. She put the receiver down on the chair. Lucy could still hear her mom talking on the phone as she walked into her bedroom and closed the door.

* * *

Over the next couple of days the phone rang nonstop. No way, thought Lucy. Her entire body tensed as she sat listening to the ring until her dad or the machine answered it.

Finally, on the third day, her dad came into her room. Lucy did not, would not, look up from where she sat in the armchair. She pretended she did not notice him. Couldn't he see she was busy with Ms. Kortum's winter-break reading?

The bed wheezed when he sat on the end of it.

Lucy continued to take notes on the Chippewa Native Americans. But beyond the sight line of her pen, Lucy could see her dad's shoes—big, brown, sturdy, reliable shoes with a shine that could only be achieved by polish and a brush. Lucy knew he would never think of getting a new pair of shoes. He had this pair and he would keep them. They were "serviceable." He liked things that were serviceable. Lucy wondered if he knew that Josephine, his wife and her supposed-to-be mom, was no longer offering any service at all when it came to being a mom, other than buying expensive presents over the phone and having store clerks sign the card.

"Your mom told me what she said."

Lucy stopped writing and decided to look up.

He met her eyes. He looked pained, confused.

Lucy raised an eyebrow. "Did she tell you she didn't want to be a mom?"

"She said she needed a break from being a mom this Christmas," he said.

"Oh," said Lucy, going back to her social studies. "That's not what she said." She kept taking notes. "For the record, Mom said—and I quote—'I couldn't be a mom this Christmas.'"

Her dad sighed. "I'm going to tell you something." The air in the room seemed to thicken into gelatin, and each breath caught in Lucy's throat. "I think she's running away from me," he said. "She is taking photos and she's probably doing great work, as your mom always does. But I think this trip is mostly about me. And her. You got caught in the middle."

Lucy wished he would shut up. She didn't want any more truths. She couldn't take any more words. Her dad's words stuck in the air, and Lucy couldn't breathe. Her mom's words replayed endlessly in Lucy's head, stinging every time. How did parents expect kids to swallow this kind of stuff? Lucy was full. She was *full*. Okay?

Lucy could feel him watching her. She bit her lower lip and concentrated on the sentence she had now copied three times from the book: "French fur trappers often relied on the Chippewa for survival in the harsh climate. French fur trappers often relied on the Chippewa for survival in the harsh climate. French fur trappers . . ."

"For my part," he said, "I'm sorry."

Finally Lucy cleared her throat. She didn't look at him.

"I can't get *caught* in the middle. I *am* in the middle. I'm the kid. I'm half you and half her. And she didn't say anything about not wanting to be a 'wife.' She said 'mom.' She said she couldn't be a 'mom' this Christmas."

Lucy realized she was nearly yelling, so she decided to concentrate on the attributes of her purple pen. She made circles on her paper. Yes, a nice thin line that never glopped. Dependable, true, honest. She ran a finger across a recently written line—huh, dried fast, too.

The bed creaked as her dad stood up. She saw him move toward her. No hug, she thought. No. He took a step backward as if he could read her mind, and then the door closed and her dad was gone.

But his words were not gone. They somehow shimmied in the air all around her, like canned fruit in a Jell-O casserole. The words seemed to soak up her thoughts, energy, everything about her. She needed to get out of this room. Lucy put on her winter clothes and told her dad she was going snowshoeing.

As soon as the frozen air touched the skin on her face, Lucy felt better. She started running on her snowshoes straight up the hill into Lookout Park.

CHAPTER 13

On Monday, January 5th, school resumed. But it was hardly school as usual. It began with a phone call to one student's parent, and then to the next parent, and then another, and another. The secretary spent the entire day on the phone—she called over thirty parents—and later had to go to a chiropractor for the kink in her neck. She said the same thing to each parent: would they come to the principal's office on such-and-such a date? Not a request—the police needed to ask their child some questions. It had to do with Wiggins Hill. Then the secretary checked the name off the list and called the next parent.

For the students, opening the principal's door and seeing a police uniform, their father in a suit and tie, their mother in the dress she wore to church, and Principal Adams's cowboy boots crossed on his desk, caused spasms of breath, a spinning sensation, and a desire to sprint. They saw the slight twinkle in Principal Adams's eyes (yeah, he was amused), and they saw his outstretched hand containing mail. They recognized the mail immediately. The postcards said *Free Wiggins Hill!*

Then Principal Adams added, as if it were necessary, "These look familiar?"

What were they supposed to say? No? Anyone could see the signature at the bottom of the postcard. Some of the kids said "Yeah," others shrugged, and yet others stared blankly, thinking about more important issues, like breath and how to get it, since they'd obviously forgotten. The jokers said, "Is there a law against postcards?"

Then the Turtle Rock police officer stepped forward. He asked each kid their whereabouts on Christmas night at about three in the morning. The police officer tried to be nice, but none of the kids trusted him, mostly because people in Turtle Rock, Minnesota, had cable TV. They had seen those police television shows, and knew that behind every nice police officer stood the mean one. (It didn't matter that only one police officer stood in the principal's office. They were sure that a second one lurked somewhere.)

While the police officer spoke, most of the kids' minds began to whirl, trying to figure out who had gotten them into trouble for sending a *postcard*, of all things!

Lucy Moon. It was as clear as that. They thought about

her standing with clenched fists and furrowed brow in the hallway: "Sign this petition!" "Stop murdering the deer!" Those braids nearly hit her knees, and that green-and-yellow hat never came off. She was a brown-eyed nutcase. Hadn't they heard that her mom still hadn't come home from that picture-taking trip? That said something.

Not all the kids felt this way, but a big chunk of them did. They remembered their friends—the ones who'd taken the postcards and signed "Lucy Moon" as a prank. If they had thought to sign those cards with her name, they would have been brilliant, but instead they'd gotten all wrapped up in the drama of it, like a baby. Sledding was for babies. They'd been duped.

It was around this point in the interview (maybe after a glance at a glowering parent) that kids began to realize that maybe they didn't want to leave the principal's office. Every kid was sure that as soon as they left, their parents would start talking about "appropriate" punishment. And then one of the parents would say something like: "No more socializing, mixing, or hanging out with that girl Lucy Moon." Well, their parents could save their breath—they'd already decided that they wanted absolutely nothing to do with her.

The afternoon of the inquisition, Lucy Moon had sat in Ms. Kortum's classroom, feeling taut and edgy. She bet all the students felt the same way. When this many parents came through the front doors of the junior high, gusts of tension were sure to blow in with them. Lucy couldn't understand why they did the interviews at school. Now everyone suffered. All day long, one student after another interrupted classes and told the teacher that Principal Adams would like to see so-and-so now. Any moment the next victim could be called. Eyes flicked to the door.

For Lucy, this tension had been particularly unwelcome. After all that had happened over winter break, Lucy felt like a side of beef dragged over rocks. She kept hearing her mom's words—"I couldn't be a mom . . ."—over and over and over. If it weren't for Zoë insisting that she get out and do things, Lucy probably would have stayed in her room doing homework. But Lucy knew she had to pull it together for school. She needed to figure out a way to get her mom out of her mind.

At least at school the phone didn't ring. Still, it would help a lot if the first days back had been normal!

Ms. Kortum stood at the front of the classroom writing notes on the board, like she always did as class began. This was a relief. It seemed like some of Lucy's other teachers had given up and turned their class into study hall. One teacher made them sit quietly and study maps for an hour. As if anyone could concentrate on the topography of Australia! Lucy found comfort in the sounds of Ms. Kortum's chalk on the blackboard, the fuzzy green cardigan she always wore, and the gray hair knotted untidily in a bun at the back of her head (a few strands drifting free, like feathers).

Another plus was that this was Lucy's one class with both Zoë and Sam. Lucy wrote a note to Zoë: *Who do you think is in the principal's office now?* She tossed it onto Zoë's desk. Zoë flattened it out, read it, and bobbed her head in the direction of an empty desk.

"Are you sure?" whispered Lucy.

Two rows away, Sam leaned over and put a finger to his lips. "Ssssssshhhhhh."

Lucy grinned at him.

"Students," Ms. Kortum said, her back to them. "I'd like you to copy this information into your notebooks *quietly*. I think you know me well enough to know that anything appearing on the blackboard also appears on my tests."

Lucy sighed, opened her notebook, and started copying the heading: "Minnesota History." For the rest of the winter and into spring, they were going to study Minnesota history. Why? That was the question. History was *el finito*, done, kaput. Life happened in the "here and now," not the "way back when." Also, history meant textbooks with names, places, and dates in bold lettering—memorization and more memorization. Who cared if there was a *story* behind Congress taking four months to approve Minnesota's application for statehood? There wasn't time for a story. No! Memorize: May 11, 1858—Minnesota becomes a state. That was history.

Still, because she had needed to keep her mind on something other than her mom, and because she liked Ms. Kortum, Lucy had read every sentence, paragraph, and punctuation mark in the winter break assigned reading. It had nearly killed her to focus on it, but she did it.

"So, can anyone tell me what put Turtle Rock, Minnesota, on the map?" Ms. Kortum put the chalk on the ledge of the blackboard. "This wasn't in your books. I want you to make a guess. The first person who gets it right gets an automatic *A* on Friday's quiz."

Hands shot into the air. Lucy shot her hand up, too. Ms. Kortum didn't mind guesses of any kind: freestyle, stab-in-the-dark, roundabout, or informed and educated. "At least guess," she'd urge.

Ms. Kortum's eyes sparkled (like her gold eye shadow) at all the hands.

"Zoë?"

"Logging?"

"Good guess, because logging was an important part of Turtle Rock history. But I'm thinking about something earlier. . . . Lucy?"

"The fur trade?" The fur trade was the least boring part of the reading, so that's why Lucy guessed it.

"That's right," said Ms. Kortum slowly. She appeared to consider something. "But before I give you the automatic *A*, I want to know which fur trading company was part of our history here in Turtle Rock. I'll even give you some help. Was it the American Fur Company, the North West Company, or the Hudson's Bay Company? Get this right and you'll be skipping Friday's quiz with an *A* in my book. What do you think, Lucy?"

Lucy glanced at Zoë. Zoë shrugged.

"No help," said Ms. Kortum.

Lucy closed her eyes, balling and unballing one of her braids in her hand. She knew she could ferret out the answer if she concentrated. The book mostly talked about the North West Company, which was French, but that was probably the obvious answer. There was hardly any information on the American Company, so maybe that company didn't last very long. . . . Hudson's Bay Company was English. Lucy didn't think there were a lot of French speakers in Turtle Rock, so that would eliminate North West. . . .

"Hudson's Bay Company?" She wrinkled her nose.

"Correct! Congratulations, Lucy."

"Yes!" Lucy raised a fist in the air.

Everyone groaned.

"Lucky," whispered Zoë.

Ms. Kortum continued: "Hudson's Bay Company established the Turtle Rock Fort on Turtle Rock Lake in 1835. After the fort was abandoned, one of the Hudson's Bay Company men, a man named Amos Zebulon, stayed in the area."

Ms. Kortum smiled at Lucy. "Good work, Lucy," she said. "Or should I say, good guess?"

Then Ms. Kortum turned to the rest of the students. "No need to worry! I've got more questions that will get you out of Friday's quiz, if you did your reading and you make some guesses like Lucy did."

Hands popped into the air, including Zoë's.

"Don't you want to wait for the question?" said Ms. Kortum, laughing.

The hands stayed in the air. Zoë stuck her hand up farther. Lucy chuckled.

But then the missing student appeared in the doorway. The hands came down and everyone stared. He looked pale. He said something to Ms. Kortum and then handed her a note.

"Lucy," said Ms. Kortum softly. "You need to go to the principal's office."

Lucy felt her heart hit her boots. She got up, grabbed her social studies book, her pen and notebook, and left the classroom. She heard chairs creak, and she knew that everyone was watching her go.

Lucy walked down the stairs into an empty hallway leading to the principal's office. What could Principal Adams want with her? The police already interviewed her! This couldn't be good. Was her dad down there? Had the police found information linking her to the fence cutting? She didn't do it! She didn't do it!

Principal Adams's secretary looked up when Lucy

pushed open the door. Lucy glanced around. No one else—not her dad, not a police officer—was there.

"Lucy Moon," the secretary said, sighing. She began massaging her right shoulder while she ran one finger down a list. "Oh, yeah," she mumbled. "Says here you're supposed to report to the school counselor, Mrs. Dee Reams, as soon as you get down here. And if you don't, I'm supposed to say that disciplinary action will begin immediately. Got it?"

Disciplinary action? What? But Lucy didn't have a chance to ask, because now the secretary's right arm was outstretched. "Go out into the hallway and make the first right. That's Mrs. Dee Reams's office. It says 'counselor' on the door. And afterward, don't you forget to stop back and get your pass for class."

Everyone called Mrs. Dee Reams "Mrs. Dreams," which was appropriate, because in seventh grade, kids got her "Dreams and Aspirations" talk, and took the career test, which had actually instructed one girl to become a clown and join the circus. Or that's what Lucy had heard. But dreams and aspirations couldn't be why Mrs. Dreams wanted to see Lucy. Not today.

In general, Lucy wasn't sure she trusted Mrs. Dreams, anyway. Lucy had seen her standing sturdily out in the hallway chatting with Principal Adams, and under thick black glasses, Mrs. Dreams smiled, which was fine, except that Mrs. Dreams smiled all the time. The smile sat there like a sculpture, as though Michelangelo had chiseled it there hundreds of years ago. It simply wasn't possible to always be smiling, especially if a person was the school counselor. (My grandma died. Smile, smile, smile? I hit my brother over the head with the vacuum-cleaner extension. Smile, smile, smile?) And also, Lucy had this thing about people who didn't have a definite hair color. Mrs. Dreams's hair was black with highlights that changed from blue to green and green to red. Mood hair.

Lucy pushed open the door. No one was there.

So she looked around. Lucy couldn't help but notice how strange Mrs. Dreams's office looked, especially for a public school office. Instead of fluorescent lights, lamps illuminated the room. The walls were painted milk-chocolate brown. A blue lava lamp sat on a table in the corner, blobbing away, sending bulging shadows up one wall. And Lucy heard the sound of an ocean, wave after wave after wave, crashing in the middle of a northern Minnesota winter. Lucy found the CD on top of the stereo: "The Say Yes to Life Series: Sigh Goes the Ocean."

Lucy thought it was all very suspicious. Everything seemed placed for maximum psychological impact. "Hmm, what have we here?" Lucy imagined Mrs. Dreams saying as she propped open the lid on Lucy's head and poked Lucy's gray jelly brains with a fork. Well, Lucy was not going to let that happen!

Still, with disciplinary action promised, Lucy wasn't going anywhere yet. She sat on the edge of the couch.

Mrs. Dreams poked her head into the room. "Oh, good," she said, and then she called out to someone in the hallway. "Yes, Lucy Moon is here!"

The next thing Lucy knew, Mrs. Dreams had swiveled her chair away from her desk and was facing Lucy on the couch with a notebook on her lap. Mrs. Dreams beamed at her.

For a moment, Lucy became like a deer in headlights under the power of that smile. Lucy thought maybe she'd won a scholarship (or at least an all-expenses-paid canoe trip in the Boundary Waters). Without thinking, Lucy smiled back and then realized what she was doing. Don't give in, she thought. She pressed her lips into a line.

Now Lucy noticed that Mrs. Dreams's thick, black glasses enlarged her blue eyes, reminding Lucy of two enormous blue fish swimming in bowls. When Mrs. Dreams blinked, it startled Lucy—blink, blink, blink. Lucy clasped her arms and concentrated. She set her face on "blank" and looked Mrs. Dreams square in the fishbowls.

"Why am I here?" Lucy demanded.

"Good," said Mrs. Dreams (blink, blink, blink). "Let's start with that! I've been asked by Principal Adams to interview you and give him a recommendation. And the sooner we start, the sooner we end. So let's get going. How do you feel about junior high?"

"Fine."

"No trouble with school?"

"No."

"The other kids don't make fun of you?"

"Not too much," Lucy said slowly.

"What about friends?"

"Fine."

Mrs. Dreams wrote something in her notebook, and then her head bobbed back up. She blinked. "'Fine' you have friends? Or 'fine' you're comfortable with very few friends?"

"I have friends!"

Did the administration think she had no friends? Lucy grabbed hold of the armrest. She watched Mrs. Dreams scribble in her notebook with a slight smile on her face. What was so amusing about this?

Lucy noticed that screeching gulls were mixing with the sound of the waves on the CD. She hated this CD. Lucy suddenly wished for Principal Adams's wagging finger. At least he got to the point, thought Lucy. Because this whole thing had to be about the postcards or the fence cutting or something.

But Mrs. Dreams seemed to be getting there, too. Her tone got softer and she leaned forward over her knees, her eyes becoming the biggest focal point in the room.

(Blink): "Why do you think you stir things up, Lucy? You have quite a reputation. It must be . . ." Mrs. Dreams paused, her eyes searching the ceiling tiles as if the right word was stuck up there like a spitball, ". . . tumultuous for you."

"I'm not living in great agitation, confusion, or excitement," said Lucy. She had just studied "tumultuous" as a vocabulary word and proudly fed the definition back to Mrs. Dreams. "I feel fine."

"So why do you organize protests?"

"Because something is wrong and it needs to be corrected. You know, justice."

"But why *you*, Lucy?" Mrs. Dreams said. And now the smile seemed almost flirty. "Why not someone else?"

"You're the counselor. You know why."

Mrs. Dreams didn't say anything. The two blue fish stared at Lucy.

Oh, give me a break, thought Lucy. "Okay, sometimes other people don't even see an issue. But other times, people see it, but won't do anything about it; maybe it's because they're afraid of saying things, or maybe because they think they don't have time, or maybe because it's easier not to do anything than to do something."

"Really?" said Mrs. Dreams (blink, blink). She was smiling and shaking her head as if she knew better. "Are you sure about that?"

"What, then? What do you think it is?" Lucy would have

liked to hear another explanation—this was the truth—but instead, Mrs. Dreams scribbled in her notebook, and Lucy imagined her making happy faces for periods and hearts over her *i*'s. Lucy sighed with the whales creaking and moaning to one another in the background, and noticed that the ivy plant on Mrs. Dreams's desk was a fake.

Mrs. Dreams looked up. "It upsets you, doesn't it, that your mother is gone?"

At this, Lucy stood up, blood rushing to her face. "What is your problem? You can't take me out of class and question me. I'm not some kind of specimen!" She reached for her social studies book and notebook. "I'm going!"

"Sit down, Lucy Moon." The voice was icy. Mrs. Dreams's smile became small, tucking itself into the corners of her mouth, and her eyes narrowed, the blue fish swimming into the back of their bowls.

Lucy sat down.

Mrs. Dreams pulled a shoe box out from underneath her desk and handed it to Lucy. She nodded to Lucy to open it.

Lucy jerked off the lid. The shoe box was filled, end to end, with "Free Wiggins Hill!" postcards.

"So?" Lucy demanded.

"Read them," said Mrs. Dreams, with an ironic smile (blink, blink).

Lucy turned them over one by one—*Lucy Moon. Lucy Moon. Lucy Moon.* They were all signed *Lucy Moon.* Some had notes: *It's mine! Lucy Moon. I want my hill back—waaaaaa! Lucy Moon.* There were several postcards signed *Lucy Moon the Protest Princess.*

Lucy felt the blood drain from her face. Could the day get any worse? She didn't need this! Lucy tried to tell herself she didn't care about these idiots sending postcards, yet other thoughts crept in: all along, kids had sent these as a joke? The kids in this school must *hate* her.

But Lucy steadied herself. The big question was *why* Mrs. Dreams showed her the postcards. It was hardly necessary. It had to be a test. Lucy decided then that she couldn't let Mrs. Dreams see her reaction. She met Mrs. Dreams's watery gaze.

"They're not all mine," Lucy said evenly.

"I thought that you might respond like this," said Mrs. Dreams, taking the shoe box out of Lucy's hands. She appeared to be enjoying herself, savoring the moment. ". . . A personality such as yours . . ." Mrs. Dreams didn't finish the thought.

Lucy desperately wanted to talk back, but she clamped her lips shut. This might be one of those times her mom warned her about, where a person should listen to find out what they were up against; otherwise they might make the situation worse.

Mrs. Dreams spoke in a voice as sweet and light as powdered sugar: "Okay, Lucy, I think you realize that you've gotten many of our students into a heap of trouble. So the administration felt they needed to do something about it and asked me to meet with you. Here's what I think: you have antisocial tendencies, and it seems that you dramatize. Situations in life aren't as important as you make them out to be, Lucy Moon. I also bet you're a bit of a conspiracy theorist." Mrs. Dreams beamed at her again (blink, blink, blink).

"It's not true," said Lucy.

"Yes, well," Mrs. Dreams said, "unfortunately, at this point you're much too combative for counseling. The simple truth is that until you realize you need counseling, there's not much I can do."

Mrs. Dreams swiveled to put the notebook and the pencil on her desk, pulled a business card out of a drawer, and then swiveled back again. "So, since counseling is out of the question, here are your options according to Principal Adams. He says you have a choice between a week's suspension from school, which will go on your permanent school record, or volunteering for the spring session of Youth Action—someone has been kind enough to nominate you. If you choose Youth Action, you will also be in detention after school until spring break. Principal Adams has phoned your father."

Mrs. Dreams handed Lucy the business card. Lucy read it:

Mrs. Myra Mudd

Cleaning Service Professional

Youth Action organizer

President, The Tiny Tims & the Healing Power of Dickens

Then the card listed several phone numbers, a fax number, and an address.

"If you haven't called Mrs. Mudd by the end of the week, Principal Adams will assume you're choosing suspension. You'll want to discuss this with your father."

Then Mrs. Dreams got up from her swivel chair and gave Lucy a hug and a squeeze. Mrs. Dreams smelled like peanut butter! Who was this person? Lucy nearly dropped her books.

The next minute, Lucy was standing outside the door under bright fluorescent lights in the hallway.

Lucy slammed the wall with her fist. She hated this place.

Settle down, she told herself. She needed to figure things out.

First, detention didn't make any sense to Lucy, since there was only one "Free Wiggins Hill!" postcard campaign and she'd already served detention for it. (And it wasn't her fault a school full of goons decided to sign her name to all those postcards.) Also, if she was getting detention because of the vandalism, well, why didn't Mrs. Dreams say so? The police hadn't asked her any more questions.

Shouldn't the opinion of the police count for something? And anyway, what did vandalism on Wiggins Hill have to do with the junior high?

And to include Youth Action with detention did not seem fair. Youth Action ran on weekends, January through April. Youth Action sounded like an honor, because kids were "nominated" to participate. But Lucy had heard the rumors. This was "youth" and "action" as envisioned by adults. Want to pick up trash? Youth Action. Want to fix fences? Youth Action. Want to polish the gymnasium floor using hot wax and your tongue? Youth Action. Yeah, anyone between the ages of ten and eighteen could sign up voluntarily, without waiting for an official "nomination," but no one ever did. Everyone knew Youth Action existed for "troubled youth," with the idea of getting bad kids so bone tired they had no energy for "monkey business." And just for the record, Lucy was not a monkey.

Lucy found her dad waiting for her after school.

"Lucy?" he called as soon as the screen door slammed shut.

Here it comes, thought Lucy. The day was going from bad to worse, but at least with her dad she knew what to expect: Lucy braced herself for nonstop talking, a good grounding, and being forced to write some sort of letter. She didn't bother to take off her coat. Lucy walked into the living room, sat down on the couch, and stared at her mittened hands.

"I'm confused, Lucy," he started.

He *sounded* confused. Surprised, Lucy raised her eyes from her mittens.

"Did you know I got a call from Principal Adams today?" he said.

Lucy nodded her head and waited.

"Well, I don't understand it, and I'm hoping there's a perfectly logical explanation. Would you please explain?"

"I didn't do anything," said Lucy.

"So you didn't send any more postcards?"

"No," said Lucy.

"And you didn't tell the other kids to send more post-cards?"

"Well, I wanted to," Lucy admitted. "But it was over after I got detention and wrote that letter."

"I don't understand this," said her dad. He looked her in the eyes. "I'm choosing to believe you, Lucy. I hope you aren't concealing something." He sighed. "It's easier not to tell me things, isn't it?"

Lucy opened her mouth, but her dad put his hand up.

"Don't answer that. I know it's true. I blame myself for it. For a long time, I was pretty content to let your mother raise you. But now I want to be part of your life.

Only, I don't know how to get you to believe it. You don't trust me."

Whatever Lucy had expected, it wasn't this.

"You know how you talk to your mom when you come home from the bakery?" he continued.

Lucy shrugged noncommittally.

"I want you to try that with me."

Lucy didn't know about that! She pulled off her mittens and scarf. She knew he'd been trying the last couple of months. In the last few weeks he'd even started making her lunches, and cooked a dinner from her mom's vegetarian cookbook almost every night. But it wasn't like she could just swap one parent for the other, especially not when he'd been so *Dad* for so many years.

"You can't replace Mom," said Lucy. "I don't *want* a mom, anyway."

"I know," he said.

"If I tell you things, you make rules about them," said Lucy. "You know you do!"

"I still might," he said. He looked down at the floor.

Then he said quietly: "Please try, Lucy. Help me. I don't know what else to do other than ask. I love you—honestly."

Lucy watched her dad rub his hands together, and decided to try to open the lid a little further than she thought was safe. "The school has a shoe box full of postcards signed 'Lucy Moon,' only, I didn't sign any of them,

Dad. I don't think they think I signed them, either. But a bunch of kids didn't take the cards seriously. They sent them to make fun of me."

Her dad didn't say anything. Then he clucked his tongue and said, "Well, they can't threaten suspension for that."

"Yeah," said Lucy sarcastically. "I would think it would be punishment enough having everybody hate me like that. You should have seen what they wrote on the postcards about me. Kids *hate* me, Dad."

Her dad gazed at her for what seemed like a long time, and Lucy was glad he didn't say, "They don't hate you," or "You don't mean that." Instead, he said: "That was wrong of them to do that." He paused. Then he said, "I'm going to call Mrs. Rossignol and see if Zoë can come for an overnight. I think it's time for an exception to that rule about no sleepovers on weeknights."

He got up and went to the phone.

Zoë was exactly what Lucy needed. It felt like old times— before all the tiny disagreements had started, and before her mom had turned into a dork. Zoë got angry about what had happened to Lucy. ("That's why there weren't more kids called into the office? Those losers!") Lucy even whispered the worst of what the postcards had said. Somehow this led into an enormous pillow fight. ("I'll give you a Protest Princess!" "Think sledders are babies? Take this!") Yes, Lucy's dad stopped the fight. And when

Zoë and Lucy stayed up discussing the intricacies of a choice between Youth Action and detention, or suspension, Lucy's dad interrupted. ("It's eleven o'clock, girls. Go to bed!") But Lucy didn't mind.

After Lucy returned home from the bakery the next day, she went straight into the living room.

"Dad, I'm going to choose Youth Action and detention, okay?" she said.

Her dad put down his magazine and pulled the lever on his lounger, sitting up. "You don't want a suspension on your record?" He smiled a sad smile.

"Yeah." Lucy nodded her head as convincingly as possible. "I mean, what if it gets in the way of going to the Peace Corps or college or something? What if they look at that kind of stuff and I didn't even do anything?"

Lucy couldn't tell her dad the true reason. She couldn't! He wouldn't let her do it if he knew why. Lucy and Zoë agreed that if Lucy got suspended, she'd get labeled, and bad things happened to labeled kids. Lucy knew one kid who ended up in a foster home, and there was another who was transferred to a school with military-style discipline. What if a social worker started sniffing around their family? What would a social worker think of Lucy's mom being gone so long? Personally, Lucy didn't think either she or her dad could handle going through that. So she wanted to do it—Youth Action and detention—and keep a low profile. It seemed like the best choice.

Her dad ran his fingers through his hair. "I don't think you should have to choose at all. I can't think of what you did wrong."

"Stirred up a hornet's nest?" offered Lucy.

He smiled. "Maybe." He continued: "Don't call Mrs. Mudd yet. I'm going to have to have a talk with Principal Adams. Enough is enough. If I have my way, you won't be in Youth Action or detention at all."

He was going to defend her? Lucy grinned at him. "Thanks, Dad," she said. If her dad got involved, maybe she wouldn't have to be punished at all. Sometimes adults needed to talk to adults to get things changed, and this did seem to be one of those times.

That night, Lucy called Sam. She'd been calling him a lot lately. But Mrs. Shipman said Sam was practicing his trombone and couldn't be disturbed. Lucy told Mrs. Shipman to tell Sam she called, and hung up the phone.

Then Lucy called Zoë on the walkie-talkie and made plans to come over.

But before she dashed out the door, Lucy glanced at her dad in the living room. He sat in his lounger with the footrest up. He wasn't reading a magazine. Instead, he tapped his fingers together while staring across the room. Lucy knew he was thinking of her. Lucy had spent most of her life thinking that a single glance would tell everything anyone needed to know about her dad—her dad had his lounger, his magazines, and the man was happy. Now Lucy knew how wrong she'd been. It was like saying you knew a town after driving through it once at twenty-five miles an hour.

CHAPTER 14

For the next several days, Lucy Moon came home from the bakery and found her dad waiting for her. As soon as Lucy hung up her coat, her dad would give her the day's progress report. On Wednesday, he told Lucy that her punishment had been postponed until his appointment with Principal Adams on Friday. "Principal Adams said he liked to see parents involved in a kid's education," he said. On Thursday, her dad pointed at the two suits laid out on the living room couch—a brown tweed and a dark blue—and asked Lucy which he should wear to the appointment. She chose the dark blue because it seemed serious, and Turtle Rock's Grim Reaper (the undertaker) always wore dark blue. On Friday, Lucy rushed home from the Rossignol Bakery to find out what happened. She found her dad leaned back in the lounger, turning the pages of a magazine, but staring out the window.

"Well?" said Lucy finally.

"Not as willing to listen as he said he'd be," her dad said.

That was that, thought Lucy. She sagged onto the couch. The refrigerator rattled on and began its wheezy whirring. It seemed particularly loud. "I better call Mrs. Mudd," she said.

"No," said her dad, yanking the handle of his lounger so the chair snapped upright. "You're not calling Mrs. Mudd. Not yet." He paused. "It just means I've got more work to do. That's what *you* would do." He looked at her. "Right?"

Lucy blinked. "Yeah," she said slowly.

Lucy was up in her room doing homework when she heard her dad make the first phone call. "Hello, Harold," she heard her dad say. "I've been having some trouble with the junior high school—something I thought the school board should know. It's about my daughter, Lucy."

Of course, Lucy and Zoë talked about everything in great detail. They were both amazed that three weeks into school, Lucy still hadn't been called into Principal Adams's office and told to start detention and Youth Action immediately, or be suspended. For Lucy, every day felt like another day of freedom, and she knew this was all due to her dad.

Frankly, her dad's industriousness left Lucy slack jawed. He'd made at least a dozen calls, followed up suggestions, and wrote letters. He made lists of ideas, and after he tried them, he ticked them off. The upshot was—Lucy felt hope. "Believe me," said Lucy to Zoë. "If my dad can change like this, world peace is a piece of cake."

And there was a side benefit to her dad being on the phone all the time—the phone didn't ring! Her mom's messages bypassed the answering machine and went straight into voice mail.

Zoë frowned when Lucy told her this. "You mean your mom is still calling?"

"Oh, yeah," said Lucy. "Last night I heard Dad talking to her about me."

Zoë didn't say anything.

"I'm feeling pretty good," Lucy continued. "It was the ringing that bugged me. With no phone ringing it's easier to pretend she doesn't exist."

Zoë's eyes widened, but she didn't say anything until they'd walked for a block or two. Then Zoë said weakly, "Good."

"It *is* good." Lucy nodded her head.

It might have seemed that everything *was* good for Lucy during this period. It was true to a certain extent. But in the week following the police interviews in Principal Adams's office, the atmosphere at the junior high had soured.

One day, Lucy got to school, opened her locker, and a

cloud of talcum powder billowed out into the hallway. Lucy coughed and waved her hand in front of her face. When the cloud settled, the inside of her locker reminded Lucy of a snow globe, with drifts of powder shifting against her schoolbooks and gym clothes. Everything smelled like a baby's bottom.

"Oh," said Lucy. "Someone's sad idea of a joke." She meant it to sound sarcastic, so Zoë would laugh. But instead, the words fell flat.

Immediately, Zoë offered to go and tell a teacher, but Lucy stopped her. "No! It'll die down."

The rest of the week continued in the same way: Lucy found a dissected frog in the pocket of her orange puffy coat. Someone threw grape soda pop all over the front of her locker. Thomas Duke and Ben Furley took special joy in running at breakneck speed toward Lucy and trying to knock her green-and-yellow hat off her head. "Score!" they yelled, when they succeeded. Lucy's braids were tugged so routinely that Lucy took to tucking them inside her sweater in the hallways. The talcum powder continued to be a problem. It got in, around, and over everything: it slid between the pages of books, ruining the bindings; it plugged the ends of pens; and when Lucy used her gym shoes, talcum powder puffed.

To Lucy, the worst was a foot-long editorial in permanent marker that appeared on the bottom half of her locker. It was titled: "Why You Should Grow Up, Lucy

Moon." And it closed by saying: "What did you accomplish, Lucy Moon? You got a bunch of people in trouble for dumb *sledding!* Good for you!"Though Lucy could not understand why no one stopped this person, who must've been sitting cross-legged in front of Lucy's locker for minutes, she found those last sentences sticking in her head. What had she accomplished?

It'll blow over, Lucy told herself. It'll blow over.

And true enough, each week, the taunts, messages, and surprise gifts came less frequently.

Still, one thing did not blow over. Sam had disappeared from Lucy's life sometime after winter break. It happened so gradually that she wasn't sure when it began. But now it was clear enough. Sam didn't talk to Lucy in the hallways or in class. He didn't call, either. When Lucy called him, one of his parents would answer the phone and say he was busy (practicing his trombone again, or at his martial arts class, or shoveling out his grandparents' driveway). No one had seen him at the Rossignol Bakery for weeks.

After obsessing about it for a few days, Lucy asked Zoë. They were at Lucy's locker, about to go to lunch.

Zoë stuck her hands in her pockets and shifted around. Finally she said, "He's not talking to me, either."

"So he *is* avoiding me," said Lucy.

"It's Sam's parents," said Zoë. "They think you're a bad influence. Principal Adams threatened Sam and me with suspension if we got into any more trouble."

"You didn't tell me!"

"I didn't want you to worry about it, and anyway, he didn't do anything except threaten us."

Lucy was beginning to think everyone blamed her for the Wiggins Hill fence cutting, except her dad, the Rossignols, and maybe the police (since Lucy hadn't seen hide nor hair of the police in all this time).

Suddenly, Lucy felt the weight of it all. She looked at Zoë. "So why are you still talking to me?"

Zoë looked at her like she was crazy. "First, because we're best friends, and I don't let principals tell me who can be my friends. Second, because no matter how aggravating you are sometimes, you make me a better person."

"What? I do not make you a better person!" Lucy said, turning away. She needed truth from friends, not this kind of stupid flattery.

Zoë grabbed Lucy's arm. "I'm not lying," said Zoë seriously. "In my heart, I'm a wimp."

"That's not true," said Lucy, but for the first time all day, Lucy smiled. "Ha!" she said.

One day at the end of January, Lucy came home from the Rossignol Bakery and found her dad absentmindedly tapping a pencil. He jumped at the sight of Lucy. Then he gave her a weak smile.

Lucy knew at once. She dropped her backpack on the kitchen floor.

"It's okay," she said.

"No, it's not," said her dad.

"You tried, Dad," she said. "You tried hard."

"There's got to be something else. I wish I were more creative, like your mom," he said.

"I don't see Mom here," said Lucy. She marched in front of her dad. "Dad, it's like this: you hardly ever get what you want. So you've got to focus on what you did do, because you did do something, Dad. I haven't had to go to detention and Youth Action once yet. It's been almost a month. You did that. You're a lot better than I thought."

Her dad guffawed.

"I didn't mean that," Lucy added quickly.

"Sure you did."

Lucy glanced at him and chuckled, embarrassed. "Okay, yeah, I did."

Her dad sighed. "Unfortunately, you need to call Mrs. Mudd tonight. I told Principal Adams you would start detention and Youth Action immediately. You'll have to do it for six weeks—until spring break. I'm sorry."

"I can do it, Dad," Lucy said.

"I know," he said.

Then he handed her a letter. It was from her mom. Lucy rubbed the postmark with her finger. On January 27th her mom had been in Boulder, Colorado.

Lucy hoped this letter meant her mom had gotten the point, and would stop calling. Letters didn't make noise.

Lucy went to her room and dropped the letter, unopened, on top of her dresser.

That night, Lucy called Mrs. Mudd to sign up for Youth Action.

Mrs. Mudd made Lucy repeat the details back to her. "Let me hear you say it," said Mrs. Mudd.

"On Saturday and Sunday, I'll be at the corner of Second and Vine Street—where the old gas station used to be, at nine o'clock in the morning," said Lucy.

"And what will you bring?"

"A bag lunch?"

"Yes, and what else?"

"Three hours of homework for the afternoons?"

"That settles it," said Mrs. Mudd. And she hung up without saying another word.

"Good-bye?" said Lucy to the dial tone.

CHAPTER 15

On her first Youth Action Saturday, at 9 A.M., Lucy Moon lined up with the other kids for a bus headed to Hopkins Lodge. Hopkins Lodge overlooked the state forest, and it came complete with a wraparound porch, rag rugs, log furniture, and a stone fireplace so large a person could stand upright in it. Lucy imagined listening to forest rangers' rescue stories and sitting in front of a glowing fire while doing homework. Youth Action was decidedly underrated, Lucy thought, except for the presence of Mrs. Myra Mudd, the Youth Action organizer, who reminded Lucy of a mosquito impersonating a human. She was long, thin, and angular, with a needle nose under a beret. A mosquito zipped up in a parka—that's exactly what she looked like, thought Lucy.

But as the bus door sighed open, and the other kids

began to board the bus, Mrs. Mudd stuck out a bony arm and pulled Lucy aside.

"You're with me," Mrs. Mudd said.

Lucy started to say that she loved Hopkins Lodge. She knew all about it, like the ladder that came down in the employee lounge and led to the attic, and the underground tunnel that burrowed under the viewing tower. Lucy could clean places those other kids couldn't even imagine!

But Mrs. Mudd cut her short. "Don't," she said. "I've got you for the entire semester. Think of yourself as my special helper."

Once everyone had boarded, Mrs. Mudd put a whistle to her lips and blew. The whistle shrieked. Mrs. Mudd nodded to the bus driver, and off the bus went. Lucy's fireplace afternoon at Hopkins Lodge turned into cold, sooty coals.

Lucy bit her lip. Well, she thought, it wasn't like this was supposed to be all fun and games. Some things in life led to great and mystical tests of character, and truly this had to be one of those times, didn't it? Surely, it did. Youth Action would only last six weekends. This was doable.

As Lucy piled into the backseat of Mrs. Mudd's sedan, Mrs. Mudd told her they were going to the VFW to clean it for next week's annual ice sculptors meeting.

Mrs. Mudd didn't say anything else.

A big box of brochures sat next to her on the seat, so

Lucy picked one up. She squinted at the cursive script and finally made out, "The Tiny Tims & the Healing Power of Dickens." Lucy assumed the badly reproduced photograph on the cover was Charles Dickens. But what was on his chin? It was either a bad smudge, or a goatee, or a— yeah—a bushy hamster hanging on for dear life.

"Ha!" said Lucy.

"That's enough of that!" Mrs. Mudd's tiny eyes flashed in the rearview mirror. "I'll have you know those brochures are brand new, and I paid good money for them, so I'd appreciate it if you kept your hands to your-self."

Okay, then, thought Lucy. Lucy turned the brochure over in order to set it in the box in the same direction as all the others and noticed Miss Wiggins's name listed at the top of a list of sponsors. That lady is everywhere, thought Lucy, as she set the brochure down. She put her hands in the pockets of her coat and ran her fingers over her walkie-talkie. Zoë had promised to keep hers on all day. Lucy wondered if the VFW was too far away for walkie-talkie reception.

Though, architecturally speaking, the VFW probably came under the classification of "lodge," the VFW seemed like the anti-Hopkins Lodge. Lucy knew that the VFW sat out on Highway 32 near Bobby's Truck Stop, but she had never been inside. As Lucy stood inside the big main room, she decided she hadn't been missing much. First, the VFW wasn't close to anything, except the highway and a logged area (scenic stubble). Second, it was about twenty times smaller than Hopkins Lodge. Third, it smelled like it housed an entire herd of damp sheep. Finally, the place seemed grandly imagined, but sort of haphazard and skimpy in the construction: the stairs came straight down from the second-floor balcony and then just stopped, the last step about three inches lower than the one above it. The banisters were simple and square, and parts felt rough. And the roof took a funny veer, making everything seem lopsided. Worse, in Lucy's opinion, was that there wasn't one comfortable place to sit. Straight-backed chairs lined the walls, and stacks of folding chairs filled one of the corners.

Mrs. Mudd drew back the twelve-foot curtains (dust billowing like smoke), and light flooded in. Lucy noticed the second-floor balcony. (Later, she'd find the restaurant-size kitchen, the bathrooms on the first floor, and the ten rooms upstairs.)

Then Mrs. Mudd left Lucy alone in the big, empty room. Lucy heard the furnace kick on, and saw the fluorescent lights jerk and startle. When Mrs. Mudd came back, she was holding a broom, dustpan, a bottle of furniture polish, and rags. She piled these on one of the straight-backed chairs.

Mrs. Mudd spoke quickly: "You're going to start by

sweeping this floor, okay? I mean every inch of this room."

Lucy nodded.

Mrs. Mudd held out the broom. Lucy took it.

"Let's see you sweep," said Mrs. Mudd. She crossed her arms. "Lots of you children don't know what you're doing when it comes to cleaning—dab, dab here and a swish and a swipe there. In my book, that's not cleaning. Sweep, Lucy."

Lucy took the broom and swept a little. This is so dumb, she thought. But then she couldn't stop thinking of the action of the broom. Did a person use circles, long drags, or little pats all in a line? Oh, this was like breathing—something that got harder the more a person thought about it! Lucy watched Mrs. Mudd's eyes skid over her sweeping handhold, then traverse Lucy's upper arm muscles, and stop at her legs.

There was a sweeping stance? Oh, good grief. Lucy tried to position her feet directly below her shoulders. Didn't everything in life require feet placed directly below the shoulders?

Mrs. Mudd moaned and grabbed the broom out of Lucy's hand. Lucy looked at Mrs. Mudd in disbelief. Mrs. Mudd thought she was a total disgrace at *sweeping*?

"Like this," Mrs. Mudd commanded. She worked in quick little sweeps in a circle, until a pile of dirt formed, and then swept it into the dustpan. "And after you've done that over every inch of this room, you do it all a second time, understand?"

Lucy nodded.

"You'll get all the corners and the cobwebs and go up the stairs?"

"Okay," said Lucy.

"We'll see how you do," said Mrs. Mudd. "Now, about that hair . . ." Mrs. Mudd grimaced as she tilted her head this way and that. She looked as though she were in physical pain, like chewing tinfoil on a filling. "Can you fit it under that hat of yours? If your hair starts shedding, it'll be murder to clean up, since you've got four times as much hair as any sane person."

Lucy tucked her two braids up under her hat. She smashed the hat down. The hat gripped Lucy's forehead like a vise, but it stayed.

Mrs. Mudd nodded. "That'll do."

Then Mrs. Mudd pulled out a round timer on a string from her pocket and hung it around her neck. "I'm going to be upstairs cleaning." She paused, pointing a finger at Lucy. "But I'll be back to check on your work, and I want it done completely. I hope I've made myself clear?"

"Yes," said Lucy. Loud and clear, she thought.

"Then I'm off." Mrs. Mudd turned the timer to twenty minutes. Lucy could hear it ticking as Mrs. Mudd raced up the stairs. Lucy placed her feet directly below her shoulders and began sweeping. A vacuum cleaner roared to a start on the second floor. Lucy sighed and began sweeping in long, long drags. She bet that Mrs. Mudd wouldn't be able to tell the difference.

Lucy swept that floor three times (Lucy's way, Mrs. Mudd's way, and a final sweep because that's how Mrs. Mudd had wanted it done the first time.) Unfortunately, sweeping wasn't the only cleaning skill Lucy lacked—it seemed she couldn't clean anything correctly.

"You're twelve years old and you don't know how to *dust?*" Mrs. Mudd said. Mrs. Mudd seemed genuinely amazed that Lucy did not automatically associate the job "to dust" with dusting the wallboards, floorboards, ceilings, and air vents. Lucy, on the other hand, felt amazed that Mrs. Mudd considered wiping air vents with soapy water to be the same as running a dry rag over something. Cleaning air vents seemed like a task of another genetic makeup entirely. "I'd like you to take some initiative, Lucy Moon. I don't coddle whiners. You're the one who accepted your Youth Action nomination."

Ah, yes, thought Lucy. Right.

Taking out the trash and recycling seemed clear enough. Lucy did this plenty of times at home. But as soon as she started to put a trash bag in the empty trash can, Mrs. Mudd stopped her, rushing across the room. "Halt! Have you cleaned out that garbage can with soapy water and rinsed it with the outside hose? That can looks dry to me."

It had not occurred to Lucy. But now that the idea was mentioned, she thought it bordered on stupidity.

"Mrs. Mudd?" said Lucy, trying to sound as polite as possible. "It's twelve degrees outside, and I heard that the wind chill is three below. I don't think it's wise for me to be cleaning out trash cans when it's this cold."

Mrs. Mudd settled her eyes on Lucy and then narrowed them. "At this temperature, it may take you longer," said Mrs. Mudd slowly, "but it must be done. Cleaning ensures health in public gatherings. The greater good is always considered first. I really can't stand shirkers, Lucy Moon. Wash out the cans."

Shirker? Did Mrs. Mudd call her a shirker? Lucy glanced at her watch, 11:30 A.M. Well, at least that was a relief—it was almost time for lunch!

So Lucy dragged the trash cans out to the back service entrance near the Dumpsters (which let off a dead animal smell even in the cold) and started to work. She swished soapy water in the cans and then rinsed them with the hose. The hose water was so icy it brought tears to Lucy's eyes when it touched her hands. (She had forgotten her mittens. She would *never* forget her mittens again.) But she continued on. A test of character—that's what this was—a test of character. Still, she couldn't help thinking that if Youth Action was voluntary, she could walk out right now. She could use one of the VFW phones to call her dad, and he'd come and pick her up.

The threat of suspension flashed in Lucy's mind. No way. Lucy stayed.

Lucy fingered her walkie-talkie out there in the service entrance, and even took it out of her pocket several times. Zoë would make her laugh, and Lucy could use a good laugh. But who knew if the walkie-talkie would even work all the way out here? Lucy had heard tales of walkie-talkies working at great distances under certain kinds of overcast skies. This sky was overcast. . . . Still, even pulling the walkie-talkie out of her pocket seemed unnecessarily risky. Mrs. Mudd might show up.

Lucy washed out thirteen cans, and by the time she'd finished, she found ice chunks floating in the ones she rinsed first. Her hands hurt, too. When Mrs. Mudd announced her lunch break with a blow of the whistle, Lucy thought she'd never heard a happier sound.

Lucy raced to the bathroom. She closed the stall door, got her walkie-talkie out of her pocket, and flushed the toilet. Water pounded out of the toilet bowl, roared through the pipes under Lucy's feet, and then rattled to a stop. Good, thought Lucy.

"Zoë?" she whispered into the walkie-talkie. She heard some static.

"Zoë?" she repeated.

The walkie-talkie jingled loudly.

Jeez, thought Lucy. Lucy quickly flushed the toilet

again. She hoped Mrs. Mudd hadn't heard that jingle! Lucy put the walkie-talkie to her ear.

But she couldn't hear a thing, only white noise. Lucy flushed the toilet a third time, turned up the volume on the walkie-talkie, and held it to her ear. She detected a breaking in the static. Was that Zoë?

But before Lucy could find out, a hand appeared over the stall.

"I'll take that." The voice, of course, was Mrs. Mudd's.

Lucy stepped backward quickly, tripping over the toilet and banging against the wall. "No," she said. Her brain sent begging thoughts to the hand: *Please, hand, go away. Go away!* "I won't bring it again," Lucy said. "I won't use it. I promise."

The hand disappeared. But the voice was still there: "Not good enough. I don't make deals. If you've had enough of Youth Action, you can quit. Are you quitting?"

"No," said Lucy.

The hand came back over the top of the stall, waiting.

Not her walkie-talkie! How would she communicate with Zoë?

"Lucy," said Mrs. Mudd's voice. "Now!" The hand furled and unfurled again in a quick motion.

Lucy placed the blue walkie-talkie in the palm of Mrs. Mudd's hand. The fingers snapped around it. Then the walkie-talkie disappeared over the top of the bathroom stall. Lucy heard the walkie-talkie jingle, and without thinking, Lucy flushed the toilet.

"And stop flushing the toilet!" said Mrs. Mudd. "I came in here because I thought something was wrong with it. Now finish up and come have lunch. I expect you to behave better from here on out. Consider yourself warned."

Lucy, feeling like a total idiot, used the toilet and flushed one last time, half convinced that Mrs. Mudd would dash back in to fire her when she heard the sound of water in the pipes. But she didn't. Lucy washed her hands and then went out into the main room to eat her bag lunch.

After lunch, Lucy sat on one of the straight-backed chairs, doing homework in the big empty room. It wasn't comfortable, but it beat cleaning. Mrs. Mudd removed the curtains from the windows, saying she was taking them home "to launder." At 3:45 P.M., both the timer around Mrs. Mudd's neck and the alarm on Mrs. Mudd's wristwatch went off, and it was time to return to the drop-off point at the old gas station on Second Street.

The Hopkins Lodge kids came back in the van, and Lucy couldn't help noticing that they were laughing and shoving one another.

Finally, Mrs. Mudd checked Lucy's name off the list.

"Lucy Moon—dismissed," said Mrs. Mudd.

Lucy walked the two blocks up the hill to her house. A test of character! Right. How could character be built through total and utter exhaustion? She wasn't building character—she was building tiredness (and she was minus one walkie-talkie). After eating dinner, Lucy fell asleep in her clothes and didn't wake until the next morning.

The next day, Sunday, Mrs. Mudd and Lucy spent the morning cleaning the VFW, and Lucy worked on homework in the afternoon. The only difference was that Lucy began the day with tiredness already draped about her shoulders.

She slept dreamlessly that weekend, and on Monday, found herself dazedly going through the motions of school. After the last bell rang, Lucy hurried down to Study Hall Room 103 and found her old detention seat. Then she got out her books and began to work. She told herself that between detention and Youth Action, she was going to be way ahead in her homework.

The next Youth Action seemed a repeat of the weekend before. As promised, Lucy was again Mrs. Mudd's appointed helper, and they were back at the VFW. This time, Lucy cleaned the mounds of dishes left behind by all those ice sculptors. She soaked, scoured, and scrubbed dishes all day Saturday. On Sunday, she cleaned toilets, and there was no pleasing Mrs. Mudd when it came to toilets. Lucy had to use a toothbrush. At the end of the day, Lucy was so tired, she fell asleep in Mrs. Mudd's car.

But that Sunday, Lucy came home and found a package on her bed. She crawled up on the bed beside it, put her head on the pillow, and picked at the tape until it opened.

A yellow walkie-talkie!

Lucy sat up.

And this was an X67 with the five-mile radius! Attached was a note: *Call me when you get home. Zoë.*

Lucy hopped off the bed and cheered. She walked over to her bedroom window. She could see Zoë's light on. She turned on the walkie-talkie. "Zoë? Are you there, Zoë?"

Zoë walked into view, waved, and picked up her own yellow walkie-talkie.

"Hey, you're home," said Zoë. "How was it?"

"Not too bad," said Lucy. "Nothing exciting, that's for sure. Thanks for the walkie-talkie, though!"

"No problem," Zoë said. "We need tools of communication! Hey, guess what?"

"What?"

"I got my period."

For a moment, Lucy held the walkie-talkie to her mouth, unable to say anything. Her first impulse was "No!" because now Zoë was light-years ahead of Lucy in terms of adolescent "development." Lucy knew she was comparing herself to Zoë again, but somehow she didn't care.

She searched her mind for something to say, but what did people say in such circumstances? At a funeral, an "I'm sorry" served just fine. At a wedding, "Congratulations." Lucy doubted she'd ever seen an "On the Day of Your First Menses" card on Tamarack Books' rack of cards "for every occasion." "Yes!" seemed strange, since this wasn't a sports event, and anyway, it wasn't how Lucy felt at all. Lucy's mom would know what to say, but Lucy was trying not to think about her.

Finally, Lucy thought of something. She pressed the button with her thumb and spoke. "Did it hurt?"

"No," said Zoë. "It was just embarrassing. It came through my pants. But Edna said that's how it happened to her, too."

"Edna? Edna was there?" This was Lucy's one thought.

"She and her mom stopped by the bakery, and good thing they did, too—otherwise I wouldn't have noticed!"

"Oh," said Lucy.

Zoë proceeded to tell Lucy all about it.

Lucy stepped away from her window and slumped on her bed. She half listened to what Zoë said, the other half of her mind listing all the things that had happened to Zoë that hadn't happened to Lucy: height, breasts, bras, and now her period. And Edna had her period, too? Edna, who also liked to make things and shop at The Wild Thrift? Maybe shopping at The Wild Thrift indicated an increase of hormones. If so, Lucy was on empty. The Wild Thrift didn't do anything for her.

As if on cue, Zoë said: ". . . So Edna and her mom went to The Wild Thrift to buy me a pair of pants, and they fit perfectly. It was my favorite color of purple, too. You know, grape!"

"Wow," said Lucy blandly.

Lucy stretched out on her bed, listening and feeling the injustice of it all. Why didn't all bodies change at the same time? Then everybody would be equal. Also, it wasn't fair that Zoë still had a life, while Lucy was in the middle of her *second* detention, plus Youth Action. Now Zoë—Lucy's best friend since second grade—was using this opportunity to make a *new* best friend. Why had Zoë even bothered buying these walkie-talkies?

Lucy inwardly moaned and let Zoë talk on, while picking up today's unopened letter from her mom. There was quite a stack on the dresser. Lucy flipped the letter over in one hand and picked at the seal with her thumb. Maybe she'd finally get around to reading one of these letters. She was starting to become curious about what her mom was writing, and the truth was, Lucy couldn't control thinking about her mom. No matter how hard she tried to stop, the thoughts stormed in and out of Lucy's mind at will, kicking furniture and slamming doors.

Finally, Zoë said: "Hey, do you want to come over?"

No way, thought Lucy. This was about all the period/Edna talk Lucy could take. "Can't," she said, yawning pointedly. "I've got stuff to do, and I'm exhausted. I'll talk to you tomorrow. Over and out."

Lucy turned the walkie-talkie off and curled into her bed.

Go away, she thought. And Lucy realized then that it

wasn't just Zoë with her wonder-body and her new friend who bothered her. Lucy realized she wanted everyone to go away: the ever-ignoring Sam Shipman (who obviously hated her), her mom (whose letters kept reminding Lucy that she *did* exist), her dad (he kept asking if she was okay, gazing at her with those sad eyes), and herself.

Yes, Lucy couldn't even stand her own self. How had she ever thought that she was gifted and talented at "stirring the populace"? Well, if the postcard campaign had been a test, then Lucy had failed it, totally bombed. Things had gotten so bad that she'd had to call in her dad to help her! At this point, Lucy should practice her typing, because it looked like the best she could hope for in life was a career in word processing.

"Go away, all of you," she whispered.

Lucy felt a muscle squeeze tight under her rib cage, and she tried to breathe deeply to get it to release, but it sat there, hard as a pebble.

So Lucy lay back on her bed, closed her eyes, and imagined sledding down Wiggins Hill. She pushed off from the top, to the right of that huge maple, lying on her belly. The hillside rushed by, and the cold air pushed against her face, making her cheeks smart and her eyes water. She tried steering using the metal handles, and when that didn't work, Lucy let her feet drag like rudders to avoid snake-grass, divots, and was that a root? She slid down, down, down. And with her eyes closed, Lucy found she could keep the sensation going on and on. She reached the end of Wiggins Hill, crossed Twelfth Street, Eleventh Street, Tenth Street, the street numbers counting down until she hit Main Street, which she crossed, too. Then she jumped a little dip behind Main Street and glided into the public park, passing the amphitheater on her right, and finally, after a bumpy moment on the rocks, she slid out, out, out onto a frozen Turtle Rock Lake. The sled sped on, in no danger of stopping. Somewhere around Turtle Rock Island, in the middle of the lake, Lucy fell asleep.

It was around this time that Lucy began to develop a genuine affection, a crush, on two activities: sleeping and academics. Lucy loved the smell of clean sheets, a freshly made bed, and that moment when a person peels back the sheets; slips between them; and, head on pillow, sinks into oblivious sleep. (Lucy did not have trouble making her bed or doing laundry during this period.) Academics were the bridge from school to bed, and Lucy welcomed pages and pages of books. The letters marched like ants across the pages, guiding Lucy to the end of one more day, one fewer day in this never-ending punishment. Very quickly, everything between sleep and studying grew dim and hazy. People skirted the perimeters of Lucy's existence.

Lucy noticed some things. In classes, Lucy noticed that Ms. Kortum seemed especially nice to her. At home, she noticed that her dad repeatedly asked her when she wanted to redeem the mukluks gift certificate, and that he bought her creams and ointments for her arms. (They were red and sore.) As for the Rossignol Bakery, well, Lucy wasn't going there as much as before. It suddenly seemed too far a walk.

One day, around the middle of February, all the junior-high students heard this at the end of Principal Adams's morning announcements:

". . . And finally, students, I'd like to remind you that hats are not to be worn during school hours. Please leave your hats in your lockers. Thank you for your attention."

That day, in almost every class period, the teacher asked Lucy Moon to remove her green-and-yellow hat. Lucy stood up and defended the hat again and again. It was exhausting, and she didn't understand why today the hat had become an issue, when she'd been wearing it since the beginning of school. At the end of the day, when her math teacher, Mr. Odegard, asked Lucy to remove her hat, she almost expected it.

Still, she couldn't help but feel disappointed in Mr. Odegard. Lucy was one of the best math students in her year (especially now that she did so much home-work).

Lucy stood up, sighing. "Sorry, Mr. Odegard, but this hat represents the oppression of the Mexican worker, and the United States businesses that hire sweatshop labor, where women do piecework for pennies. Also, this hat is made of hemp, which should be legal."

Lucy sat down. She put her head on her desk and closed her eyes.

"Lucy," said Mr. Odegard. "Did you hear what I asked you to do?"

Lucy pulled her head off the desk and gazed at him. "Yeah," she said.

"Take off your hat?"

"Sorry," she said. She shook her head and said, "No."

"You'll have to see Principal Adams, then." Mr. Odegard sighed.

"Why? You never cared before," said Lucy.

In response, Mr. Odegard pointed at the door.

"Now?"

"Now."

When Lucy got to the principal's office, she found the secretary waiting for her. The secretary pointed to the principal's door, and when Lucy entered, Principal Adams swung around in his chair and put his hand out.

"The hat," he said.

"How did you know it was about the hat?"

Principal Adams didn't answer. Instead he smiled that principal smile of his and said: "I'm waiting." His hand remained outstretched.

"No," said Lucy. She put a hand on her hat. "This hat

represents the oppression of Mexican workers. . . ."

"I've heard about it, Lucy," he said. "Now give it to me."

"What are you going to do if I don't? Give me more detention? I mean, you've done everything to me and I haven't done anything."

"How about suspension?" said Principal Adams. "This isn't an idle threat, Lucy."

"For a hat? I'm going to get suspended for a hat?"

"By the time I count to three, I want that hat in my hand." He paused, raised his eyebrows, and continued, "One . . ."

"Do you want my boots too? What about my socks? It's a piece of clothing—a simple, lousy piece of clothing. I'm keeping it!"

"Two . . ."

"Maybe I walk funny or I'm too short? Or what about the fact I don't wear a bra? You should suspend me for that. I certainly don't fit in here."

"Thr—"

"Okay!" said Lucy, throwing the hat Frisbee style. "It's yours now!" she yelled. "Are you happy?" (Lucy was embarrassed about yelling in the end—mostly because Principal Adams knew he had gotten to her—but there was nothing she could do about it.)

Principal Adams caught the hat out of the air. Then he walked to his closet, the one where he kept confiscated items, opened it, and tossed the hat inside. Lucy felt sick.

"And now I want you to go home," Principal Adams said. "You're not suspended, but you are this close to it." He pinched his thumb and forefinger together. "I tried to warn you that this was not elementary school."

Principal Adams got up from his desk and held his office door open for her.

Lucy grabbed her backpack and decided to walk directly down to the Rossignol Bakery. She was tired of all the peace and quiet at her house, and at the Rossignol Bakery at least she'd be around people. On the walk down, the image of her hat spinning into the dark mouth of the confiscation closet played over and over in her mind. Principal Adams had no right to do that, thought Lucy. He shouldn't have done that!

But as Lucy walked down the hill into town, other thoughts crept in. Oh, who cares? Let it go. Why fight it anymore? And she found herself agreeing. Yeah, wasn't this enough? At least hatless, there was no reason for Lucy to attract more attention. She didn't know how much attention she could take.

"Where's your hat? And why aren't you in detention?" Zoë demanded when she arrived at the bakery and saw Lucy doing homework hatless.

"Principal Adams took the hat and he sent me home, so I came here," said Lucy.

Zoë gasped. "He took your hat?"

Lucy looked up at her and felt irritated by Zoë's outraged expression.

"Don't worry about it," said Lucy. "It's just a hat. Maybe it was time to stop wearing it anyway, you know?"

"It matters," Zoë said. She stopped in front of Lucy, her right foot tapping. "And I know it matters to you, too. I know it does. I just don't know what's gotten into you. It's like you're drugged."

"Look, whatever," said Lucy, tossing her pencil down on the coffee table and stretching out on the red couch. "Do you think your mom would mind if I slept here for a bit?"

"You are not going to sleep!" said Zoë. "How can you be going to sleep at a time like this?"

But Lucy pretended not to hear her and kept her eyes shut.

"Anyway, I was going to ask you if you wanted to go to The Wild Thrift with Edna and me."

Lucy shut her eyes firmly and let her breathing go slower and deeper. Edna and Zoë, Zoë and Edna, Edna and Zoë—la, la, la, la, la.

"Fine," said Zoë. "Be that way. And for the record, I know you're not asleep."

Lucy drifted off a few minutes later.

* * *

Lucy woke with someone shaking her, someone who smelled like cinnamon, coffee, chocolate, and . . . Lucy opened her eyes . . . someone whose aproned bosom was in her face. Mrs. Rossignol.

"Lucy . . . Lucy . . . wake up, dear."

Lucy scrambled to sit up.

"Sorry, Mrs. Rossignol," she said.

Lucy noticed that the storefront portion of the bakery was dark, except for the fluorescent lights in the back, and that all the chairs sat on top of the tables with their legs in the air. "What time is it?"

"It's closing time," said Mrs. Rossignol, pushing Lucy's hair out of her eyes, "and I expect your father is waiting for you. You can call him as soon as I let you know about one little thing." Mrs. Rossignol sat back.

"Okay," said Lucy. She wasn't sure what this meant.

"Now, I wouldn't be telling you this if I didn't love you, correct?"

The words "love" and "wouldn't be telling you" in the same sentence? Not good. "Okay," said Lucy in a small voice.

"Zoë spent all of her savings on those yellow walkie-talkies so that she could talk to you, and from what I can tell, you've only used them once or twice. Is this true?"

"I don't know," said Lucy. She didn't know. It hadn't been a lot, but . . .

"Now, I don't care about walkie-talkies," continued Mrs. Rossignol. "What I care about is friendship. My Zoë misses you, Lucy, and you've been treating her . . ." Here, Mrs. Rossignol sighed and picked at a spot on her apron. ". . . Well, you've been treating her not so good. She has gone out of her way for you again and again. And I don't know what's gotten into you, Lucy."

Lucy started to protest, but Mrs. Rossignol put out her hand and stopped her.

"Oh, yes, I know things have been tough for you," said Mrs. Rossignol. "But you're feeling sorry for yourself— poor, poor Lucy—and I won't have it." Mrs. Rossignol's voice became soft: "I'd be lying if I didn't say we've all been worried about you. Because we all are, believe me." Then she leaned back. "But I want to see some fight in you, Lucy. Where's the Lucy that stuffed the deer hunting boxed lunches with those indecent flyers? Where's the Lucy that got my Zoë to swim out to Turtle Rock Island? Do you remember that? I thought the two of you were going to die! Where's the Lucy that sneaks out of her house at all hours to go sledding, and takes my Zoë with her? Make some effort." Mrs. Rossignol poked Lucy in the side. "Or is all the yeast gone out of you?"

Lucy started to get up. She wanted to get out of there. She didn't want to be poked and prodded by Mrs. Rossignol.

"No, you sit down," said Mrs. Rossignol.

Lucy sat down.

"When my husband died, I thought I'd died, too. I sat

for days, only wanting to sleep, just like you, Lucy. . . ."

Why was Mrs. Rossignol telling her this? This didn't have anything to do with Lucy's situation. She wasn't married. She didn't have a husband. Lucy desperately wanted to get away.

". . . And Zoë went through a bad time, and thank God I realized it. Thank the Good Lord that He woke me up and told me I had a daughter, because I almost forgot. And right now, your mama is gone to who-knows-where, and that principal up at the junior high has decided to make you the scapegoat for the trouble on Wiggins Hill, but you have to fight! Do you hear me? Fight! And I want you to make some effort toward Zoë. At a time like this, you don't want to lose your friends." Mrs. Rossignol leaned back and straightened her apron. She sighed. "Also, I want this to be the last time you sleep on my couch. You stay home and in bed if you're too sleepy to sit up. This is a bakery, not a hotel."

Lucy's face turned red; tears pricked at the back of her eyes. Mrs. Rossignol had never spoken to her like this before. Why was she doing it now? And what business was it of hers? No one asked her to care. Leave me alone, she thought as she grabbed her coat and books. Leave me alone.

"Thanks for the encouragement," said Lucy. "I'm going now." She headed toward the front door.

"Lucy?" said Mrs. Rossignol. But Lucy wasn't going to turn around. "Lucy!" Who cares, thought Lucy as she pushed open the door and felt the blast of cold, winter air. *I don't.*

That night, Lucy put her yellow walkie-talkie in the Rossignol mailbox. She didn't leave a note. And before she went to bed, Lucy did one more thing—she drew the shade on her bedroom window because it faced the wall of the Rossignol house and Zoë's bedroom window.

So that was how, near the end of February, Lucy began avoiding the Rossignols. She walked to school an hour early. She skipped lunch. And she didn't go to the bakery. Lucy decided she didn't need anyone—a good bed and lots of homework served her just fine.

CHAPTER 16

It was the last weekend in February when Lucy Moon arrived at the old gas station for her Youth Action assignment to find Mrs. Mudd ticked off at her.

"Ms. Kortum at the Turtle Rock Historical Society says she needs you to help her," said Mrs. Mudd. She tap-tap-tapped her pencil against her clipboard. "She won't have anyone else—and I offered *everyone*—but she said you're the best student in her social studies class. So today, you're to report to the Grundhoffer House. Do you know where that is?"

Lucy nodded. It was one of Turtle Rock's claims to fame—an eight-sided house built in the 1800s. The Historical Society gave tours of the house every weekend.

"It's on Third Street. Four blocks that way," said Mrs.

Mudd, pointing. "Don't get lost. If you don't show up, it'll be worse for you next week."

Mrs. Mudd paused and then said, "I hope you're not up to your sly ways, Lucy Moon. This was all very suspicious. You'd be just the type to weasel out of Youth Action."

Lucy felt confused. She could barely weasel her way out of bed these days. But who cared? For once, Mrs. Mudd was headed one way and Lucy in another!

"Go on," said Mrs. Mudd. "And you'd better pray I don't hear one bad report about your behavior."

Lucy opened the door to the three-season porch of the Grundhoffer House and saw a sign on a desk: RING FOR TOURS. Lucy rang the bell.

Lucy half thought this was all a strange mistake. How could Ms. Kortum work at the Grundhoffer House? She had a full-time job at the junior high already! More likely, someone about two hundred years old, wearing knickers and a puffy shirt, would show up, hand Lucy a pickax and steel wool, and gesture toward the water closet. Lucy would give the toilet its first cleaning ever, probably in honor of some freaky event like the sesquicentennial. (And didn't the word "sesquicentennial" sound like chunky peanut butter being squished from a tube? How could anyone celebrate that?)

Still, a decrepit toilet away from Mrs. Mudd was a toilet of pure pleasure.

Lucy glanced at her watch. She rang the bell a second time.

"Coming . . . Coming! Just a minute."

And there she was: Ms. Kortum, wearing sparkly aqua eye shadow and smiling widely.

"Finally, Lucy Moon!" Ms Kortum said. She put her hands on her hips. "Boy, do I need your help."

Lucy's eyes widened at the sight of her teacher, but she got right to the point—no use pretending this was a social call. "It's the toilet, isn't it? You want me to clean it, right?"

Ms. Kortum's face screwed up. "When have I ever asked you to clean a toilet, Lucy Moon? I need your brain, not your brawn! Let me show you."

Ms. Kortum beckoned Lucy to follow, talking all the way through the Grundhoffer House and down the dark steps into the basement. "I knew as soon as I heard from your father that you were exactly the kind of help I needed. But Mrs. Mudd wasn't willing to give you up. She made me fill out all sorts of ridiculous paperwork. But here you are!"

Her dad did this? Lucy hadn't seen him working to improve her situation since January. Then Lucy got it—he hadn't wanted to get her hopes up. He'd been secretly steadfast for weeks. Lucy's eyes started to water. Now was not the time! Lucy blinked back the tears and pinched the back of her hand.

At the bottom of the stairs, Ms. Kortum turned on the

lights, and Lucy saw chairs around a banquet table, and on the table, a huge box. AMOS ZEBULON, PAPERS 1 OF 14 read the words on the side of the box.

Ms. Kortum handed Lucy a pair of white gloves.

"Okay, I want you to put these letters and papers into acid-free sleeves." Ms. Kortum held up a plastic sleeve. "Then I want you to put them in order by date as best you can. And be careful, because this is the oldest history of Turtle Rock we have. Then we'll have lunch at twelve, and then you've got homework to do—and I've got my grading. If you don't have homework, I'm a crack cribbage player, and I'd like to have a game."

Lucy nodded her head.

"Oh, and here's the best part," said Ms. Kortum, smiling. "Anything interesting you find, you must read aloud. I'm sure we'll find all sorts of things in these boxes!"

Ms. Kortum seemed to want Lucy to smile, so Lucy smiled.

She shouldn't get used to this! If she got used to it, next week with Mrs. Mudd would be a million times worse. Lucy could work with Mrs. Mudd and not take it personally—just do the work in a zombie trance. It had taken several weekends to develop the zombie trance, and Lucy didn't want to lose it now!

Lucy swallowed hard. "How long do you think you'll need help?" Lucy hated that she lacked the gumption to ask this in a casual way—in a way that didn't sound like begging, pleading. But right now, she was a lobster without a shell, all soft and raw.

Ms. Kortum showed no signs of noticing. She looked at the box. Her brow furrowed. "For sure until spring break," she said. "This is only one of fourteen boxes, Lucy. I can't imagine us going through them quickly, can you?"

Lucy bit her lip and smiled unsteadily, wave after wave of relief crashing through her.

Ms. Kortum glanced at Lucy. "You know," said Ms. Kortum, "I could really use some tea. Would you like some tea, Lucy?"

Lucy shook her head.

"Well, I'll go get a cup for myself, then. Be right back."

At the sound of Ms. Kortum climbing the stairs, Lucy glanced at all her good fortune, then sat on a chair and started to cry. It didn't last long, and when she was done, Lucy felt ready to work.

That first weekend at the Grundhoffer House was the first weekend Lucy hadn't felt like sleeping during the day. And though it was painful, Lucy let the first green stalks of spring poke up through her frozen heart. Maybe she'd make it until spring break. Yeah, she could make it.

CHAPTER 17

At the junior high, opinions about Lucy Moon grew more generous as daylight lengthened, stretching toward spring. The kids had finished their punishments. The police left them alone. And as a result, the kids' anger at Lucy Moon began to subside incrementally each day.

Most kids' lives got on in a normal fashion. They got their allowance (and tried to figure out how to ask for a raise). They saw their friends after school (and wished they were old enough to drive a car). Teachers gave homework freely (without any concern about students having a life). Principal Adams stood in the hall between classes, pulling boys into headlocks. "Come on, come on—I've seen you move faster than that," he said every day. The Big Six— Kendra, Brenda, Didi, Gillian, Chantel, and the Genie— crowded on the third floor in the southeast corner, as they'd always done. And boys lined up in the back hallway to dump wrappers in the southeast corner trash can, or slurp a drink from the southeast corner water fountain. It was normal. All was normal.

Except for one thing: Lucy Moon. Lucy Moon's new behavior caused the school equilibrium to shift subtly, and it felt like a pebble in a shoe—sometimes not even evident, sometimes slightly irritating, and sometimes downright painful. Normally, Lucy beamed with the intensity of a searchlight. Sitting next to her, people sometimes felt the heat of her concentration. When Lucy listened, the person suspected that she took in more than what they'd actually said. Lucy Moon giving a book report meant calling the room to action. And Lucy didn't *talk* in class, she *challenged*. She believed in big issues, stood up for them, and took on everybody in her path: students, teachers, Principal Adams—even Miss Wiggins. There was something . . . well, admirable about it. What did they believe in? Their television shows? Lucy reminded them all (sometimes like a brick to the head) that there was another way. Maybe they'd never do things the way Lucy did, but in the end, no one wanted to be without her. Lucy's extremism was a standard, a bookend to judge their own behavior. So when Lucy dimmed during the winter—when she dragged, and barely paid attention—it felt wrong.

Kids started talking. The "lobotomized Lucy" they called her. They found out that Lucy *still* had detention for the "Free Wiggins Hill!" postcards, even when they'd heard that Sam Shipman came up with the idea in the first place! In addition, Lucy had been forced to join Youth Action. That was way too harsh.

It had something to do with the adults. Why were they paying all this extra attention to Lucy Moon? Was she *that* special? Yeah, she was weird. But she'd been weird forever! Suddenly, adults wanted to hear the Lucy Moon stories: How Lucy bit Brian Gellman when she saw him bite his little brother, in order to teach the kid not to bite; how Lucy lined the edge of a mining pit with red sand and put up signs that said THE LAND BLEEDS; how Lucy took water samples from elementary-school drinking fountains to test for lead. Kids heard parents repeating Lucy Moon stories on the phone, or an aisle away in the grocery store, or at the gas pump. What was the deal?

And so the kids at the junior high had begun to feel the invoking of that ancient line in the sand that separates kids from adults: the us and them, the out-of-the-know and the in-the-know, the powerless and the powerful. At first it had felt like a faint background noise, but when Lucy Moon came back to school without her green-and-yellow hat . . . well, that was downright wrong. No green-and-yellow hat? This was not okay. Lucy Moon may have been a weirdo, but she was *their* weirdo.

Even the Genie, of The Big Six, noticed. Several kids

overheard the Genie say, "Lucy Moon may be a freak but you know she doesn't deserve this."

That was when Gillian put her arm around the Genie. "You're not feeling well," she said.

"Do we need an emergency online shopping intervention?" Kendra asked.

"Yes!" Didi and Brenda squealed together.

In the end, all the kids agreed: what was so wrong with Lucy Moon trying to get the truth out about Wiggins Hill? As kids thought about the chain-link fence around Wiggins Hill, they began to agree that fencing a good sledding hill and arresting sledders were things that simply defied rational behavior. In fact, what kind of "enlightenment" (a period of scientific thought they had studied in school) had society reached if this was the end result? Pitiful. It was pitiful.

In addition, there was the irritating fact that Lucy Moon's homework had become so detailed—with additional sources and outside reading—that she made the rest of them look about as intelligent as slobbering bulldogs. Something needed to be done. Lucy Moon had way too much time to do homework.

With the Grundhoffer House Youth Action assignment, Lucy Moon began to shake off the haze of cleaning, school, books, homework, more cleaning, school, sleeping, sleeping, sleeping. And as she began to feel more like herself, she found—surprisingly—that she was angry.

Lucy thought she should be happy. Don't get her wrong—she felt much better at the Grundhoffer House than during the three weeks she'd cleaned with Mrs. Myra Mudd. It's just that she wasn't that happy. Relieved? Yes. Not so tired? Yes. Having a better time? Things were a hundred percent better. But Lucy felt angry.

See, when Lucy thought about all the things that happened because of Wiggins Hill—stacked them up, shuffled them, looked at them front to back, back to front, and upside down—she couldn't find one thing she did wrong. All she had done was ask questions, raise an issue. And this is what she got: a double-length detention at school for her part in the postcard campaign, a Youth Action assignment that involved solitary confinement with a toilet and a toothbrush, and finally, she seemed to be shouldering the blame for the Wiggins Hill vandalism. In addition, her green-and-yellow hat now lived at the bottom of Principal Adams's closet as feed for the neighborhood silverfish!

On top of this, her mom had gone from stalking Lucy with phone calls to stalking Lucy with thick letters. They came in the mail more and more frequently now, and Lucy had finally succumbed. She read a couple. *Dear Lucy*, they started. But Lucy thought they should begin *Dear Diary* or *Dear Confessor*, since her mom used the letters to chronicle the minutia of cloud-photography life, and confessed things like *feeling guilty about feeling so free*, or *finally I can breathe.* Then she'd gush on and on about how sorry she was about Christmas. Right. The postmarks clearly indicated that Lucy's mom steered her car as far away from the northern Midwest United States as possible, driving along the tattered edges of the southern states. Any farther away and she'd need a submarine! Lucy decided that collecting them, unopened, on top of her dresser, was a good idea.

Finally, Lucy felt angry because she no longer had any friends. And this, she thought, was her fault. No friends except Ms. Kortum and her dad, and did they even count? Ms. Kortum was paid by the school to be nice to her, and her dad was her dad. Yes, she'd say he was a friend now, and a good one. It's just that he was clearly a dad first.

Lucy desperately wanted to talk to Zoë, but how could she? Scenes panned through Lucy's mind: putting the yellow walkie-talkie in the mailbox, trying to get Zoë to hand out postcards in the school hallways when she didn't want to do it, and pretending to be asleep in the Rossignol Bakery when she could hear every word Zoë said. Lucy even admitted that all this time she'd kind of wished she had a body like Zoë, with all its new bells and whistles. (She was so sick of having to shop in the little boys' department for jeans!) Also, Lucy had a vague recollection of not even giving Zoë credit for *The Turtle Rock Times Shuts Its Eyes.* That one hurt.

But Lucy felt so angry, she wasn't sure now was a good

time to talk to anyone. Someone might say the wrong thing, some little ping of a thought, and Lucy would respond, *ka-boom!* Not good, no, not good—especially if there was any chance of winning Zoë's friendship back.

Lucy decided to concentrate on the Amos Zebulon papers at the Grundhoffer House until she felt less angry. This was despite that fact that old papers held no excitement for Lucy, except for their recycling potential. (True, Ms. Kortum made Minnesota History an okay topic in class, and Lucy had written a couple of A+ reports, but it was time to move on.) So Lucy surprised herself when, during the second weekend, she became intrigued.

On that Sunday, Lucy picked a leather-bound journal out of the box. Lucy thought she would figure out the beginning and ending dates and file it somehow, but Ms. Kortum insisted that Lucy read it. "It's part of the fun," she said.

Lucy sighed and opened it up, and began searching for something entertaining. It wasn't the kind of journal that recorded lots of thoughts—more like a simple record of the day's activities. A typical entry recorded the date and said something like this:

Fine weather. 8 beaver, 3 mink. Set out traps.
Spent rest of day working on fort with other men.

Not the most exciting read, but Lucy soldiered through it.

After being bored cross-eyed over lists and lists of animals trapped, it occurred to Lucy that Amos had killed *a lot* of beaver, tons, it seemed. Lucy had never heard of that many beaver. She mentioned this thought to Ms. Kortum, who sat across from her sorting correspondences. Ms. Kortum smiled at Lucy and said, "Imagine what the birdsong must have sounded like in the middle of the nineteenth century."

And that started an avalanche of thought: Yeah, what were the woods like then? If there were more birds, the woods must have been noisy! How many beaver lived then? Bear? Fox? And what about animals that were extinct now? Did passenger pigeons fly over Minnesota?

Lucy read on, beginning to piece together Amos Zebulon's story. As Lucy had learned in class, Amos Zebulon had worked for the Hudson's Bay Company, an English fur-trading company. He was only fifteen or sixteen when he joined, and in his mid-twenties, he came to Turtle Rock to help with the new fort the Hudson's Bay Company built. He wasn't in charge, but he'd had a lot of responsibility. He was good with a canoe, an excellent trapper, and could carry a tune.

Then came this entry:

March 22, 1836: The Chippewa invited the men

from Turtle Rock Fort to the sugar bush today. They are harvesting the sugar, and it is a festival of sorts. We came bearing gifts for the Chippewa—bells, ribbons, and tin cups. (We were in dire need of festivities, for during the long winter we have been among ourselves.) The Chippewa spike the tree, collect the sap, and boil it. Most they save for later, but some goes into ducks' beaks and birch bark cones. When it is cool, the children suck the hardened sap and laugh.

I must also confess fascination with Rippling Water, the daughter of the head of the Chippewa clan. She has been married once (and abandoned), cannot bear children, and the Hudson's Bay Company will not recognize unions between their men and the Indians. Men of other companies find an Indian wife useful in this wilderness. I find I cannot forget her.

Lucy read the section to Ms. Kortum.

Ms. Kortum clapped her hands. "Oh, that's exactly what I thought," she said excitedly. "You must tell me if they get married. I've suspected for years that Amos Zebulon married a Chippewa Native American!"

"But what is this 'sugar bush'?" Lucy put down the journal. "I keep telling Amos that there's no *bush* growing *sugar* in Minnesota, but he keeps saying it!"

Ms. Kortum started laughing. She pulled off her reading glasses. "A 'sugar bush' is a grove of sugar maple trees. You make maple sugar out of sugar maple trees."

"Well, why don't they call it a bunch of sugar *trees* or something? A tree is not a bush."

"I don't know, Lucy," said Ms. Kortum. "Maybe you should look it up. It might make an interesting paper for class. . . ."

"I'm not *that* interested," said Lucy, hurriedly picking up the journal.

Amos returned to detailing daily life. The men worked hard on building the fort and solidifying their relationship with the Chippewa.

Then this:

May 20, 1836: Fine weather. Established Rippling Water's bride price with her father: 3 moose, 10 blankets, 1 hatchet, 5 kettles. Two of the other men in the fort think it's a mortal sin marrying an Indian, and the others (including the Chief Agent) say nothing. I suspect the Chief Agent knows that we will all benefit from my family bond with the Chippewa, especially with the Sioux warring.

Lucy read this section to Ms. Kortum.

"Oh, see if there's more," said Ms. Kortum. "I want

definitive proof!" So Lucy continued on, and then finally she reached this entry:

July 8, 1836: Killed last moose today. Smoked the Calumet with Rippling Water's parents. It is done. We are married in the Chippewa way. I consider myself lucky to have found a wife.

"You have to tell the social studies class," said Lucy.

Ms. Kortum smiled. "Yes, I do!"

Then the little bell dinged upstairs, and Ms. Kortum jumped up.

"Tour!" she said. "Be back in an hour." She dashed up the stairs.

Lucy continued reading. Rippling Water taught Amos to speak Chippewa, as well as Chippewa customs and manners. She made Amos (and the other men in the fort) snowshoes and moccasins. She caught and dried fish, harvested wild rice, and made sugar from the sugar bush. She gathered fruit and berries, and snared small game.

Then a fight broke out between the Chippewa and Sioux. Two of the men in the fort were killed, and the fort was abandoned. The Hudson's Bay Company ordered Amos Zebulon to travel to a fort near Lake Superior. But Amos Zebulon was married, so he decided not to go. He settled in Turtle Rock. He thought he could make a living trapping and working as a guide and interpreter.

Then Lucy read this:

September 22, 1836: I hope to record this faithfully. I do not trust my grasp of Chippewa. Rippling Water told me that before we met, she dreamt about the sugar bush. In the dream, song vibrated around and through the big tree in the center of the other trees. She says it wasn't the tree singing, but something larger, all encompassing, far-reaching, overall. The song passed through her body as if she were water for the song to wade in. She could not move for a long time afterward. Two days she lay. When she moved again, she felt budded with spring. A few months later, she met me at the sugar bush. She says I am part of the dream. I do not understand this. But I record it in the hope that someday I will.

Lucy let the journal fall on the table and stared at the basement wall. Weird, she thought. As soon as Ms. Kortum came back from her tour, Lucy showed her the passage, watching her read.

When Ms. Kortum looked up from the page, Lucy asked, "What do you think?"

"I don't know—it's strange," said Ms. Kortum. "But he doesn't seem the romantic type at all. I wonder why he recorded this. It must have touched him deeply." She rubbed her hands together. "Maybe our Amos was falling in love," she said.

Our Amos? Lucy didn't know what to say about that, except that it was just like an adult to get all mushy and blame everything on love. "Isn't it time for lunch?" said Lucy.

Back at school on Monday, Lucy found a note in her locker: *Do you still want to be friends? Sam.*

Her heart leaped.

Then Lucy got embarrassed. Could she be any more pathetic? Look at her getting all hyper and happy. It was just chicken scratch on a piece of notebook paper. Lucy turned the paper over in her hands. Her name wasn't on it—just "do you still want to be friends." Sam probably made a mistake. Even if it wasn't a mistake—he ignores her for months and then tosses a ratty note in her locker? Wimp.

Lucy scribbled a message on the same note: *Did you mean this for me? Lucy.* She slipped the note in Sam's locker and tried to forget about it.

But the next day, the note appeared in her locker with another line written: *Yes, the note was meant for you, Lucy Moon.*

Lucy wrote back: *So everything is fixed now? You ignored me for months.*

Over the next few days the note moved between the two lockers.

Sam wrote: *I'm sorry. My parents went ballistic.*

Lucy wrote: *Yeah, well, no one talked to me. Maybe you noticed.*

Sam wrote: *What's going on with you and Zoë?*

Lucy decided not to answer that note. What business was it of Sam's?

Several days passed, and then Lucy found another note in her locker: *I was a wuss with my mom and dad. Sorry about that. Do you still want to be friends? I do. Sam.*

Lucy held the note in her hands, considering. What did she want? If she said yes, Sam could ditch her again and that would hurt. But she missed Sam, and he was the one approaching her, and not the other way around, and he had admitted he was wrong. Everyone deserved a second chance, right?

Maybe Zoë would give Lucy another chance, too—if Lucy had the courage to ask for it.

Okay, wrote Lucy. She was careful to write that *okay* casually, without exclamation marks, or pressing too heavily with her pen, or underlining it. Her heart wanted to do all of these things—in fact, if her heart had its way, Lucy would have underlined "okay" three times.

The following weekend, Lucy sat across from Ms. Kortum in the basement of the Grundhoffer House, holding a packet of papers tied with string. Lucy picked at the knot until it gave way.

The first piece of paper looked like a will. It donated land for parks in Turtle Rock. Most of this land overlooked Turtle Rock Lake. It appeared that Amos's house was on the property, but Lucy couldn't recall ever seeing anything there. It must have been torn down. Then she turned to the next paper.

Agreement between Amos Zebulon and Sebastian Wiggins Concerning the Sugar Bush, the first line read. She peered at the drawing and then read the description. That's when she finally saw the name. Sebastian *Wiggins*? She looked closer at the drawing. Lucy let out a little squawk.

All this time she'd been reading about "the sugar bush" and not once had she thought . . . She'd never considered . . .

Ms. Kortum looked up from her letters.

"What?" she said.

Without thinking, Lucy handed Ms. Kortum the paper.

CHAPTER 18

Ms. Kortum read the document—trapping it, capturing it in her fingers.

Or so it looked to Lucy Moon, who berated herself for handing it over. An adult asked, and Lucy obeyed without thinking? Giving away one of the most important documents she'd ever encountered in her life? Did she lack brains? Lucy knew about adults, and though there were a few good ones, a lot of times they talked a kid out of things. Mostly, adults did what they wanted, taking everything out of a kid's control.

Lucy struggled to contain herself. She wanted to snatch the document out of those fingers—spidery fingers, now that Lucy saw them properly—and run somewhere, anywhere, away from here!

Calm down, she told herself. Ms. Kortum might

give it back—if she didn't realize the significance.

How could she *not* realize the significance?

Ms. Kortum pushed up her bifocals and then turned the paper over to gaze at the drawing. Lucy's hope went out with a feeble fizz.

"This is Wiggins Hill," said Ms. Kortum.

"Yeah," said Lucy. She tried to smile, but her face felt stiff, like new cardboard. "Funny, isn't it? Ha! That's history for you." She stuck out her hand for the document.

Ms. Kortum folded the document along its original fold lines and stuck it in a sweater pocket.

Lucy's heart beat a quick *cha-cha-cha*.

"What are you going to do with that?" said Lucy.

"I'm not sure yet," said Ms. Kortum. She stood up and pushed in her folding chair.

Lucy stood up with her.

"Could I make a photocopy of it?" Lucy said as casually as she could, but her voice cracked, pitching up two octaves. "It's one of the cooler things I've found."

"I'm not sure that's a good idea, Lucy," said Ms. Kortum. She took a step toward the door.

"Where are you going? What are you going to do with it?"

Ms. Kortum put a hand over the sweater pocket that held the document. "Lucy, I know very well that you'll want to publicize this document, that it goes along with those postcards of yours. . . ."

"What's wrong with that?"

"Look, I want to think about what to do with this."

"What do you mean 'what to do with this'? You mean burn it, don't you? You're going to burn it so that you don't have to deal with it. You think it'll cause too much trouble. But think about this: Wiggins Hill isn't supposed to be fenced!"

"I would *never* destroy history," said Ms. Kortum, turning red.

"I'm sorry, Ms. Kortum, I shouldn't have said that. But please do the right thing. Please!"

"I need to think what to do," said Ms. Kortum. "Why don't you take the rest of the day off? I won't tell Mrs. Mudd. This is for me to decide, okay?"

This is for me to decide. There it was—adult presumption.

"No, it's not okay," said Lucy. "And it isn't for you to decide. I saw that document with my own two eyes. I'm not forgetting it. Why do you get to decide what's important in life? Because I know you think sledding isn't important, but that document right there shows that there is more than sledding involved with Wiggins Hill!"

"Lucy, take the day off," said Ms. Kortum. "I want you to give me two weeks with this document, and during that time, I don't want you to ask me about it. I promise not to destroy it. Can you do that?"

"I don't have any choice, do I? You won't just let me

make a photocopy?" Lucy gave Ms. Kortum her most pleading look. "I'll keep you out of it. I promise."

"And that's exactly what I am worried about—that you'll keep me out of it. Lucy, give me a chance to think about this. The document will still be here in two weeks."

"You promise?"

"I promise."

Lucy grabbed her schoolbooks and her coat, but before she left, Ms. Kortum called out to her. "Happy spring break, Lucy!"

"Thanks," said Lucy reflexively, already halfway up the basement stairs.

Then she stopped and turned around. She walked back down the stairs.

"Did you say 'spring break'?" asked Lucy.

"I did," said Ms. Kortum, smiling.

Lucy was still angry, but this was confusing, because if it was spring break, that meant . . .

"This is our last time together?"

Ms. Kortum nodded.

"And I'm done with detention, too. . . . I made it." She said this softly. Where had she been? She'd lost track of time.

Ms. Kortum smiled at her.

Lucy could feel the Zebulon document sticking out of Ms. Kortum's sweater pocket. It hurt her, knowing it was there, and unattainable. But how could she leave without saying something? This was her favorite teacher.

Or at least she was before she did this!

"I've got to go," Lucy mumbled. "Thanks for this." She gestured at the table and boxes. "It was a lot better than Mrs. Mudd." She paused. "See you in class, I guess."

"Bye, Lucy."

Lucy left the Grundhoffer House thinking about what an idiot she'd been. If she had used her head, she would now be carrying a photocopy of that document! Ugh, ugh, and triple-ugh.

She was halfway up the hill to Fifth Street before she realized that spring break meant that she could walk down to the bakery with Zoë again—if she and Zoë were friends. That was unlikely, wasn't it?

But friends or not, Lucy needed to speak with Zoë. It was time, because no matter how Zoë felt about Lucy, Zoë needed to know about the Amos Zebulon document.

Lucy marched up to the Rossignol house and rang the doorbell. As the doorbell pealed out its church hymn, Lucy's courage sputtered, did a last pirouette, and died. What was she doing? It had been too long. Zoë would never talk to her. But if she tried to run, someone would see her. So Lucy took a deep breath and stuck her chin in the air. Friendship was secondary. She was here to pass on important information. That was all.

The door opened, and there stood Mrs. Rossignol.

"Lucy Moon!" she said with a wide smile. "Oh, we have missed you. You have no idea how boring life is without Lucy Moon!"

Lucy glanced up, balled her fists, and said what needed to be said in a burst of words: "I'm sorry I ran away that night."

"Yes, your running away did hurt my feelings some, but I understood. You've had a hard time. You're forgiven, love," said Mrs. Rossignol. She patted Lucy on the head. "But you will talk to Zoë, won't you?"

It was more an order than a question. Lucy felt Mrs. Rossignol's strong hand guide her inside and give her a gentle shove. She had little choice but to climb the stairs leading to Zoë's room.

Zoë's door was open, so Lucy walked in. Zoë lay across the bed with her feet crossed at the ankles. She was reading a comic book. Everything looked the same, except . . .

"Is your hair red and . . . purple?" said Lucy. Lucy hadn't planned on this being the first thing she said to Zoë, and she vowed then and there to learn to control her mouth.

"What's it to you?" said Zoë, without bothering to look up. "I thought you were ignoring me."

"I was," said Lucy.

Zoë turned a page of the comic book and sighed.

Lucy swallowed and said, "I'm sorry. I want to make up."

Zoë leaned her head against a hand and kept reading.

Lucy continued in one long gasp of breath: "Okay, I didn't care at all how you felt and all I thought about was how I couldn't believe this was happening to me and how tired I felt and then your mom lectured me and I just wanted everyone to go away and so I avoided you and gave you back the yellow walkie-talkie." Zoë seemed very still now. "I know I can't be your best friend," Lucy added.

Zoë pushed herself off her stomach and sat cross-legged in the center of her bed.

"Why today?" Zoë said. "Why are you telling me this today?"

"Because today I found something at the Grundhoffer House about Wiggins Hill, something that could really make the difference. Ms. Kortum took it away. And that made me realize that there was only one person I wanted to tell. I wanted to tell you, because you're my best friend, because you're the one person who'll understand. I'm really sorry."

Zoë didn't say anything. She stared out the window at the Moon house. "You drew your shade," she said.

"Yeah," said Lucy.

"I think I hated you for a while."

Lucy didn't say anything.

"You wrote tons of notes to Sam, but not to me. Lots of people saw you and Sam dropping notes in each other's lockers. You like him, Lucy."

Lucy didn't know what to say. What did Sam have to do

with her friendship with Zoë? Lucy spit out: "What about you and Edna? Are you best friends now? You replaced me with her pretty fast!"

"So that's what this is all about—you're jealous of Edna!"

"You're jealous of Sam!"

Zoë smiled then. Lucy laughed a little.

Zoë's tone softened: "What about you and Sam? Do you like him?"

Lucy sighed and thought about it. Images compiled and came together: the night at Gustafson's Wild Nature Gallery when Sam held her hand, the talks as they walked down the hill, mongoose-cobra, all the planning for the "Free Wiggins Hill!" campaign, his smile.

"I don't know . . ." Lucy began.

"Look," said Zoë, "if you're not going to tell me the truth, we can't be friends—"

"No," said Lucy, interrupting. "I mean, I don't know. It's yes, maybe, sometimes—all of them. I want to be his friend. I know that."

Zoë pulled at a string on her bedspread.

Lucy stared at her friend and thought, it's now or never. "Is Edna your best friend now?"

"No," said Zoë quickly. "You were always my best friend until you returned that yellow walkie-talkie and dumped me."

"Oh," said Lucy.

"But she's been a good friend, especially since you haven't been around. I was so nice to you, too. I tried hard to be nice."

"Well, you didn't have to get punished like I did."

"No, I had to watch my best friend get unjustly punished and turn into something as interesting as oatmeal paste."

Lucy hadn't thought of that.

There was a pause. The pause stretched into silence, and suddenly the silence seemed insurmountable, a barrier between them. Lucy stared at the floor and realized there was one more thing she wanted to say, whether it made any difference or not. "There's this other thing, too," she started. She paused, and continued. "There's been this little part of me that thought you didn't really want to be my friend because people like you, and I'm this puny, bra-less wonder with a big mouth. I mean, you've got to admit, it doesn't make sense. Why would you want to hang out with me? You could hang out with anyone."

"Is that true?" said Zoë. Her face broke into a smile. "You've been thinking this all year?"

"A little," said Lucy, feeling hopeful at Zoë's smile.

"How often have I told you that you are my best friend?" said Zoë.

"A lot," said Lucy.

"So will you promise to believe me this time?" said Zoë seriously.

"Really?" Lucy felt a bit of hope.

"Yeah, I want to be friends—even best friends," said Zoë. "But I've got some rules for you this time: One, you can't make fun of my sewing and knitting. Two, it's okay if sometimes I like making things more than I like protesting. You've got to deal with that. Three, if you get mad at me, you have to tell me! Deal?"

Lucy swallowed hard. Then she nodded. "Deal."

"I want to be best friends," said Zoë. "But don't ever dump me again!"

Lucy blinked as Zoë's words struck.

"I really missed you," said Zoë. She looked away, wiped her eyes, and then said, "So tell me what you found out about Wiggins Hill, and we'll call Edna, Lisa, Quote, and Sam to tell them."

CHAPTER 19

"It looks like the sunniest spring break on record," said Ken, on WBRR, North Country Radio. "Temperatures may hit forty-four degrees around noon!"

"And remember, the junior high could use your pocket change for that new gymnasium. Help 'Fill the Pencil with Lead,' folks," said Julie. "Now, in honor of spring break and spring fever, here's 'Sandals in the Snow,' sung by the Obertob Sisters."

Lucy Moon reached up and switched off her radio alarm clock as the three-part harmony began, her mind filling with images of hair scared stiff into bouffants and matching, ruffled dresses—nothing like WBRR for waking a person up in the morning.

Then she realized this was the first day of spring break and Zoë was her best friend again. "Ha!" Lucy grabbed the yellow walkie-talkie off her bed table and turned it on.

"Zoë?" she said. "Are you up?"

When there was no answer, Lucy sang into it: "Lullaby and good night, la, la, la, la, la, la, la." (She couldn't remember the rest of the words.)

Lucy took her thumb off the SEND button and waited.

The walkie-talkie jingled, and Zoë's voice came on: "I'm sleeping!"

"Come on, get up!"

"How much time do I have to get ready?"

"Twenty minutes?"

"Okay. Over and out."

That's how spring break began and how spring break continued—at a breakneck pace. There was a sleepover at Zoë's and a sleepover at Lucy's. There were meetings at the Rossignol Bakery with Sam, Edna, Lisa, and Quote, and explorations along the side of the lake and up the bluff. Of course, Lucy got her mukluks. It took an entire day to drive to and from the Burnum mukluk store, and Lucy had to spend half a day admiring her new mukluks, talking *ad nauseam* about their superior comfort, and jumping in and out of every drippy snowbank to test them. Mrs. Rossignol scolded Lucy: "Don't blame me when you start sniffling!"

Lucy didn't do one lick of homework over break, and she didn't touch a sponge, vacuum cleaner, dust rag, or any sort of cleaning powder, spray, tablet, or liquid. In fact, she refused to get down on her hands and knees for any reason. Lucy talked on the phone and ate Puddle Jumper Cafe pizza. She had made it. She had made it!

The only thing that would have made spring break perfect was having that Amos Zebulon document safely in her possession. It was killing her! Zoë slugged her in the arm, telling her to buck up. "It's only two weeks," she said. Lucy calmed herself by keeping a tiny notebook in her back pocket for document-rescue plans and any other ideas that occurred to her.

It was also during spring break that Lucy came downstairs one evening and found her dad sitting at the kitchen table. Lucy saw neat piles of credit-card bills, handwritten notes, letters, and postcards surrounding him. She watched him pick each piece of paper up and then mark something on a car atlas map of the United States. Lucy moved around the table to see what he was doing, and then realized it might be private. She backed away, but her dad saw her and said, "Go ahead," so Lucy leaned in for a look.

The United States map had sprouted lots and lots of notes. Pink highlights followed the veins of highways, Post-it notes leafed the pink highways, and short notes like *breakfast*, *2 nights*, and *Rebecca Silver* were connected by a single line to the highway, or daisy-petaled around the dot of a town.

"I'm using the credit-card statements and the postmarks

of letters to see where your mom has traveled," he said. "I've got where she's paid for gasoline, ate lunch, slept in hotels, and stayed with friends." Her dad picked up another bill.

Lucy thought about the pile of letters spilling across the top of her dresser. Mostly, they remained unopened. Words, words, words—*finding my wings*, *the first time*, *spectacular*, *awe-inspiring*, *wonderful*, *beyond belief*, blah, blah, and blah. A postcard for Lucy had arrived two days ago. One side showed a Louisiana bayou. The other side read: *Lucy—please, honey, would you talk to me? I love you and I miss you. I know you're on spring break. Mom.* If you want to talk to me you have to see me, Lucy thought.

Lucy watched her dad work and realized that he seemed relaxed in a way she hadn't seen him for a while. Maybe it was the slope of his shoulders or the way he breathed, but he seemed focused, and . . . content.

A strange thought found its way into Lucy's head: it seemed like her dad wanted to rewind time. She imagined time, from this moment, running backward: snowstorms sucking snowflakes off the ground and tucking them in foggy pleats, snowplows winding backward through the Turtle Rock streets leaving fresh-fallen snow in their wake, the carcasses of holiday turkeys and hams growing flesh on their platters, the Wiggins Hill fence unraveling (the sun setting in the east), and finally, finally, finally, "Wind that there's," someone would say.

Lucy imagined her dad would stop time right there: it is an October 3rd afternoon. Snowflakes fall. A light-blue compact car drives away from a red house on Fifth Street, the music of Bach is playing on the car stereo. Only this time, Don Moon sits beside Josephine Moon.

Without a word, Lucy rushed up the stairs. She sat on her bed and caught her breath. Lucy realized she hardly ever thought of how her dad felt, or thought of her parents as people who loved each other, choosing to be together before Lucy even existed. What she'd witnessed downstairs had little to do with her, and everything to do with her dad's feelings for her mom. And if old receipts were as close as her dad could get to his wife, well he'd take it. Lucy went to her dresser, piled the postcards and letters in her arms, and went back downstairs.

She handed her dad the letters and stood by his side, leaning against him. Her dad put his arm around her. Then Lucy did something she never did—she climbed into his lap.

"Aren't you getting a little big for this?" he said, though Lucy could tell he was pleased.

"You're not strong enough?" Lucy countered.

"We'll have to see, won't we?"

And so the two of them began to work. With his arms around Lucy, they plotted the postmarks of her letters.

When they finished that night, they ripped the map out of the car atlas and pinned it onto the kitchen wall to have a look at it. And then together, the two of them stood side by side, quietly thinking.

All those places, Lucy thought. She put her finger on the pink-marker line and traced it. Lucy's mom had driven from Turtle Rock, Minnesota, into Wisconsin, then Illinois, Iowa, Nebraska, Wyoming, Montana, across the Canadian border into Alberta and British Columbia. Then into Washington, Oregon, down the coast of California—on and on she drove—Nevada, Utah, Arizona, New Mexico, Colorado, Oklahoma, Texas—until the last postcard from Louisiana. Her mom had let the screen door slam, stepped into a car, and had driven away from their little red house. She had driven wherever whims and clouds took a person. What was that like? Lucy couldn't fathom it.

As her dad cleaned up, putting his bills and letters into a shoe box, Lucy noticed a police ticket. She picked it up and laughed.

"Reckless driving, Dad? You? What were you thinking?" she said. The man drove slower than farm equipment. Lucy held the ticket up.

Her dad squinted at it.

"Oh, that's your mother's," he said. "Your mom apparently forced Miss Ilene Viola Wiggins's car into a ditch. Or at least that's what Miss Wiggins claims. Remember that snowstorm the night your mom left? The ticket's paid, so that's that."

Miss Wiggins again? Lucy stood dumbfounded.

"You're saying the night Mom left, she had something to do with Miss Ilene Viola Wiggins going into a ditch?"

"Supposedly," said her dad. "Your mom said she remembered seeing Miss Wiggins driving her Cadillac, and that when she tried to pass, Miss Wiggins drag-raced her up the hill. All she knew was that she passed her. She says she didn't hit anyone. There's not a scratch on our car." He put the lid on the shoe box.

Lucy handed the ticket over to her dad, said she was going to bed, and went upstairs.

Lucy shut the door to her room, sat in her chair, and went through the details. Okay, on the night of the big October snowstorm, Miss Ilene Viola Wiggins claims she was run off the road by her mom. This is also the night the sledders are arrested on Wiggins Hill. Then later, Miss Wiggins's donation makes it possible for Gustafson's Wild Nature Gallery to turn her mom's studio into gallery space. So her mom is kicked out of the studio.

Weird.

Was it possible that Miss Wiggins had still been angry about whatever had happened on the road when she decided to make the donation to the gallery? Was the gift of the gallery an act of revenge in some way? Could Miss Wiggins be making Lucy's life harder? The thought shook Lucy a little. No way, she thought.

But Lucy couldn't stop thinking about it.

It was true that Lucy felt Miss Wiggins's presence everywhere—in the newspaper, at the gallery opening, on the back of The Tiny Tims flyers in Mrs. Mudd's car. Before this year, the only time Lucy had thought about Miss Wiggins had been when she was figuring out when to go sledding on Wiggins Hill!

And it was true that Miss Wiggins probably didn't like Lucy much after all those "Free Wiggins Hill!" postcards arrived at her house signed with Lucy Moon's name. And there was that postcard Sam had left on Miss Wiggins's pillbox hat at the gallery opening. But Lucy had apologized.

It was true Lucy was Josephine Moon's daughter. . . .

But what was the connection between Lucy's troubles at school and Miss Wiggins?

This was all a big coincidence. Since taking on the fight for Wiggins Hill, it was only natural that Lucy would notice Miss Wiggins's name more . . .

. . . or Mrs. Dreams was right. Lucy was becoming a conspiracy theorist!

Lucy picked up her yellow walkie-talkie to call Zoë.

CHAPTER 20

What later became known as the "Easter Bonnet Incident," began with the Genie of The Big Six strolling into Turtle Rock Junior High the Monday after spring break wearing a straw hat with green-and-yellow silk flowers attached to the brim. Several of the boys gave her regal bows, or tipped imaginary fedoras as she stepped on by, climbing the steps to her third-floor locker in the southeast corner. The Genie was known for making statements with fashion, so it was not altogether unusual for her to appear wearing a hat with silk flowers. The surprising part was that the Genie did not leave the hat in her locker. The Genie wore her hat after the day's first bell rang.

Several people witnessed the hat traveling on her head into the Genie's first class—math. According to others in the math class, the hat stayed on top of her head during the class, and many witnessed the flowers on the brim of the hat bobbing through the hallways on the way to the Genie's next class—band. The band teacher said nothing. (Though the trumpet section did try to blow the flowers off by aiming their gusty notes in the hat's direction.) During gym, the Genie removed her hat, but brought it into the gymnasium and set it prominently on a front bleacher. After gym, the hat was seen like a small island of spring on top of the sea of heads moving toward yet another class.

To anyone who questioned her, the Genie said, "People should be able to wear hats in school if they want." Then she'd look the questioner in the eye and say, "In fact, I think we should all celebrate Easter with green-and-yellow Easter bonnets—don't you think? I think *you* should wear one tomorrow."

The Genie did not mention Lucy Moon.

All became clear, though, when the sixth-period study hall monitor asked the Genie to remove her hat. According to several firsthand witnesses, the Genie said, "This hat represents the oppression of hat wearers everywhere, and is a stylish reminder that Easter bonnets should be worn on Easter Sunday."

Then she sat down.

For a moment, everyone was silent, and then two or three people broke into applause; others started laughing. One person chanted: "Moonie! Moonie! Moonie!" The Genie curtsied.

"Eugenie Sovil," said the study hall monitor, holding out his hand. "Your hat?"

The Genie got up and gave the study hall monitor her hat. That was the end of the straw hat with green-and-yellow silk flowers.

The next day, the Genie came to school wearing a green baseball cap with a yellow silk flower attached. And Didi—another third-floor, southeast-corner girl—came wearing a yellow bandanna around her head. The Genie made it to third period before giving up her hat, and Didi was seen without her bandanna after fifth period. According to eyewitnesses, both the Genie and Didi stood up and said the hat represented "the oppression of hat wearers everywhere," and each added their own tags about Easter bonnet fashion. It was said that, after this speech, the Genie was sent straight to the principal's office.

The next day, five people came to school wearing hats; all of the hats were either green or yellow or both.

The day after that, ten people were wearing green and yellow hats of various sorts, and the day after, there were twenty. The number of hats kept increasing until it seemed that every other head sported a hat in various sizes and shapes: bowler hats, plastic St. Patty's Day hats, felt hats, woven hats, baseball hats, knit hats, berets, and kerchiefs.

Teachers' closets began to fill with hats collected from students. In addition, if a teacher asked for a hat, the student stood up and gave their reason for hat-wearing: "This hat represents the oppression of plastic molecules by forcing them to become plastic St. Patty's hats and toy barnyard animals." "This hat represents the oppression of triangle-headed people everywhere. . . ." (The speaker wore a tricornered hat.) "This hat represents the oppression of those who happily heap food on their head." (This was a hat made from a piece of foam shaped like a wedge of Swiss cheese.) Teachers could not stop the students from making statements.

Eventually, the teachers sighed and tried to ignore the hats in their classroom. They had lessons to teach, and if they did not mention the hats, the class remained relatively calm. Teachers sent fewer people to the principal's office, and hats wobbled on the tops of students' heads in the hallway.

Lucy Moon came back from spring break and watched the green-and-yellow hats paraded through the hallway. What was going on? Lucy understood how kids might grow bored with yanking her braids and scrawling graffiti across her locker. But to come back to school and find everyone engaged in a *protest*? Over Lucy's green-and-yellow hat? It made no sense—no sense at all.

Zoë grew happier and happier as the week progressed. It seemed that every time Lucy saw Zoë, she was dancing—winging her arms out and skipping in circles. Unbeknownst to Mrs. Rossignol, Zoë had contributed the following hats to the junior high school collection: a green sombrero, a fish-shaped *Minnesota Loves Walleyes* hat, and a Green Bay Packers stocking cap (which Zoë said was left by a Wisconsin relation, and its presence so embarrassed the Rossignols, they couldn't throw it away on the off chance that the garbage man saw it and *assumed*).

Lucy tried to figure it all out until Zoë finally said, "Hey, don't knock it—enjoy!"

So Lucy decided to enjoy. She liked being on the outside (hatless) for once. Here was a protest that she, Lucy Moon, had nothing to do with (and everything to do with). No one could accuse her of organizing it. The idea certainly wasn't hers, and the very style of the protest wasn't anything that could have originated in Lucy's brain—an Easter bonnet protest? Brilliant! And who in their right mind would have expected anyone from The Big Six to do this? Lucy had to admit that there was more to the Genie than she'd originally thought. Various people, including Sam Shipman, promised to get Lucy's green-and-yellow hat back, but she didn't think much of it. To Lucy, the Easter Bonnet Incident was well worth one three-year-old, green-and-yellow hat.

The *Turtle Rock Times* came out on Thursday, April 1st, and it was such a good read that folks thought that it must be an April Fools' issue. Not that the *Turtle Rock Times* had ever done a spoof of itself, and the paper that day included rather boring things like lists of speeding tickets issued, three or four "won't last long" ranch-style homes for sale, and yet another recipe for meatball goulash. (Though the news that Abbey Sable scored over 200 in junior bowling made everyone pause. Abbey Sable made bowling balls skid down lanes like deep-freezer hams.) Readers called each other to consult. "Oh, that funeral for Mary O'Hannigan was as real as can be—don't think someone made that up. Her obituary's right there in section two, page three." The suspicious minds then said: "Say, what if the newspaper planted fake stories *with* the boring ones?" And the loyalists replied: "They wouldn't do that. They are *so* nice at the *Turtle Rock Times*. But now that you mention it, there's that *new* reporter from St. Paul. . . ." In the end, readers decided that truth or fiction, the paper had never been such good reading, and the *Turtle Rock Times* took in twenty-three new subscriptions on April 2nd.

The first too-good-to-be-true story was on the front page. "Girl Gang Cuts Wiggins Hill Fence," the headline blared. A gang of girls? In Turtle Rock, Minnesota? Oh, this was too much, said folks, chuckling, some putting the newspaper down on their laps so they could wipe their eyes. The article, continuing in all seriousness, said that the police had finally tracked down a group of female junior-high students who had admitted to cutting the fence. "We are discussing the situation with the owner of the fence, Miss Ilene Viola Wiggins," the police chief was quoted as saying. "This act is a potent example of the persuasive and pernicious power of peer pressure." (Many thought the repeated use of the letter *P* was rather clever, since the police chief was known to pop *P*'s in his speech whenever he got worked up. In person, it was always wise to check the police chief's coloring and demeanor before stepping too close—his apoplectic plosives had sprayed many a pair of glasses, and ruined more than one good silk blouse.)

Then in section one, page two, there appeared this article:

Youth Action Project Leads to Wiggins Hill Discovery!

Ms. Polly Kortum, longtime curator of the Grundhoffer House and member of the Turtle Rock Historical Society, said that Youth Action volunteer Lucy Moon made a discovery last Saturday.

"I'd given Miss Moon the task of organizing the Amos Zebulon papers," says Ms. Kortum. "On Saturday, she showed me a document she'd found—an agreement between Amos Zebulon and Sebastian Wiggins concerning the Chippewa Indians' sugar bush. I am so excited about this historical discovery!"

The discovered document clearly indicates that Wiggins

Hill was once a grove of maples the Chippewa Indians used to make maple sugar. In addition, Amos Zebulon laid out clear conditions for the use of the Wiggins Hill land.

An early settler of Turtle Rock, Amos Zebulon helped found the Hudson's Bay Company fort at Turtle Rock and married into the local Chippewa clan. When the fort failed, Amos Zebulon stayed in Turtle Rock. After his wife died in the mid-nineteenth century, Amos Zebulon became noted for reclusive behavior. He also owned a lot of land. At his death in 1901, he donated much of this land to the city.

Many people know that Amos Zebulon donated the bluff and the city lakefront property. What is not commonly known is that Amos Zebulon owned Wiggins Hill. He called the land the "sugar bush," and several years before his death, he gave this land to Sebastian Wiggins under a strict agreement. The document is entitled "Agreement Between Amos Zebulon and Sebastian Wiggins Concerning the Sugar Bush." Sebastian Wiggins's and Amos Zebulon's signatures both appear at the bottom of the document.

The document reads:

"Being that the sugar bush is a land that was sacred to my wife, Rippling Water, of the Chippewa, and was the location for collecting maple sugar by her clan, I give this land with great reluctance. But being old (and without children), I must choose someone, so I choose Sebastian Wiggins. In taking this land, Sebastian Wiggins indicates that he is *not* a landowner, but a guardian, a steward of the land. By which I mean that he is to take care of this land, but leave it for others to enjoy. (I've listed my restrictions below.) No money has changed hands, as I do not want Sebastian Wiggins to think himself an owner but a *steward*.

If his signature be found at the bottom of this document, Sebastian Wiggins has agreed for himself (and for all following generations who may inherit the title) to act as steward of the sugar bush. These are the terms he has agreed to (in no particular order):

• He may build a house at the top of the hill where the land is already cleared (see drawing). But this is the only place he may cut into the land.

• Any road must be built according to the drawing below. He may not remove any of the sugar maple trees.

• The land must remain in its wild state. No fences, no cutting, no clearing of the land can occur. A fallen limb may be removed to the edges, but it should be left to rot, as I've noted that many birds find homes in rotting limbs. All brambles and other such plants must be allowed to stay. I find the eagerness with which this generation harnesses the land until it matches the pitiful vision in their head detestable. Let there be wild places.

• The big sugar maple in the center must be protected at all costs. It is a blessed tree and sacred to my wife.

• The Chippewa must always be welcome in the sugar bush. They must be allowed to stay as long as they like, and harvest the sap as they choose. I doubt very much that they will return, but I want the land to always be open to them.

I am an unlearned man who loved his wife. Let Sebastian Wiggins refuse to sign this document if he does not intend to follow this agreement. Let Sebastian Wiggins sign under witness of heaven.

When called for a comment, Miss Ilene Viola Wiggins said she did not remember her father having any agreement like the above mentioned, and refused to make any further statement.

Contact Ms. Polly Kortum at the Grundhoffer House for more information regarding the Amos Zebulon document.

This article caused readers to pause. It was not like the newspaper to poke fun at Miss Ilene Viola Wiggins—especially not with all the trouble surrounding that hill. This caused them to think that the newspaper might be telling the truth, after all.

Still, all that about Lucy Moon had to be nonsense! Wasn't it a little unlikely that the girl causing all that ruckus about Wiggins Hill would find an old document supporting her claim?

And a girl gang? Now, that didn't make one iota of sense—not in Turtle Rock, Minnesota.

After the confusion wore off, nearly everyone wondered what Miss Ilene Viola Wiggins thought of all of this. But no one knew. Eventually, it got around that Miss Wiggins called her secretary at Wiggins Faucet on

Thursday, April 1st, and said she had "pressing business elsewhere." Miss Wiggins was gone for the week.

Of course, Lucy and Zoë racked their brains trying to figure out the identities of the junior-high "girl gang" members. This was after Lucy's mild panic attack upon reading the article. She had looked over the newspaper at Zoë, her face frozen. "They're going to think it's me!" she whispered. She'd get suspended. They'd enroll her in Youth Action for the *forever* semester, chaining her to Mrs. Mudd. Zoë calmly pointed out that Lucy hadn't seen the police in a very long time, and that if they had a "gang" it would include Sam Shipman, and he was definitely a boy. "Oh, yeah," said Lucy, breathing again.

But if it wasn't them, who could it be? As far as they knew, they were the only ones in the junior high passionately worked up about Wiggins Hill. Both Lucy and Zoë thought of Mrs. Dreams's shoe box full of "Free Wiggins Hill!" postcards—it had to be full of clues! But neither Lucy nor Zoë wanted to step near that office.

They even halfheartedly tried to figure out if one of their female friends had gone bad: hadn't Lisa Alt flipped out when her mom refused to replace the powder-blue ski jacket? Lisa had been forced to spend her allowance on a used coat from The Wild Thrift, since she refused to wear the granny coat her mom had offered. Or what about Edna? Edna was the one who'd called them about the arrested sledders. Maybe she'd been there that night and now harbored a secret rage! (Lucy and Zoë knew that Edna had found out because she lived next door to Lisa Alt.) As for Quote, well, they couldn't even imagine her sledding. All of Quote's shoes were pointy and nontread. But maybe *this* was the perfect cover! Truthfully, the thought of any of their friends involved in a fence-cutting only made Lucy and Zoë laugh. They figured that eventually they'd find out who belonged to this "girl gang." It would all leak out sometime.

Anyway, this was the conversation that occupied Lucy and Zoë on Thursday, Friday, and now, on Saturday afternoon, as they walked home from the Rossignol Bakery. They had left early. Zoë had complained of "rolling-pin wrist," right after Mrs. Rossignol left to run an errand. "We'll let the hired help run this place for once," Zoë had said as they scooted out the door.

When they got close to Third Street, Zoë halted in midstep. "Should we stop at the Grundhoffer House? You know, to thank Ms. Kortum?"

"Yeah—let's!" said Lucy.

Ms. Kortum sat behind the tiny desk on the four-season porch, warming her socked feet on a space heater. She seemed to be working on a crossword puzzle.

Lucy banged open the door. Ms. Kortum jerked upright.

"Thank you!" Lucy yelled. She ran behind the desk

and wrapped her arms around Ms. Kortum. Ms. Kortum shrieked a little, but smiled on seeing Lucy.

Then Ms. Kortum gave Zoë a look, raised an eyebrow, and said, "Shall I?" When Zoë nodded, Ms. Kortum dinged the "Ring for Tours" bell.

Suddenly, Lucy heard singing. It was "For She's a Jolly Good Fellow."

"It was your dad's idea," said Zoë.

Lucy ran inside and found her dad, Mrs. Rossignol, fresh veggies, cheese curds, and a big bowl of cherry punch. Zoë and Ms. Kortum joined them. Then they all raised paper cups to Lucy.

"To Lucy, for persistence and historical discoveries," said Ms. Kortum.

Everyone took a sip.

"You did it, Lucy," said her dad.

After a good twenty minutes of stories about postcards, Wiggins Hill, Miss Wiggins, and the Zebulon document, the adults began to talk among themselves, leaving Lucy and Zoë to explore the Grundhoffer House on their own. As Lucy and Zoë crept from one room to the next, Lucy realized that, along with all the happiness she felt, she still felt unsettled. Something wasn't quite finished. She tried ignoring the feeling as they toured several of the upstairs rooms. She turned her back on it, even stepped on its tail to make it yelp, run, and hide, because, for heaven's sake, shouldn't she be feeling happy? But the unsettled feeling was stubborn, and the more Lucy struggled with it, the more she felt it.

It was in the Grundhoffer sewing room that Lucy knew what it was all about: Wiggins Hill. Of course. Lucy tried to talk her subconscious out of whatever it was considering. Everyone knew about the Amos Zebulon document now. Wasn't that enough?

But deep down, Lucy wanted to confront Miss Wiggins about Wiggins Hill one more time—to finally close the matter. It was an instinct, the kind of instinct Lucy had followed in elementary school again and again.

She felt so tired, though. Why not leave all that elementary-school stuff behind? Why not step into the river that was adolescent brain chemicals and peer pressure, and let the current take her to something else, something new. Why did she have to assume that it would all be bad? And anyway, she couldn't fight it completely. Bodies changed. Facts were facts.

Still, Lucy didn't want complete metamorphosis, larva to butterfly. She didn't want to lose track of herself, to doubt herself, consider all her past actions babyish. They weren't! And Lucy wouldn't allow Mrs. Myra Mudd, Mrs. Dreams, Principal Adams, Thomas Duke and Ben Furley, oozing hormones, or even her mom's absence to define her. Lucy would step into the river, yes, but with her arms wrapped tightly around what was truly hers: her self. It was easier said than done; still, what choice did she have but to try?

This instinct to do one more thing about Wiggins Hill was part of her past, but Lucy wanted it as part of her present, too. Maybe she wasn't gifted or talented. Maybe she'd fail all the time. But it was part of the way she was, the way she thought, and Lucy decided she wanted to fight for it, come what may.

But what would Zoë think? Lucy needed Zoë, and Lucy had been so horrible, and Zoë didn't need a crazy activist friend, did she?

But Zoë called Lucy her best friend. Zoë knew Lucy. That was the truth.

Finally, after Lucy and Zoë had made their way back downstairs and into the parlor, Lucy decided to ask her. Lucy watched Zoë as she stared up at the portrait of Mr. Grundhoffer. What if Zoë said no? Lucy couldn't seem to open her mouth to say the words.

But Zoë took the matter into her own hands. She tossed a mohair scarf over her shoulder and said, "Out with it, Lucy Moon."

Lucy spoke with the speed of a cheetah: "I want to do one more thing about Wiggins Hill."

Zoë held her gaze on the portrait. She smiled a little and then picked at something in her teeth. "Look at that," she said finally. She pointed at the portrait. "That is *not* real hair. He's totally toupee-ed."

Lucy frowned at the portrait. "It's real. It's a comb-over." She turned toward Zoë. "I want to organize, too," she said.

"Yeah?" said Zoë. A Mona Lisa smile was plastered across her face. "How do you know it's a comb-over?"

"In my gut," said Lucy. She smacked her stomach with a fist. "Right there. And I think it's Easter Sunday. Easter Sunday is the big day." Lucy felt breathless now.

"The Easter Egg Hunt?"

Lucy nodded.

Zoë paused for a long minute, leaned to look into the dining room where Mrs. Rossignol, Lucy's dad, and Ms. Kortum were picking up, and guffawed.

"That's exactly what I've been thinking!" whispered Zoë. "I can round up a little support, too. Want to hear my idea?"

Then Zoë told Lucy about what she'd been thinking. Lucy listened. Then Lucy told Zoë what she was thinking, and together, they came up with a plan that combined the best of their ideas.

CHAPTER 21

At one o'clock on Easter Sunday, Sam Shipman handed Lucy Moon her green-and-yellow hat. They stood in front of Lucy's little red house on Fifth Street. They were waiting for Zoë, Edna, and Quote, who had all opted for a last-minute bathroom break.

Lucy gaped. "My hat," she said.

Sam grinned.

Lucy took the hat from Sam and turned it over in her hands. It was the hat made of hemp; the hat that stood for the injustice of women doing piecework for pennies; the hat Lucy had worn every day since her mom returned from that photo trip in Mexico City. Lucy remembered the brightness of the colors and how it had smelled of incense when she had first pulled it from her mom's suitcase. But now she saw the hat as it was—lumpy and misshapen, the colors faded. It was kind of ironic that the hat had returned to her but her mom had not.

Lucy curled the edges of the hat over her finger and stretched it out. It was still her hat, and it was one of the nicest gifts Lucy had ever received. "I don't know how you got this. . . ."

"It wasn't easy," said Sam.

"Well, thank you," said Lucy. She paused and said, "Why did you do this?"

"You needed to have your hat, Lucy, and . . ." Sam glanced up at the sky, took a deep breath and said, ". . . I like you."

Lucy looked away.

There were the words.

Lucy knew that the words meant being "more than friends," but she wasn't sure exactly what being more than friends meant, practically speaking. Did this "I like you" mean that Sam wanted her to be his girlfriend? Or did he think of her as some sort of extraspecial friend? But people didn't say "I like you" if they were friends. There was no point.

Lucy's heart began to race. What would her mom say? Lucy imagined her mom sitting on the kitchen stool chopping vegetables, and tried to manipulate the scenario so that her mom talked to her. But the only thing Lucy imagined were tears streaming down her mom's cheeks, and that was probably because Lucy had put an onion on her mom's imaginary chopping board.

Meanwhile, Sam seemed to be waiting for a response. She was supposed to say something!

Sam sighed and shook his head. "It's okay," he said. "You don't have to say anything. I ignored you for months. I wouldn't like me either, if I were you."

But Lucy considered: Sam had seen her in action. Remember when she had broken her promise about parents not finding out about *The Turtle Rock Times Shuts Its Eyes*? He was still her friend. He had even seen that lacy pink dress. All he had done was say he "liked her." How complicated did she want to make this?

But it could become complicated. Feelings were complicated. People said one thing and meant another and then tacked on a few dozen assumptions for good measure.

Lucy spoke quickly (before she lost her nerve): "I like you, too."

With those words, Lucy felt a surge of feeling. It caught her by surprise. It was as though she'd stepped off dry land onto ice floating on a lake. Lucy wobbled a little. She didn't know how to stand on two feet anymore. Worse, how did a person get back to dry land?

Sam smiled. Oh, no—could he tell she could barely stand?

Lucy tried to smile back, but instead ended up frowning

and crossing her arms over her chest. "This better not screw up our being friends," she said. "You better promise!"

"Okay, okay," said Sam, holding his hands above his head. "I promise."

There was an awkward pause.

Lucy put the green-and-yellow hat on her head, and the act steadied her somehow.

That's when Quote, Edna, and Zoë finally clambered out of the Rossignol house.

Zoë noticed right away. "Your hat!" Zoë said to Lucy. "How did . . . ?"

Lucy pointed at Sam.

Zoë stopped midstride. She stared at Sam. She stared at Lucy. "What's going on?" she said.

Quote gave a knowing look, but Edna was oblivious. Edna was struggling with a scarf that didn't want to be tucked into a coat.

Lucy started to laugh, and shook her head. She was happy to see Sam blushing. "Are you guys ready?"

Zoë's eyes darted between the two of them. "I guess so," she said.

"Yup," said Sam.

Quote announced: "'Once more unto the breech, dear friends!' That's from *Henry the Fifth*, Shakespeare."

"No wait, this is better," said Edna, finally tossing the scarf over her shoulder. "'Let us ride to Camelot!' You know, from *Monty Python and the Holy Grail*?"

"Oh, let's go," said Zoë. "'I deserve a break today.' That's Ronald McDonald—or close enough."

Lucy smiled at them, feeling very lucky all of a sudden. "Okay, let's see how many people we've got," she said.

The five of them set off for the ruins of the old sanatorium, which sat on the backside of Lookout Park. They'd told anyone who was interested to meet them there. Lisa Alt said she would be there, and they had hopes of more.

Turtle Rock was a town holding its breath. More than the usual number of residents turned up at the Easter Egg Hunt that year, despite the chilly weather and a storm cloud suggesting snow. Change was coming to Turtle Rock—a person could feel it in the town's pulse. Mixed among parents (whose children were lined up at the start line) were the elderly, wearing winter boots and leaning on walkers or canes; construction workers with thick backs and callused hands; dog walkers who'd "happened" that way; and high schoolers making snide remarks but waiting all the same. These were the people that could read the events of the previous fall and winter as some people watched the sky to read the weather, which explained the large gathering of gossips. Others simply wanted entertainment of sorts. Anyway, it didn't take a genius to know that the coinciding of the Amos Zebulon document and Miss Wiggins's sudden departure on April Fools' Day meant something was up.

Whatever was "up" would be revealed, they hoped, at Miss Wiggins's yearly Easter Egg Hunt Address, always given right before the hunt.

And if Miss Wiggins didn't show up for the event? Well, that would be a story in itself.

(Many noted that the *Turtle Rock Times* had sent out a reporter and two photographers, instead of just a photographer. So they weren't the only ones thinking this might be a newsworthy occasion.)

Then someone in the crowd spotted Miss Wiggins's Cadillac. They all turned to watch as the mayor, dressed in a lilac-colored suit and a pink top hat, rushed across the lawn to meet her. Miss Wiggins stepped out of her car, and the two of them walked briskly toward the platform.

Yes, it looked to be a fine gathering for the Easter Egg Hunt (if only the weather were a little warmer and less threatening). Yellow and purple streamers snapped in the wind, and the fifteen-foot plywood Easter Bunny thumped against its supports. Children gathered by the start ribbon; a group of older children elbowed each other for the best position, and there was a crowd of about two hundred adults standing in front of the platform, waiting for Miss Wiggins's address, bundled in their coats and drinking coffee and hot chocolate from thermoses.

That's when they heard something that sounded like a great group of squirrels chattering, but far, far off.

The mayor leaned into the microphone. "Happy Easter,

everyone!" he said. "The Easter Bunny has outdone himself this year—there are five Golden Eggs hidden in the park with gift certificates to some of Turtle Rock's finest business establishments!"

Someone called out from the crowd. The mayor responded: "Carol says there's a twenty-five-dollar gift certificate to Tamarack Books!"

That chattering sound behind them grew louder. It wasn't squirrels. It sounded more like an assemblage of chanters—a roving band of monks? People began to turn around, away from the platform where the mayor and Miss Wiggins stood, squinting to see if they could spy anything back at the edge of the park. They knew it was rude to look away while the mayor spoke so sincerely, but surely no one expected them to pretend such a racket did not exist.

And then they saw them: they were coming up over the edge of the bluff, from the unused path that ran by the old sanatorium. They appeared bit by bit: carrying signs, wearing hats, either green or yellow or both. There must have been sixty of those junior-high kids, yelling and chanting, with signs pinned on their shirts, hanging off their green-and-yellow hats, and mounted on hockey sticks: FREE WIGGINS HILL! IT'S THE SUGAR BUSH NOT WIGGINS HILL! SLEDDING FOR EVERYONE!

They scanned the group to pick out that girl Lucy Moon—the green-and-yellow hat, the braids so long that one fell into each pocket of the orange puffy coat. She must be here somewhere, they thought.

And there she was: Lucy Moon stood right near the front with that Zoë Rossignol. They were leading the chanting, sign-bearing adolescents toward the podium. When they got close, they circled the podium and the crowd in front of it. The noise was deafening.

Some of the audience members smiled to themselves, because this was shaping up to be much more interesting than they'd ever expected—this wasn't news, this was a human drama of epic proportions! (Or as "epic" as a situation got in the polite society of a small town located in northern Minnesota.)

Heads began to pivot between Miss Wiggins, the mayor, Lucy Moon, the junior-high protesters, and back again. The mayor continued talking, but later, no one could recall a word he said—not a soul had listened.

The two photographers from the *Turtle Rock Times* scuttled around, shutters clicking.

The junior-high students chanted so loudly, they effectively masked the sound of the mayor's voice over the speakers. "Steward—not owner/Wiggins Hill's a loaner!" "Take down the fence! We want recompense!" "No one owns it! No one owns it! No one owns it!"

It seemed Miss Wiggins wasn't paying a lot of attention to the commotion passing by at ankle-level. She looked as though she were truly listening to the mayor, but one couldn't help but notice how her lips seemed pinched together.

The mayor tried to wrap things up. "And now, before we begin, a word from Miss Wiggins . . ." he said, nearly dropping the microphone as he swatted at a protester's sign, ". . . who nourishes our souls with the mulch of her composting verbiage on the eve of spring!"

Miss Wiggins raised an eyebrow at this. A few people chuckled at the introduction, since the poor, befuddled man had just said that Miss Wiggins's words stunk to high heaven.

But Miss Wiggins took the microphone graciously, all at ease, it seemed. Then she searched through the faces of the chanting adolescents. She found the girl she wanted— Lucy Moon—and she said this directly to her, in the gentlest voice anyone had ever heard Miss Wiggins use: "Could I have a moment to speak, please? I think you'll like what I have to say."

Lucy Moon finished her chant, ". . . Wiggins Hill's a loaner!"

"Please," said Miss Wiggins.

Their eyes connected. For a moment, the tension between them was so palpable, it was easy to imagine a squirrel traversing it like a telephone wire.

Then Lucy Moon nodded. She stopped marching, put down her sign, and signaled to the others. It took a minute, but soon they were quiet.

Miss Wiggins smiled at the protesters and began. "This year, my Easter Egg Hunt Address will be personal in nature."

The reporter from the *Turtle Rock Times* opened her notebook. The photographers focused their lenses on Miss Wiggins. Folks in the crowd glanced at each other expectantly.

"I've come to a time in life when I need to make some decisions," Miss Wiggins continued, "and since I've been so intimately involved with Turtle Rock, I feel I should announce them publicly." Miss Wiggins glanced around. "There are three announcements: First, as you know, Turtle Rock's hospital attracts people from all over northern Minnesota because of our first-rate staff and medical technology. I've decided that there needs to be a complement to the hospital in the form of a luxury retirement community. This has been a dream of mine for a long time, and I've had the blueprints for several years. So, with the blessing of the hospital, I'm happy to announce that we'll begin digging this spring. The first resident will be me."

"This means that, secondly, I will be spending fewer hours at Wiggins Faucet. I don't expect to ever give up work, but I will be allowing more time for travel, seeing friends, and reading historical treatises."

"Thirdly and lastly." Miss Wiggins twisted around so she spoke directly to Lucy Moon. "I must thank Lucy Moon and Polly Kortum for discovering the agreement between

Amos Zebulon and Sebastian Wiggins concerning the sugar bush, a thing I knew nothing about until I read it, with all of you, in the *Turtle Rock Times*." Miss Wiggins paused, and then continued: "Wiggins Hill will be donated to the city of Turtle Rock as a public park. The fence will come down as soon as I hire a construction crew to remove it."

Miss Wiggins held an open hand in Lucy's direction. She began to clap. "Thank you, Lucy Moon."

The crowd gasped, and then began clapping, too. The protesters began to cheer, throwing their signs and hats into the air.

"And now, I suppose we should begin the Easter Egg Hunt." Miss Wiggins seemed to say this directly to Lucy Moon.

(Later, a few folks suggested that Miss Wiggins's smile seemed strangely triumphant, but others said, "Oh, no, that wasn't it at all; though I will say she stared at that girl for an awful long time.")

Still, when they glanced at Lucy Moon to see how she took that look, they saw Lucy meet Miss Wiggins's gaze steadily, her lips a straight line. That girl had courage, some thought. Others wondered how a junior-high girl had found the perseverance to keep at this Wiggins Hill issue all this time. A town could do worse than having a few more Lucy Moons around.

Then the mayor handed Miss Wiggins a megaphone,

and Miss Wiggins aimed it at the children waiting to begin the hunt for chocolate eggs.

"Ready . . ." she said.

Several children put one foot over the start line.

"Set . . ."

The children leaned forward, gritted their teeth, and tried to focus on this year's egg-hunting strategy.

The elderly in the crowd reflected that things didn't go this right very often in a lifetime. Then they smiled, watching those children. If Miss Wiggins didn't say "go" soon, someone would likely be impaled on an elbow!

As snowflakes began to drift from the sky, the word came:

"Go!" said Miss Wiggins.

CHAPTER 22

Through big flakes of snow, Lucy watched the little kids break through the ribbon and spill out over Lookout Park. Lucy Moon felt her happiness flee with them.

All around her, junior-high students were jumping up and down, hugging each other, and screaming. They tossed their green-and-yellow hats into the air, trampled on their signs, and threw the bits of cardboard sign up, and up again. Some students ran to Miss Wiggins and *thanked* her. It seemed to Lucy that Miss Wiggins shrugged them off (of course), but it was stupid, stupid to go *thank* her, treating her like some sort of hero, after all the wrong she had done. She had fenced the hill even after her father had signed an agreement promising not to do it. Had everyone forgotten?

Lucy put her hands on her hips.

And then, Miss Wiggins had used Lucy in her speech to make herself look generous! She'd *used* her!

Sam and Zoë grabbed Lucy's hands and dragged her around in a circle. Then they hugged her. Lucy submitted with the enthusiasm of overcooked spinach.

The impression Lucy had of Miss Wiggins's announcement was of someone doing a dance step—step here, step there, do a twist, and walk away.

At the very least, Miss Wiggins should have said these three words: "I am sorry." But she hadn't said them. No, instead, Miss Wiggins made the announcement sound as if it were her idea all along: to give a gift of Wiggins Hill to the itty-bitty children. And everyone cheered. How was this possible? This was all wrong! "I'm sorry" was what Miss Wiggins needed to say!

Oh, Lucy couldn't stand it! She stomped her foot. But since Sam stood right next to her, she ended up stomping on his foot, hard.

"Ouch!" he said. He began rubbing his foot, pain scrawled across his face. "What did you do that for?"

"Oh, sorry," Lucy said. "Really sorry, Sam!" The only boy she'd ever liked, and she'd stomped on his foot.

Lucy realized then that she, Lucy Moon, had just apologized. Yes, Lucy was the first one to say "sorry" in Lookout Park at the Easter Egg Hunt.

She was getting a pain in her head. Lucy rubbed her temple and watched Miss Wiggins walk up the hill to her car. She stopped here and there to shake hands. A photographer hovered around Miss Wiggins like a gnat, until the mayor opened Miss Wiggins's car door. She stepped in, closed the door, and drove away. Just like that.

"I'm leaving," Lucy said to Sam and Zoë. She started to run. She ran as hard as her lungs let her. She pumped her arms and legs like pistons in an engine. Her braids flip-flopped against the back of her coat, and Lucy ran and ran and ran and ran.

Lucy ran past the parked cars, out of the park, and into the neighborhood. *Thank you, Lucy Moon.* Lucy heard it again and again, like a mosquito hovering near her ear. *Thank you, Lucy Moon. Thank you, Lucy Moon.*

Lucy yelled, "AAAAAAAAaaahhhhhh!"

Then she bent over, panting, and realized what she had done—she had just screamed in the middle of a neighborhood on Easter Sunday. What was she thinking? She glanced around between breaths. In each of the shoe box–style houses, people began to gather in the rectangular windows, peering out.

Lucy tucked her braids, her most recognizable feature, into the collar of her orange coat. She was happy to note it was snowing harder now, making it more difficult to see.

She needed to get out of here, but where could she go?

Then she got an idea. Yeah. It was a little out of the way, and she didn't want to walk on any major roads, because someone might see her, give her a thumbs-up, or want to talk to her. Still, she could get there.

So Lucy lifted a line of barbed wire with one hand and bent underneath it. She'd start by cutting across this field.

Lucy thought of her dad then. He'd expect her home any minute now. Reluctantly, he'd let her go to the Easter Egg Hunt, and only after Lucy had begged for an hour, promising a peaceful protest (like Gandhi and Martin Luther King). Lucy was pretty sure he thought it was only going to be six of them holding signs. (Lucy truly hadn't expected all those kids, either.) She was supposed to return home right afterward for Easter dinner (vegan stuffed peppers). But nothing had turned out the way Lucy had expected, and she didn't want to go home. She wanted to be alone.

Lucy ignored the eerie sense of déjà vu all this wanting to be alone gave her. She had spent weeks avoiding people, being alone. That hadn't gone so well. But so what? There had to be times when people needed—like oxygen, water, food, and sleep—to be alone, right?

It was snowing quite hard now. Lucy reached up to take off her hemp hat so she could pull on her knit one, and that's when she realized that the green-and-yellow hat wasn't there. Where was it? Lucy spun around in one direction and then the other.

The hat was nowhere to be seen. It must have fallen off when she was running, or maybe it had gotten caught on that barbed wire a while back. Tears gathered in the corners of Lucy's eyes. But she would not lose control. Lucy pulled on her knit hat, wiped at her eyes with her mittens, and kept on walking.

This would not, should not—*will not* be the end, thought Lucy. It couldn't end this way. Lucy remembered the last weeks: the Genie wearing green-and-yellow hats day after day, and then everyone else doing it, too. The Genie—of all people! When Zoë, Sam, and Lucy gathered people for the Easter Egg Hunt March, tons of kids had shown up. They'd swarmed up the side of that hill, chanting, signs held high. It was all so right, so how could it have ended so wrong?

After walking through a grove of pines, sprinting discreetly through the backyards of a few houses, hauling her body over a fence and onto a neighborhood street, Lucy finally reached the end of Twelfth Street. She walked to an opening in the trees and saw it—Wiggins Hill.

Even fenced, the hill took her breath away. The light through the falling snow washed the scene with the palest blue, and the giant sugar maple looked like an etching. Everything else—the five smaller sugar maples, the brambles, the top of the hill—dropped away, suggestions only, hidden behind a lace of snow.

Lucy felt better immediately. She began to jog the perimeter of the hill, sticking out her mittened hand to bump it along the chain link.

That's when it occurred to her: this fence was coming down. Next time, she'd be able to dash across this hill and tag the big sugar maple if she liked.

It was as if she'd been struck by lightning. A surge of joy shook Lucy's body. Yes!

Why had it taken her this long to see it? Why did she have to be physically present at Wiggins Hill to understand the celebration at the Easter Egg Hunt? Yes, Miss Wiggins had fenced the hill. But Miss Wiggins was donating the hill to the city for a park. She was giving it up! That seemed a fair trade for a document that probably wouldn't hold up in a court of law. Suddenly, Miss Wiggins's using Lucy to look good didn't seem like such a big deal anymore. Miss Wiggins could thank her morning, noon, and night! Lucy wanted to . . .

"WHOOOHOOOOOWEEEEEYAAAAAAAA!"

Lucy began dancing an Irish jig (or what she thought an Irish jig looked like). She clapped her hands over her head and sang a made-up song: "Ha-ha-ha-ha . . . freedom! Freedom!"

They had done it!

"Who's there?" a voice called from the top of Wiggins Hill.

Lucy froze.

She squinted up the hill. She could barely make out a woman standing near the top, and if it weren't for the big solid boots on the woman's feet, Lucy would have said it was Miss Wiggins. The woman shaded her eyes with her hand and peered down the hill. It *was* Miss Wiggins.

Surely, Miss Wiggins saw Lucy in this bright-orange coat, but Lucy didn't say anything. She had wanted to see the hill, not Miss Wiggins. And now she saw that coming to the hill hadn't been the brightest idea since, of course, Miss Wiggins lived at the top of it.

Lucy was reminded again of all the times Miss Wiggins's name had popped up over and over the last few months, and how it seemed like she was connected to Lucy's life. But Lucy was sure she wasn't. Still, Lucy couldn't get Miss Wiggins out of her head. She'd read the newspaper and see her name and photo everywhere. Miss Wiggins was either on the board of some organization, or donating money, just like she donated that money for the gallery space that replaced her mom's studio, or for Mrs. Mudd's new "The Tiny Tims & the Healing Power of Dickens" brochures. She probably even gave to that dumb "Fill the Pencil with Lead" fund-raising campaign for the gymnasium at the junior high. . . . But what did Miss Wiggins get in return?

That's when it occurred to her. Lucy stood stock still, hardly daring to breathe, until one by one her thoughts slipped into place. Could it be?

Well, there was only one way to find out. . . .

"It's Lucy Moon!" she yelled as loud as she could.

Lucy climbed through the hole in the fence and half jogged up the hill toward Miss Wiggins.

Miss Wiggins waited for her at the top of the hill, her arms crossed over her chest. And though Lucy was out of breath, she summoned every bit of strength to begin talking as soon as she came near enough to be heard. "Was it a *coincidence* that Gustafson's Wild Nature Gallery got a donation from you after you'd had some sort of run-in with my mom on the road? What about the junior high needing a new gymnasium and looking for donations? Is that why I got a double-length detention, a psychological examination (a lame one, by the way), and a recommendation for Youth Action? Was it a *coincidence* that Mrs. Mudd had decided to make me her special cleaning companion around the same time she got a donation from you for those new 'Tiny Tims & the Healing Power of Dickens' brochures?"

Lucy didn't know what she expected to happen, but in a rush of insight, she knew that if Miss Wiggins had any sense she wouldn't answer. And she didn't—or not with words. But for a split second, recognition seemed to cross Miss Wiggins's face. Miss Wiggins knew something; she had *done* something, but what? The look passed, and a more polished demeanor took its place.

Then it occurred to Lucy that the situation might be more complicated than she had thought. (Lucy wondered why sometimes it took saying a thing to make this realization.) It was complicated because when someone had money, people did all sorts of things to please them. Everybody knew that Lucy was involved with *The Turtle Rock Times Shuts Its Eyes* and the "Free Wiggins Hill!" postcards. Maybe people punished her because they thought it would please Miss Wiggins. Or maybe it wasn't something as harsh as punishment—maybe it was as simple as not giving Lucy the benefit of the doubt. Not getting the benefit of the doubt could lead to all sorts of things—things like Youth Action and unending detentions. All of this could have happened without Miss Wiggins knowing about it at all. And, hey, maybe Miss Wiggins believed that reading Dickens healed people.

Oh, come on, thought Lucy. No one was going to convince her that Miss Wiggins believed in that kind of baloney!

"You did something," Lucy said.

Miss Wiggins snorted. "Just because a person has the money to pay for anything they want doesn't mean they'd do it, Lucy. I'll have you know I have strict principles and I adhere to them."

Lucy sighed. As predicted, Miss Wiggins wasn't going to admit to anything, though Lucy felt slightly vindicated by whatever she had seen on Miss Wiggins's face. Still, it was time to let it go. She'd never know. The only thing Lucy did know was that she didn't completely trust Miss Wiggins.

Lucy nodded at the hole in the fence. "I didn't have

anything to do with that, you know. I would never do something like that!" Miss Wiggins wasn't the only one with principles.

Miss Wiggins's eyes trailed to the hole. "No," she said. "That was the work of Miss Eugenie Sovil and friends."

Lucy's mind spun. The Big Six cut the fence? They were the junior-high "girl gang"? The fashion-enhanced wonder-waifs of the third floor?

"Whoa," said Lucy.

"Lucy, is it against your belief system to converse normally? It seems you prefer confronting people with your wild accusations—in their own backyards, for heaven's sake."

"I was only asking some questions," Lucy said.

Miss Wiggins ignored her comment. "I take a lot of pride in this town. I do things that benefit everyone. I want you to understand that."

"I care, too," said Lucy. She balled one of her braids in her fist.

"I know," said Miss Wiggins. "And you're about as persistent as a biting fly."

"You've got to have everything your own way," Lucy shot back.

That was when Miss Wiggins chuckled a little. After a beat, she said: "Funny, I would've said the same of you."

There was a pause, and the two of them stared at each other for a long moment.

Miss Wiggins tucked her scarf in around her neck. "Good-bye for now, Lucy Moon."

And then Miss Wiggins turned and strode over the lip of the hill, toward her blue house.

Miss Wiggins is wearing work boots, thought Lucy.

On her way back down the hill, Lucy stopped at the giant sugar maple. She put her hands on its bark, feeling the furrows under her mittens. She listened to the wind, and then turned and leaned against the tree. She stared out down the long hill, finding the sketchy outline of Turtle Rock through all the snow.

The Big Six cut the fence? It was about time Lucy stopped thinking that their heads were filled with cotton candy. Miss Wiggins wore work boots? And that conversation . . . yeah, there were ways that Miss Wiggins and Lucy were alike. (But also very different, too, thought Lucy defensively.) No one seemed to be who Lucy thought they were.

It was too much! With a rush of emotion, Lucy desperately wanted to have the sense that she knew somebody, like you knew grape jelly. You read the label—"grape jelly"—and that was enough to know that it tasted great on bread, time and time again. Would it be so bad to wish for people to be as dependable?

And shouldn't moms be more dependable than anyone? Lucy didn't even know who her mom was anymore.

At this point, all she wanted was for her mom to apologize in a way that felt like an apology. She didn't want to hear, "I'm sorry, but the opportunities have been once in a lifetime." Or, "I'm sorry, but I've had it bad, can't you understand?" Confessions and explanations were only meant to show Lucy that she hadn't considered what was going on with her mom, that in essence, Lucy was a shallow and insensitive daughter—the kind of daughter that forced mothers to apologize when they'd done nothing all that wrong. Lucy didn't buy that! "I am sorry," was what Lucy wanted to hear. Lucy wanted her mom to admit that she had done Lucy a wrong.

Huh, thought Lucy. She guessed Miss Wiggins's apology wasn't the one she wanted to hear today—not really.

Lucy snorted. Well, no matter what she wanted, she'd bet she wasn't going to get an apology from her mom anytime soon. She'd be lucky if her mom made it home by summer. Heck, her mom might never come home.

It was as if the thought had simply been waiting backstage, and now it was making its appearance. Lucy hadn't thought it once. She hadn't *wanted* to think it. She'd just been trying to ignore her mom's existence all this time.

If Christmas, her dad, Lucy, couldn't bring her mom home, *nothing* would.

Nothing.

Lucy slipped down the side of the maple tree and started to cry—great, loud barks of cries.

Slowly, through her tears, Lucy began to understand one thing: if the choice was between an apology and her mom driving circles around the great state of Minnesota forever . . . well, she'd take her mom back on almost any terms.

"Just come home," she whispered into the snow.

Lucy thought then of Amos Zebulon's wife, Rippling Water, and the song Rippling Water felt around and through this sugar maple, from somewhere else, somewhere larger. The song had passed through Rippling Water "as if . . ."—and Lucy found she had memorized this part—". . . she were water for the song to wade in." Lucy closed her eyes and imagined her body being water, and for a moment or two, she thought she felt the thrum of song. Lucy envisioned her words carried along in the song, and realized, with a start, that she was praying.

It was either a lifetime or one long minute later when Lucy opened her eyes. The snow fell, fell, fell. Her breath puffed and unraveled. Her nose was numb. Her butt was cold.

Her mom might not come home.

The realization made everything seem dull. It was like seeing in shades of gray instead of color, or feeling the smoothness of plastic sheeting everywhere, on everything.

Still, Lucy stood up and brushed the snow off her pants. She straightened her knit hat. She cupped her hands in front of her face and blew into them to warm her nose.

Then she told herself the truth: without her mom, Lucy had survived the worst school year she could remember. She had friends (Zoë especially), and with friends, a person could be stronger than when all alone. Her dad had turned out to be pretty dang heroic in his efforts to help her, and he never gave up. Her dad wouldn't give up on her. She knew this now. And Mrs. Rossignol and Ms. Kortum cared about her. Plus, it seemed like Sam might be her boyfriend (if she hadn't screwed it up by stomping on his foot). Lucy's face grew hot.

Okay? Lucy told herself. You are not alone.

It was a good thing people weren't grape jelly, because grape jelly couldn't surprise you in a good way, either—like her dad had.

And, Lucy thought, this hill—the one we fought for—is free!

At first, Lucy forced herself to spin around, winging her arms out with an image of Zoë in her mind. But the first surge of dizziness made her smile, so she spun a little more. And pretty soon, Lucy lifted her face to the sky and spun as fast as she could, until she fell and found herself rolling down the hill. When she stopped, somewhere near the bottom of Wiggins Hill, Lucy laughed. "Ha!"

* * *

Thirty minutes later, Lucy turned left onto Fifth Street and spotted her red house. She knew she was in for it. She was late coming home, she was outside in a snowstorm, and who knew how her dad would respond to the news that so many kids had joined the protest. Still, she felt content with the sort of weariness and relief that a good cry leaves behind. Lucy noticed that the porch light had been left on for her, and smiled.

There were two cars in the driveway: one was the station wagon, and the other was an unknown minivan with what turned out to be Florida plates. Well, so be it, thought Lucy. She was headed toward a lecture from her dad, and she was too tired to care if someone else got to enjoy the show. She just wanted to be home.

Lucy walked up the sidewalk and through the front door. The screen door banged shut behind her.

"Lucy?" called her dad.

Then a woman appeared.

Was it . . . ?

As Lucy's eyes adjusted to the indoor light, she saw it was.

Her mom's face seemed all angles and hollows. She wore a thick, blue-and-burgundy sweater that Lucy had never seen, and her hair now hit her shoulders. She held out Lucy's green-and-yellow hat. "Looking for this?" she asked.

Confused, Lucy took the hat out of her mom's hands

and stared at it. "How . . . ?" she started. It was the second time today the hat had been returned to her. And by the last person Lucy expected.

"Zoë and Sam came by," her mom said. "They said you dropped it in Lookout Park. They want you to call them."

Lucy looked up then, saw her mom's gray eyes, and that's what started it.

Lucy set the green-and-yellow hat on the kitchen counter and rounded on her mom. "What are you doing here?"

"Lucy!" said her dad sharply. Lucy had forgotten he was even present. But there he was, towering behind her mom, suddenly very apparent.

"No, Don." Lucy's mom held her dad back with one arm. Then she spoke softly to Lucy. "I wanted to surprise you for Easter." She sounded sad, as if it hadn't worked out like she hoped.

"Well, I don't need you anymore," said Lucy. "If you're not a mom, I'm not a daughter."

Lucy was happy to see her mom pale at these words.

The anger was red hot and slashing. Later, Lucy was ashamed of the violence she'd witnessed in herself, especially after praying on Wiggins Hill, but right now, it felt like scratching something that had itched for months. Lucy wanted her mom to feel what she had felt, every knifelike bit of it. Lucy continued: "You left me! You said it was all about photography, but in the end it was all about escaping Dad and me. You ran away! You don't even know how bad this year was for me, do you? I wanted to run away, too, but I didn't. I stayed here and worked it out."

Lucy turned her back to her mom. Her mom touched her shoulder, and Lucy whipped around. "Didn't you hear me?" Lucy said. "I worked it out *without you*. I don't need you. Go away."

But then something Lucy hadn't foreseen happened. Her mom reached out and pulled Lucy into her arms.

Lucy's body revolted. "Don't touch me!" she said.

Her mom held on. "I'm not letting my *daughter* go," she said. "I made that mistake once."

The words mixed with the familiar scent of outside air on her mom's sweater, and Lucy felt her head bump her mom's shoulder, like it always did when they hugged, and she started to cry. Lucy hated herself for being naked, soft, and pink, because she wanted to be cold and impenetrable, like steel, to show her mom that she had grown strong, like a skyscraper—all alone, all by herself. Still, Lucy couldn't stop crying.

Oh, did she miss her mom. She did.

And that's when Lucy heard these words whispered in her hair: "What I did was wrong, Lucy. I'm sorry. I am so, so sorry."

The words were simple, unembellished with excuses, and Lucy knew the words were true.

It was enough for a beginning.

Before even an hour had passed, news about the Easter Sunday protest was on North Country Radio, WBRR. Ken and Julie interrupted programming to give "eyewitness accounts" (callers who'd phoned in), "news updates" (confirmations from "insider sources"), and a special "Biography of a Rebel" (Ken's epic poem about Lucy Moon, in rhyme that clunked along like a car over potholes). Of course, Ken and Julie tried to get both Lucy Moon and Miss Wiggins on the phone. Eventually, Miss Wiggins called them, the producer patching her through immediately, interrupting a Theremin version of "Here Comes Peter Cottontail."

"I asked you to stop calling me," came the voice over the air. "Now get back to that fiddle-faddle music of yours. Poetry certainly isn't your strength!"

"Yes, ma'am," said Ken. The Theremin started up with a blurt.

As the days passed, the excitement died down. But for a few folks in Turtle Rock, something else replaced it—a thoughtful pondering of the story of Wiggins Hill and Lucy Moon. These folks thought about Lucy Moon while they waited for the microwave to heat up a little leftover hot dish, or while they stood on the front porch watching for their ride. Mostly, they thought about themselves. What would they fight for? Was there something they